WALT

WALT

A NOVEL

RUSSELL
WANGERSKY

SPIDERLINE

This edition published in 2014 by
House of Anansi Press Inc.
110 Spadina Avenue, Suite 801
Toronto, ON, M5V 2K4
Tel. 416-363-4343
Fax 416-363-1017
www.houseofanansi.com

Distributed in Canada by
HarperCollins Canada Ltd.
1995 Markham Road
Scarborough, ON, M1B 5M8
Toll free tel. 1-800-387-0117

House of Anansi Press is committed to protecting our natural environment.
As part of our efforts, the interior of this book is printed on paper that con-
tains 100% post-consumer recycled fibres, is acid-free, and is processed
chlorine-free.

18 17 16 15 14   1 2 3 4 5

Library and Archives Canada Cataloguing in Publication

Wangersky, Russell, 1962-, author
Walt / by Russell Wangersky.

Issued in print and electronic formats.
ISBN 978-1-77089-467-9 (pbk.).--ISBN 978-1-77089-468-6 (html)

I. Title.

PS8645.A5333W34 2014   C813'.6   C2014-902743-5
                                               C2014-902744-3

Cover design: Alysia Shewchuk
Text design and typesetting: Alysia Shewchuk

Canada Council   Conseil des Arts   ONTARIO ARTS COUNCIL
for the Arts   du Canada   CONSEIL DES ARTS DE L'ONTARIO

*We acknowledge for their financial support of our publishing program
the Canada Council for the Arts, the Ontario Arts Council, and the Government of
Canada through the Canada Book Fund.*

Printed and bound in Canada

For Leslie

CHAPTER 1

We needs
Cereal
Bread
Choco & White Milk
Cat
Yougurts
Toilet paper
Deorant
Shampoo
Oranges
Banans

Hard to forget a list like that—hard to forget the girl, too. Her name's Alisha. Skirt right up to there, the kind that makes you wish you could be somewhere nearby and watching when she finally has to sit down. Just to see how she'd manage it, scissoring those long legs at the knees without showing you anything else. Not getting caught looking, of course. But if you're not supposed to be looking, then why's she wearing it, anyway? Her hair dark and short and cut in tight next to her face, and she's got that beautiful-girl way of looking back at you when she does catch you staring—I'm not saying she looks right through you, but that somehow she looks right around you, as if light rays can be bent and you're the kind of a person that she just doesn't need to be seeing right now.

And you know she's not single, it's right there in the note that she's got to be part of a couple—that's easy to figure with *We needs* right there at the top. She dropped the list by the bin at the cash registers, the one that's usually full of torn coin rollers and the receipts that people shed before they're even out the door. Just try returning the wrong-sized batteries without that receipt, mister. I already know her name, and her Facebook says she's "In a relationship," too, but I'm getting way ahead of myself.

Timing is everything—I empty the bins almost before there's anything in them, so connecting the scraps of paper to the people who discarded them is easier than you might think. And her note, tossed down there, well, the spelling's a mess, and the *banans* makes me wonder if she's French or European or in some other way just not from here. The *cat* part gets me, too, because she doesn't look like a pet person. Not at all like a pet person, not like she's ready for the mess or the bother.

There's something about the way she's done up that makes you think she's not going to put up with something that's going to always be shedding or hooking your clothes with its claws.

"Done up like a stick of gum." That's the saying, whatever that's supposed to mean. She's all about the clothes, right down to the way she opens one button on her coat, just the right button, when she swings her legs into the cab. Always a cab, too, and that's gotta add up to some coin for sure — five bucks each time even if you're barely going around the corner, and who always has five bucks to throw away?

Kev told me where she lived when I asked, because he drives for Co-Op — the yellow ones that always pick her up — and I've known Kev since he was five, so it's not like he's going to keep something as harmless as a name and a neighbourhood away from me. Little two-storey house, one in from the corner, white with rusty-coloured trim, and when you look inside from the front, even if you're staring from across the street, you can see there's art up on the walls, and the cat looks out the front window almost all the time, sitting there like it's stuffed, or more like everything outside is a movie it's barely interested in.

After that, bit by bit, it wasn't that hard to track down more information.

I go on the Internet and check Facebook to see if she's put up any new pictures. She likes pictures of herself, likes putting them up. I'm not her Facebook friend or anything — I've never asked to be; she doesn't even know I'm out here — but she doesn't have all the privacy stuff done, and I think that maybe she likes the idea of someone having a look at her stuff, like it's not necessarily a bad thing to be noticed or desired remotely.

Well, she must like it, judging by the pictures she puts up. Once, one of her in the shower—dressed in a T-shirt, all right, nothing perverted or anything. But she was in the shower, the water streaming down so that it looked like long threads, like she was surrounded by a tepee of straws or something. It's crazy. Her friends leaving notes right there under it, like it's so ordinary that everybody does it every day, piling into the shower and letting the water come down on you until your clothes are clinging.

I go in every day or so just to see if she's got another picture up there, and what it is she's doing this time. It's addictive enough. It always makes me wonder when she'll be back to the grocery store.

You probably think a grocery store is big and anonymous, with its ruler-straight aisles of canned goods and pet food and laundry soap. And it is—to a point. Anonymous to the point that there's no real personality to it, no matter how hard they might try to make you think it's a neighbourhood or something. Because neighbourhood's in your head.

The store's anonymous until you've lived somewhere long enough to start making familiar paths, until you start making routes from here to there so that you carve your own small space out of the bigger place.

With a city, you make your trails by choice. Same flower shop where you always get flowers, same Thai place for hot and spicy soup, same video store where you know almost every single one of the titles and where they'll be on the shelves. Anonymous is nice, but it's better when at least a few people behind the counters start to recognize you, when they give you that smile and nod that says you're familiar, maybe even read the patch on your shirt and start calling you "Walt."

It's the same in the store, the way you learn your place. The way it turns out you like the same cereal as the stock guy with the black hair, the way you learn you can be saucy with the cashier with the piercings and she'll be saucy right back, whether or not there's a manager lurking around.

Maybe the first time you're here—maybe the first ten times—you're a stranger to me, but come in often enough and I'm going to start remembering you. I'm good with faces. Anyone can be, if they see someone enough. Think about it: there's a red-haired girl here who's always working the flower counter. I bet you're probably picturing her right now, and you probably even know the way she usually does her hair—always pulled back, isn't it?—and you know that because you've got to go by her counter with your cart on the way to the parking lot every time, and there she is, almost every time.

Well, it's a two-way street. Maybe your coat's familiar. Maybe it's your hair, or the way your mouth smiles but you manage to keep your eyes diffuse, unfocused. After a while, you're familiar even if no one makes an effort to point you out.

You're familiar, and the things you always put in the cart are familiar, too.

Some people make a different kind of mark. The brusque ones and the cold ones who can't even bring themselves to smile back when you make a particular point of smiling at them — they're bad enough, but there are worse.

Me, I can't stand the people who think they own the place. It's stupid, I know, because it shouldn't mean anything to me. Not my problem, not my profits. But the ones who just pick up a bunch of grapes and eat them as they go, the ones who peel a banana and stuff it in their mouth, leaving the emptied peel in their cart before they've even paid for it — I can't help but get angry with them.

Can't help wanting to go right up to them and set them straight.

It's like someone walking in through your front door without saying hello and going straight to your fridge.

Someone did that at my parents' house, years ago. They were having a party, and I opened the door when the bell rang. A man walked right by me, down the hall, and into the kitchen. He opened the fridge and had a good look around at the beer and the single bottle of white wine lying on its side, and when he turned to me, the very first thing he said was "Have you got any Coke or what?" It's stuck with me ever since, so maybe I'm just overly sensitive. And I know you're going to say that the store isn't my house, that it's not my food, but I kind of feel like it is, in a way, with the number of hours I spend here.

I'll cut you some slack if you're in a rush or something, if something about you says hurried and harried and unable to keep it all together. If you're so pressed that it looks like you don't even have any idea what you're doing. It's different

6

if you just don't care, if you drop scraps of trash from your pockets or your purse right there on the floor just past the broccoli. The amount of balled-up tissue I pick up in the run of a week would simply amaze you. And I know some of it is accidental, stuff just falling on the floor when your hands come out of your pockets, and that some of it is because people are always in a rush. But a lot of it isn't.

If I think you just don't give a damn, if I'm sure you're doing it on purpose, I'll give you the hard stare—as if that makes any difference—and I'll also make it my business to follow you around the store after that, as if I'm supposed to be keeping tabs on you. Not much more I can do than that.

But it's strange how unsettling some people find that— some middle-aged guy trailing them through the grocery store, just daring them to drop something else.

You wouldn't believe what people do. I've found fresh chicken breast quarters left high and dry on a tideline of popcorn packages in the snack aisle, and it's not like you can just look at them, shrug, and put the package back in the cooler.

You don't know for sure how long something like that has been there. If it's not cold—and I mean really cold, like I've found it right after someone changed their mind and dumped it there—then I have to throw it out, and it goes down in inventory as "shrinkage," which is, on the accounts, in exactly the same place as shoplifting.

And the thing is, you're paying for it anyway. You and everyone else, paying because you're too lazy to go back and put away something you didn't want after all. It's built right into the price. Everything's built in there, right down to the wages of the guy who's picking up your used tissues. Me. You just don't see me spelled out word for word on your grocery receipt.

Maybe you should.

Because it's funny how quickly out of sight can become out of mind.

CHAPTER 2

Sept. 26 — Dear Diary: Is that stupid or what?
So maybe not a diary really — just keeping track.
Writing stuff down to see if I'm blowing things out
of proportion. Rain today. Got groceries. Fed the
cat. Called Mom, and she asked about Daniel —
again — like always, asking if we are getting serious.
So here's the short version of chapter and verse on
Alisha Monaghan; all boring. I wish I was writing
about moving to France to teach English as a Second
Language or starting to work on a master's degree or
having sex on a train or something. If anyone read
this, what would they have? A detailed record of just
how dull my life is. Wake up, go to work, buy groceries. I mean, I'm twenty-five years old — a quarter
century, if you want to look at it that way. I should
have things sorted out by now. I should be getting
on track. I should be working in another province,
living a bigger life — except my parents would still
want me to come home for dinner every Sunday.
A degree in French and Spanish, and I'm living in

a province with almost no use for either of them. I can just see my future, everything stretching out one plodding step at a time, achieving nothing but surviving. That's not enough. And something else— I'm writing this part down because I can't shake it. Just a feeling, but almost constant. You know that "not alone" thing they always talk about in ghost stories? That first clue before the scary stuff actually starts? That's where I am, all shook up and nervous, and I have no idea why. For weeks now I've been on edge, looking over my shoulder, second-guessing. Twenty-five years old and I'm worried about the bogeyman. I wish I could shed the feeling, because it's just plain stupid.

CHAPTER 3

garlic (minced)
Russets
sour creme
Oranges
chips
gatorade

Sometimes, you just don't get enough to figure anything concrete out. Part of a meal, maybe, certainly only a fragment of a life. But I'm good at fragments of life.

I look around my kitchen and about the best I can think of it is that it looks just how anyone would expect a lonely middle-aged man's kitchen to look. Big white fridge, and it has a kind of grumble to it every time the motor stops, a kind of double rattle followed by a single, heavier thump. I hardly even hear it any more. When I do, I'm convinced it's actually going to stop right then for good, and I'm going to wake up in the morning to thawed frozen vegetables and a bunch of stuff gone to mush. But, then again, at least it will be defrosted—first time in a long time for that.

The rest of the place sort of echoes that half-stepping, old, and potentially failing fridge. There's the linoleum, curling up right there where it meets the front of the cupboards—the dirt gets caught there if you get right down and look at it close. Not that anyone would. It doesn't really bother me, so I'm not going to get down there with a toothbrush any time soon.

There's usually a plate or two in the sink, unless I've just done the dishes that day. But don't think I'm grubby like "the place is a risk for food-poisoning" grubby. The fridge is pretty much empty, because it has only the things I like and nothing else, and it almost always has a shelf or two that has nothing at all, a wasteland of shelf. Beer, when I want some—and that's not very often.

There's usually a coffee cup on the wooden kitchen table, off-centre where I leave it, and I don't take milk or anything, so even when the cup's dirty, it's almost clean. Well, clean enough.

I always find that cup in the same place, even though I never once think about putting it there. It's like the bones in my arm are a particular length, like my muscles and tendons prefer to unspool in the same familiar way, and the table itself has all its edges in the same place always. The same lever, the same pulley, the same fulcrum, so why wouldn't my cup wind up within fractions of an inch of where it always does? It's not like anyone else is trying to mark out their own space on the surface. The only motions here are my own.

I bought that table, unpainted and unassembled, years ago in a big-box hardware store on the edge of the city. I pulled the pieces out of the long, flat box that was exactly like fifty other boxes stacked up right there at the store. I put the bolts for the legs through the brackets under the tabletop, spun on the nuts, and tightened them with the crescent wrench. I put the varnish on it, too, four coats, and I can't go through the kitchen even now without dragging a knuckle across the top, just to feel the way it's supposed to feel. And I swear sometimes I can smell the raw wood still, just the way I could when I opened the box.

There's a spot, right near one end, where someone smacked a beer bottle down hard enough on the wood to leave a little half-circle of dents. That probably would have been me.

Hardwood, too. Aspen — I think that's what the box said — thin strips of it all glued together to make one big, wide surface. Strips from maybe thirty different trees, and all of them coming together to be something that stands in my kitchen all day long while I'm somewhere else. The whole thing made in some Pennsylvania town with a German-sounding name, "some assembly required," and opening the box brought a small waterfall of sawdust, as if it had been packed up the moment they had finished working and shut the planer down, the tabletop sliding right straight out of the machines and into the box without so much as a final dusting.

And that beer bottle mark on top?

I know it by heart, even if I have no idea exactly when it happened. I sometimes let my index finger run over the top of it, the even little "bump-bump-bump" of it, the order reassuring in its regularity. Each dent corresponding to a ridge on the bottle, like cold-stamped, inverted Braille.

What I'm saying, I guess, is that there's a whole lot of information that's right here in this house, right out in the open. Sometimes silly little keys can unlock far more than anyone thinks. There's information all around, all about me, if anyone cares to look. Just like there's information out there about all of us.

The old cabinets in the kitchen are white laminate — slick fronts and a dark wood strip along the bottom with a groove where you put your fingers to pull them open, real 1980s stuff. If they were open, all you'd get to see are the handful of plates and cups and glasses I've got left. I don't need anything fancy for company, because there isn't going to be any.

The kitchen cabinets are worn and out of style, but there's a way of holding your eyes, a way of dialing things up in your memory so you can see it all just like it was when it came out of the box — as if buying stupid kitchen cabinets was somehow like putting down mooring lines and tying yourself safe and fast in place.

I remember when we went out to buy the range and that stupid grumbling fridge. The two of us were in the Sears store at the mall and we could see the sales guys angling toward us from all over the appliance section like there was blood in the water or something. Two or three of them made their way around and through the familiar maze of the furniture display, and they looked at us and back at each other, trying to figure out the shortest route to reach us first.

Commission sales. I couldn't stand it, myself, even though I tried it once or twice before I found my feet at the store. I was doing it before we were married, making good money. I suppose for the right people, it's just like a sport or something. But I couldn't stand the customers or the other salesmen.

I know how they think: here comes another young couple with stars in their eyes and their futures all caught up there in their heads, probably money in their pockets or at least willing to sign up for the payment plans. Sharks, turning sharp and fast — ready to hook their teeth right in, to try to make you think about how nice your place is going to be with your new appliances and the smell of pot roast and scalloped potatoes curling in around your near-perfect brand new life. It's a particularly tawdry kind of magic, but it's magic just the same. If they could pump that smell of roast and potatoes into the furniture store, I don't doubt for a moment that they would.

That range is still here — white, the enamel chipped in a few places, and I've replaced a couple of the burners myself and had someone in to do the thermostat in the oven once when it burned out. But pretty much it's still exactly what it always was.

Everything else, too.

The sink's right there so you can look out the back window, centred in the counter, the window above it four feet long and looking down the back garden toward the fence. The kind of window that makes a dishwasher unnecessary, because you can stand there for hours and just look outside, even if you're looking at nothing, your hands doing whatever it is they're doing, and it's not like work or chores or anything. It's like humming while you're doing something else — you just slip into doing it, because everything feels so comfortably right.

Mary never liked humming.

Hated it, actually — for some reason, the sound of it just grated on her like nobody's business. Like it was hard to accept that anyone could be happy when she wasn't. Or maybe she wasn't happy and just hadn't figured it out yet, so the lack of her own humming was meant to be some kind of clue. Humming? Bad enough. Only whistling was worse. Introverts hum. Extroverts whistle. All of them irritate. That was her theory.

Mary.

Yeah, I was married once, for a while — that "a while" was almost eighteen years.

Not my decision, any of it — not the getting married part, not the splitting up part either. I always felt like a cork in an ocean in that marriage, tossed around in all directions by different winds and currents that were impossible to resist but that had nothing at all to do with me. I never felt it was completely my fault, but I imagine some of it probably was.

So, Mary. Her last name was Carter — one of the Carter girls from up in Rabbittown — and she kept it after we got married. Four girls before Mrs. Carter had a boy by Caesarean, going under the gas with the blunt message for her doctor that "Boy or girl, I don't care, but for God's sake tie my tubes while you're in there. And don't you dare tell Frank."

Rabbittown is a hard little St. John's neighbourhood, the kind of place that's more than capable of taking care of its own, the kind of place well experienced with the skill of turning its back on everyone else like they don't even exist.

Mary came out of there fast, like a refugee sprung from a rough bare-ground tent camp somewhere, never once looking back, although they were sure willing to open the gates and take her back quickly enough afterwards, I'll bet. Or at least I suppose they did — it's not like I ever saw her again. Small neighbourhood, everyone tight. It's the kind of place I was barely tolerated when we were a couple, and where I certainly wasn't, once we weren't.

We were rocky, always. I got tossed around, but so did she. She drank, I drank. She hit, and I did that, too. I'm not proud of it, but we were pretty evenly matched, even if I had twenty pounds on her. Because she didn't hold back, ever. She threw herself right into it, every time, flat out, the same way as she argued — fists and slaps and raking you with her fingernails without a moment's thought if you gave her the opening.

We made up, fought again, made up. In fact, we made a kind of specialty of having the same old fights each time, like we were two trains permanently set on the same tracks — always aimed head-on at each other, quite able to see the big staring headlight but completely unable to do anything but charge blindly forward. We'd crash, get up bruised, set ourselves right back on the same tracks, and do it all over again. The same old starting places, every time. And every time, we revved up faster, cut to the chase quicker, and managed to go for the soft spots every married person knows their spouse has, only faster, each and every time. Like shorthand.

That's that definition of crazy, isn't it? Doing the same thing every time and still expecting it to turn out different? Or better? Or something?

At least once a week, you can see a couple just like we used to be in my grocery store: zero to fury in six seconds flat, and if you stand there and listen, you realize pretty quick that the words they're trading back and forth mean a lot more to them than they do to anyone else in the store. When "Did you forget the milk again?" can get a response like "Shut the fuck up," you know they're mining a strip of the pure ore and not messing around with the dross.

We were like that. Fast and sharp and hard. All in, every time.

If I have to give her credit for anything, I'd say the thing Mary was best at was making the hard decisions — because I didn't. I'd put things off, think about deciding on something later. Mary just went ahead and did it.

Really, both of us had the right to leave first — both of us had reasons.

Except she actually did the leaving.

But that's not the way it started.

CHAPTER 4

Limes
Salt
Tequila

In the beginning, Mary threw herself straight at me — and that's something, boy, that's something downright incredible if you've never had it happen to you before. And I hadn't.

Makes you confident in a hurry, makes you think that you're a lot more than you really are. Puffs you right up, even if you're not the kind of person to get puffed up.

It started at a house party just on the edge of Rabbittown. The house belonged to a guy I was working with then, Robert, and I remember that I had a new shirt on, right straight out of the plastic package and onto my back as I was going out the door, and one of those stupid little silver straight pins they use to hold the sleeve just so on the front of the package had found a soft spot on the inside of my wrist. It was a wonder that the cardboard from inside the collar wasn't still stuck there on my neck. I had my wrist up to my mouth, trying to stop the

19

constant little flame of bright-red bleeding when I first saw her. It was a Mexican party, margaritas and tequila and limes and people staggering around way too fast because they were drinking hard and we were all really only used to beer.

I caught her staring at me from the living room. I was in the kitchen where all the noise was at the time, two blenders and the hard-edged, jagged drinking laughter you hear right before the falling down and the crying. It was darker where she was — the living room lit mostly by big fat candles with guttering flames and too much melting wax, and one lone dull floor lamp in a corner near the couch — and the light from the kitchen was reflecting brightly back to me in the pupils of her eyes.

She was a pretty girl, gorgeous, really, and she was like a sprinter, out of the blocks all at once and running right straight at me.

It's funny what you remember and for how long. The way some details are carved right into you and all the rest just fade away.

Robert was having a goodbye party because someone was leaving town. Back then someone was always leaving town for work or for school or because they were just plain fed up with the weather. It was a cold summer night, and it was raining like it had been for all of June and most of July that year, the street outside sharp silver and completely running with water. But inside it was warm, with that heavy damp feeling of too many people packed into a small space, talking too loud and breathing too much. Everyone had brought tequila and we were already running out. Two girls locked themselves in the bathroom upstairs, laughing and who knows what else. Everyone was drunk, and I'll always remember the feeling of nacho chips crunching on the floor under my sock feet because the bowls had been knocked over once or twice, and nobody really noticed or cared.

It was a long time ago; it's almost silly now, thinking about it.

But Mary.

It's flattering, sure — you're out in a crowded place with a bunch of people and there's a pretty girl (hell, a lovely girl) who only ever looks at you, her eyes big wide circles and staring all the time. I got sucked in so fast. It's hard to recognize, hard even to believe, that it might all be for show, or at least that it all might have been done on purpose. When you're a young guy, you never think of a girl standing in front of a mirror, making her eyes open wide like that, practising just in case she might need it. I didn't even realize what was happening.

If nothing else, Mary could make up her mind. It can be a very bad thing, getting yourself hooked up with someone who already knows all the answers, someone who's written your life story complete with all your lines, all of it without even giving you a chance to speak.

I always figured I'd meet up with a Katie or a Linda or a Leslie, something exotic or different, or something, someone with high, sharp cheekbones that scream out "I'm not from here." Not a Mary — not a hard, local, familiar Mary, that serious and religious name, like a stern upper lip and no time for jokes here, buddy.

Seriously — in this town, a Mary?

But the next thing I knew, I was walking her home, the road all bright with the streetlights reflecting in water and that metal smell you notice in the air when it's summer and there's rain.

The houses crowded too close together so it was like they were leaning in to listen to whatever it was we were talking about. She was telling me she had three sisters and a brother, that she lived with her parents in a too-small house where they were all packed in on top of each other, and that she couldn't wait to get away. We passed a hard guy out in front of a red house, and he was watching us and smoking a cigarette right down tight to the filter like he'd never be able to have another. We crossed the street in front of a car stopped at a stop sign, and as soon as we were out of the way, it peeled out fast, accelerator right to the floor and holding it while the tires spun and the back end of the car swung back and forth. Sharp, precise memories, like important points on a map, coordinates, and every time I think about that night, I think about every single one of those things, like the particular order of them is essential for everything that came later, because that was exactly the route for how we got from there to here.

We were in front of her parents' place pretty quickly and then she was in the door and gone. A straightforward night, and I turned my face up toward the sky after she went in, feeling the rain pecking down, sharp, cold drops, not caring one bit about getting wet.

22

Each passing week things just got better.

I kick myself a little now, wondering just how simple a sap I was. She wanted me, and only me. Looking back, I think my mistake was believing that I was the end, rather than just the means.

We'll leave it at that for now.

I'm Walt and she was Mary, and she's somewhere else now.

Good riddance, I guess.

I'm fifty, and I'll admit I'm not in the best shape, a bit of a gut out in front of me for all my sins, which mostly err toward two — gluttony and sloth — if they go anywhere at all. Pretty small sins, all things considered. Only deadly the way gravity is — inevitable and waiting. Not deadly like speed, the way you rush toward that. Not like falling, like sex. I don't have that many sex sins, not just now. Adultery? You've got to still be married for that, and I'm not, even if she keeps coming up in my head at the strangest of times.

My hair's pretty much all grey and I keep it short now because of that, because distinguished looks better than just plain unkempt and old. I've still got all my own teeth — my mother would want you to know that. Teeth were important to her, for some reason. She was the kind of lady who would just grab your chin and twist your mouth open to have a look around, as if she didn't trust a word you said and had to check things out for herself. She took me to the dentist two weeks before Mary and I got married. He finished things up all neat and she paid, like she was washing her hands of me right then and there. Bought me all new underwear, too, ten pairs.

My mother's been dead three years now. She died hard and long, so there's not ever one little bit of doubt in my mind that she's really gone, or that she's better off. Dad's been gone longer, so I hardly even think about him now. But her words still have a way of echoing around inside my head, like she's always going to live there or something. Just another unbidden planet caught in orbit too close to me.

Every couple of days, something my mother said will creep into my thoughts. Sayings were so much a part of her that it sometimes seems to me she was more like a great ball of sayings—all wrapped up on itself like yarn or those thin rubber bands inside a golf ball—than a person.

Maybe that's what we all are—lists of stuff preserved in the memories of other people. Collections of scraps, ordered in our own particular ways.

So, if you want to add me to your list, here I am: a little paunchy, grey, old, flat-footed, and a bad back the next time, every time, I have to shovel wet snow. I'm not hard to get along with. I have a sense of humour—or I think so, anyway. Someone who knows me better would probably have a few memories to kick around, or would remember stuff I said that might have made someone else laugh.

But I don't think I could pick out who that person is anymore—that person who knows me better. You move further and further away from people when you stop even trying to stay close.

Which is hard.

But when you're gone, when you're dead, that's all that will be left of you — the part that lives in other people's heads until they're gone, too. And that's a much smaller package than you really are, like the way your ashes are so much less than your body.

It's not even like you're distilled, like the world ends up left with some essence, some essential you. Memories are more like leftovers — the pieces other people think are worth keeping, at least for a little while.

I'm not sure why I'm going on like this. When I'm the only one talking, I go off on tangents, because there's no one to shut me up with some snide comment or to just haul me back into line.

What I mean is that memories are fine, but things are always better right when they are happening, when they're fresh and sharp and complete and you're wearing them out there on your skin, feeling and smelling and tasting them. Everyone knows that. Leftovers are what's in the fridge after everyone goes home. I guess you get used to them, and make do with what you have.

CHAPTER 5

(St. John's, NL)—The Royal Newfoundland Constabulary (RNC) will
hold a press conference at 11 a.m., Nov. 12, at the Fort Townshend
headquarters to announce a new government policing initiative.
The chief of police will be joined by the minister of justice for the
announcement. Media are requested to be set up by 10:45 a.m. All
media are required to present police-issued identification.

At Maddox Cove, just about as far east as Inspector Dean Hill
could drive and still be on land, the big Atlantic swells rolled
in the fall's sharp sunlight, hiding the white teeth of their
peaks until they were practically upon him.

Standing by the car, he was thinking about leaving his
last job—the one he'd had before the limbo he was caught
in now, the one where he'd run stats for the Major Crimes
Division. Leaving that job had also meant leaving the office
he'd had for so long, the office with the tall tree outside, taking up precisely one-third of the window. The sort of image,
he thought absently, that photographers pointed to when they
talked about the law of threes. He'd liked the work there, the

easy rhythm of crime stats and neighbourhood maps, the patterns that seemed to jump out at him when all the work was right and everything fell into place. He watched the waves, part of his mind pulling up the pattern of building crests, five up and then two falling back, thinking about it without even really thinking about it. It still felt like a loss: he'd come to love the patterns of that job, the way pieces just slipped into order. It didn't help, either, that it had all happened at once: the loss of his job and the loss of his marriage. Julie had come at him out of the blue, a suitcase waiting by the back door even as she was telling him she was leaving, and it wasn't a trial separation either. It was, in her words, "a done deal," though she'd reached up to kiss him on the cheek as he stood there, dumbfounded, by the open back door.

Dean looked at the car—an unmarked beater from the police pool, one of those dark, low-slung Dodges with no hubcaps. The driver's door was open, the keys in the ignition and the warning bell ringing steadily, almost apologetically, against the wind.

Winter ducks, saltwater fish–eating ducks, were lurking along the edge of the foam, bobbing backwards over the crests without seeming to move, escaping before the waves had a chance to break over them.

He heard the radio through the open door of the car—Communications asking why their calls to his cellphone were going straight to voicemail.

"Doing interviews," he said sharply into the microphone, already regretting the weight of the lie. And then they told him to come back in.

He put the microphone in its silver bracket on the dashboard and looked out through the windshield at the water for a little while longer before putting the car into reverse.

Back at the station, an almost dead-eyed senior lawyer from the Department of Justice had explained the new assignment matter-of-factly: "It's you and Sergeant Scoville, and it's nothing sexy like a cold case team or anything. There aren't enough cases to make that worthwhile. Call it a bag of best practices. You'll be devil's advocate on other investigations, picking holes in cases, and you'll fill in the rest of your time looking at old cases that have gone nowhere so that the files stay open. It's just going to be the way it's going to be."

The lawyer stared at him steadily, as if daring him to say anything.

"It's the minister's idea, and it's probably because of something he saw on television some night. And then the chief agreed to it, because, when it's the minister's idea, you just go with it and get some results that will look good in the paper. It's politics, and you're pawns. And the other cops are probably going to hate you, because you'll trample all over their work and they'll think you're just out for the glory."

The minister. The chief. Dean didn't know either of them well — he'd met the chief only a few times — but he did know from experience about police departments and priorities. Stats and profiling had been a priority for a while, and then it wasn't, and that's how he'd lost that office, tree and all.

Dean also knew about how you could measure those priorities simply by looking at the office space you got and the furniture that came with it. And the message he and Scoville were clearly being sent was that they shouldn't expect anything. They had cast-off desks hauled up from the basement of the station instead of the new modular stuff, and those desks were crammed into an office that had previously held one detective and now held two. No windows at all.

"You guys are here because you're supposed to be self-starters. Or you're low maintenance. Or something like that. But don't make any mistakes: your job is to make sure your ties are straight and your jackets buttoned. Stand back there and let the chief and the minister answer the questions. You're not to do any talking."

The lawyer looked at the two detectives as if he didn't expect any talking from them either. And there wasn't any. After he left, Dean looked down to make sure that his tie was, in fact, still straight. He'd heard a similar speech before, back when they'd taken him from Robbery and plunked him down on his own with a computer and a textbook on spreadsheets. He'd been called a self-starter then, too.

It was quiet in the office, the lawyer's words hanging. Dean looked across at Scoville, who had been in arson and who was now here, holding a coffee. Dean watched him stretch his blunt-fingered hands up over his head.

"Low maintenance?" Scoville said. "Mostly that means we won't complain. Been there."

The minister might want results, but Dean had already

decided that the chief couldn't really care less. That's why he and Scoville were on the squad. Dean knew his results from stats had been almost impossible to pin down empirically — and Scoville was a stubborn cop no one ever wanted to work with, not even in Arson, where the work was dirty and cold and endless. A place where Jim Scoville could happily dig around up to his knees in wet charcoal and never have to speak to another living person. Because Scoville didn't like talking — in fact, he didn't seem to like anyone or anything outside the job. Maybe that wasn't completely a bad thing: lately, Dean didn't like talking either.

Dean knew they'd made a team out of two cops who didn't even really want to be in the same room with each other. From the outside, it must've looked like a science experiment — the kind that wouldn't work.

CHAPTER 6

Nov 15—You know how sometimes you'll just stop and be sure there's someone watching you, but you look around and you can't see anyone? I feel like that a lot, and I can't seem to shake it. I don't know. It's unsettling, and I don't like it at all.

Sometimes, I think I catch a glimpse of someone, but I'm not sure. And then when I look around, everyone's just so ordinary. Maybe it's living alone: Daniel's here when he wants to be, but there's a lot of time he's not. When there were three of us in the house, it was a lot of fun, but Heather and Sue got jobs away, and they both wanted out of the lease. I got them to pay a bit to let them out, and I like having the place on my own, but it's right at the edge of what I can afford. I worry about that. But I worry for a lot of reasons. Maybe I'm just being paranoid.

CHAPTER 7

Pasta
pasta sauce
peppers
cucumber
spinach
green onion
tomato
bagels
garlic bread?
chick peas
olives
snacks for work
cream cheese
cheese (cheddar)
milk
diet pepsi

Sometimes, you can just read a list and immediately get the whole picture, not only of what's for dinner, but the whole darned thing, the big ball of wax that's their lives—who they are, what kind of house they live in, what kind of money they make, the little box of a car they drive, even the kind of magazine subscriptions that would show up in the mailbox out front.

Even the little breaks on the list tell you something—those parts where there's a little indecision, some hesitation, like the person's trying to do something just a little bit different but isn't sure they actually should. Those are the parts you work on most, the ones you worry at like a piece of loose thread on the sleeve of your shirt, the ones that offer the best information when you set your mind to decoding them. In any relationship there are unspoken rules, and those critical marks show the lines we're afraid to step over.

That question mark after garlic bread, like someone's trying to decide if it would be too much—or the brackets, just to make sure you don't fuck up and pick the wrong kind of cheese, and someone gives you that face. Sometimes it's the small things that actually complete the story.

I can see her in my head—I know it's a her, and not because of the Diet Pepsi, either. I know because that list was in red ink and because of the wide loops curling down under the *g*'s, just the shape of them, big and full and swinging wide. I know it as well as if I had seen the shopping list laid out flat on the counter with a pen beside it before she went to the store, as if she were going out shopping for me and I looked up from the table and over at her and said, "I guess I know what's for dinner."

I know something else, too: I know I could skim through that list and then go out and fill the cart with a whole bunch of other things, and that I could wheel it up to the front of the store for her and know that every single extra thing I chose would be right.

What the note says for sure: spaghetti for dinner, a side salad, the cheat of pouring the sauce right out of the jar but then bulking up easy and fast with fresh vegetables. Garlic bread from the deli counter, tossed into the oven and pulled out hot like it was a "Good Housekeeping" magic trick or something. Nothing wrong with that, other than the fact that she feels like she has to do it.

I'm sure it's a woman on her way home from a full-time job, already busy enough to be more than pissed off over the fact that she's the only one worrying about dinner. There are little bits worth underlining: almost everything on the list is there to meet someone else's needs. I see it all the time; I can pick out ten women working from lists just like that in the store at any one time. Drink boxes they never drink out of, oven-cooked French fries they don't actually eat because they are afraid of packing on a pound or two, cookies resolutely without nuts to pack in lunches sent to schools with endless allergy rules.

You can see their world if you let your vision go kind of soft: I feel like I'm right there — like I could find my way to their bathroom blindfolded, a bathroom in a house I've never been in.

That's me sitting on the kitchen countertop, watching,

when she gets home. That's the way I imagine it, as if I'm sitting right in the middle of the action and the conflict and the clipped little sentences that married couples start to bat back and forth so sharply, those sentences where only the two of them can hear the weight of the dropped words and the importance of the slipping, downhill intonation. Words flying right over the heads of the youngsters spooling around their legs, kids asking for one more snack because they can't wait even another minute for dinner.

"How was your day?"—but with the sentence dropping down flat at the end so you know the speaker couldn't actually care less about the answer. Drive in a car with those couples on a highway road trip, even without the kids, and the same old lines of conflict are inked in the fact that he wants a chicken sandwich and she wants a place that can at least make good coffee: "I've already had two bad cups of coffee today," like it's a scorecard and she's just plain owed.

You can't top two bad cups of coffee, the acid, roiling nastiness of them, even with a pair of chicken sandwiches, so you fold your hand at the first real coffee place you see. Well, you should fold your hand, but often the stakes don't let you. There's too much riding, for each of you, on being the one to win the hand.

And you're keeping score. It's not easy to admit it when you're looking right at the person you're playing against, but late at night, I'm sure our ceilings all look the same, hovering up there in the dark, and the best you can say is that the counting is quiet and precise, and that the grand totals are underlined every bit as clearly as if a legion of accountants had been at work, making sure the totals are perfectly correct on both sides of the ledger.

Maybe there's a way out of that.

Mary and I never found it.

But I still wonder: maybe if someone's willing to come out of their own little fortress for just a minute or two, take that step or two forward. Maybe be the first one to back down (but not absolutely always the first one to back down, because that's just surrender). Maybe that would be the way.

Looking at the note again, I imagine she's a store regular.

There are so many of those women moving through the store, travelling in their close-held, personal little bee-dance patterns, it's like loose schools of fish, so much the same and yet keeping a distinct and constant distance between each other. As if they can recognize themselves.

Sometimes I think I can only hope that they don't all get together and make a vicious little club — imagine that.

They'd have the same set of frustrations and complaints, they'd be facing the same unfair, uncaring world, and you know it would mean they'd build up on top of each other like a thunder cloud, complaint on complaint like a wobbly tower reaching right up into the stratosphere, coiling around on itself and only growing more intense and unpredictable.

Picking out how the men in their lives had let them down.

Now that's a club where you'd want to avoid being the only invited male guest, let me tell you: women with the corners of their mouths pulled down hard and the lines growing fast enough there for you to know it's an attitude that's quickly becoming permanent, ingrained. I've seen enough of that to know exactly what it means, to know that it doesn't ever run in reverse.

Mary was like that, eight years in — the mouth-turned-down part, I mean.

I think it arrives at the moment when sheer, unstoppable disappointment trumps everything else, trumps it and overwhelms it and buries it in the backyard after killing it with the sharp edge of a shovel.

Because there's a line you cross where the weight of disappointment becomes overwhelming.

A point where it just comes at you from all directions whenever you think about doing anything at all.

I look back and think that it happened fast in our house, faster than it probably should have, just a handful of years in, when married life should either still be a long-running, unrecognized honeymoon or a nest of squalling accidental kids.

Eight years in was when Mary realized The Grand Plan wasn't all it was cracked up to be.

The Grand Plan.

Part One — get out of Rabbittown, preferably married.

Part Two — make just enough appearances with the man to let everyone in the old neighbourhood know just how good you've got it, then hightail it right back out of Rabbittown once you've shown it all off. Even if you don't really have it good at all. Then have kids quick, settle down. For us, Part

Two was where it all hit the rocks.

Part Three—I don't think we ever got close to Part Three.

In fact, I don't think I was ever close enough to make out what Part Three was even supposed to be—and I think that was exactly where the big disappointment came from for Mary.

My gears slipped. And at just the wrong time.

CHAPTER 8

bananas
Butter
Whipping cream
ginger ale

Everything about that list just says "comfort food." Or dessert. Something with a hint of "please rescue me." Sometimes, there's no one coming to the rescue. I see them more often than you'd think, grocery lists that read like life rings. From all kinds of people; I mean, you might expect desperation from some people — tired, worn out, stressed housewives maybe. But it's anyone, really, picking up chips and dip or crackers or instant pizzas. I can look out my front window and anyone walking by might be lugging their own particular safety net home, filling no hole, solving nothing.

Home for me?

McKay Street in east end St. John's, nothing that special, row houses up and down both sides of the street, an older neighbourhood forced to fancy up fast to try and keep up with the house prices. And I don't really have much truck with anyone who lives down here, I have to tell you. I really don't have much time for the effort of being neighbourly. I keep to myself, and the only time I see anyone is when I'm in the backyard, going out the front door, or having a look at the emergency vehicles—police or fire or ambulance—pulling up to someone else's door, someone else unwillingly spilling the details of their private life right out there in front of me all over the pavement.

Out back, there's just a little postage stamp of yard, the remaining scrap of geometry left over when all the ordinary pieces have been cut out of an irregular city block. Everyone else with full rectangles of yard, us, midway through the block but still stuck with the leftovers. The backyard used to be Mary's space—I was in charge of the lawn mowing and the occasional large fallen tree limb, but she did the flower beds and planted the tall currants that still stand all along the fence in the back, idiot red repeating berries that come back every year and shrivel away into tight little knots when no one picks them but the birds. Gardens: there's a little bit of the resurrection in the whole thing, right? Every time the poppies rip open red in the early summer, or in the fall when the dead-heads of the old flowers are standing around waiting to be knocked flat by the snow, I think of her out there with the dirt on her hands and on her knees.

That was a sight, for sure, Mary rising up from the edge of the garden and the soil and coming toward me. I don't know—she had a way of just letting whatever was in her hands fall, forgotten, arms limp as if they didn't matter at all, and I never knew, would never know, whether that was device, design, or the way she really felt. But it would shake its way right into me, every time. Take my breath literally away.

She'd look straight at me, raising herself up from the dirt, and it made me feel like there wasn't another single thing in the world that mattered to her.

She shed things, and walk straight toward me, the only man in the entire universe.

There are a lot of things I may have forgotten, but I haven't forgotten that.

And the yard? I may be trying hard to forget all about it, but it certainly hasn't forgotten Mary.

Flowers have a way of setting their roots into you. A couple of years might go by when I don't see anything at all out in the yard except the poppies, and then a spindly little columbine, some refugee from one of Mary's constant past plantings, will shoot up and open its flowers like a bunch of staring eyes and rude little mouths, and it will drive me right out of the yard all over again. Can't even stand to look at them, like they're accusing me of something.

Big maples throw their branches in over the sides of that yard like great open hands with far too many fingers—there is not one single maple tree in my yard, but the shade from their crowns cuts over the fence in semicircles onto the grass in half a dozen places. Every one of my neighbours has one, and year after year, their offspring try to set up shop in my yard as well. Every spring, it's a regiment of brave little stupid maples lifting their heads up above the grass, reaching always up, those two blunt little seed-leaves first, and then the pair of unfurling flags they wave to prove they are maples, after all. And every year, I mow them down, one clean sweep from house to fence and back again and they're done, no second chances until next year's brigade comes ashore.

There's a clothesline that reaches from the corner of my house just into the neighbour's yard, attached with an old hook to the trunk of the maple nearest to our property line, and I don't think I've ever hung anything on that line at all. But that line of string is the closest thing I get to owning one of those big trees—Mary convinced our neighbour to let us tie the clothesline to the hook. The hook predated us, rusty and beckoning.

You don't see maple trees like that in this city much. Not big like these.

Neighbours? Down at the end of the yard is one neighbour with two cats that piss right on my back door and manage to look insolent even when I catch them in the act. Then there are the neighbours on either side, the guy on the left with the dogs that still bark at me even though they've seen me out there in the yard for at least five years, and the couple on the right who bought one of those outdoor fireplaces that make you keep the windows closed at night in summer or lay there choking on someone else's smoke right in your own bedroom. You can call the city to complain, but really, where's that going to end up? I'll tell you where — in the kind of bad feeling that never fades.

I wave to them all, I make involved small talk about the weather if I'm forced to, and if they have something more on their minds, I find someplace else I suddenly have to be. The bare edge of politeness is what I've got, if I'm pushed to it, because there's not really much margin in it for me now.

I'm sure they get along much better with each other than they do with me — I see them sometimes, talking to each other over the fence and across the no man's land of my yard, and they always seem more animated, more interested, than they ever do when they're talking to me.

Like most things, that's probably a two-way street, the kind I'm just not all that used to driving on. Sometimes, I look outside at them and tell myself that I should try harder — that I should go out and listen to whatever it is they're talking about, that I should at least try to work up some interest. But I can't find the energy I'd need.

I like it better inside, upstairs, looking down on the street as people go by. They don't look up; they never look up.

The front room upstairs, I call it the study. It's a fancy name, but really it's just another bedroom. It faces right out on the street, no front yard or anything, just the sidewalk, and I'm sure it would be hard to sleep in there with the noise, especially since they changed the bus routes around and now I've got an express downtown going right by the front door every twenty minutes or so. I mean, they start at seven and sometimes I like to sleep a little later than that. I might not have gotten off work until five on the overnight swing—hell, I might not have gotten home from walking around the city until seven, so the buses would be coming on full service just as I was getting into bed.

We mix shifts at work. Sometimes I'm on during the day for the simple cleanups: the bottles of olives that get dropped and the toddler who throws up all over a cart—and there's always the trash bins and all of that, the stuff out back that people don't ever think about. The crushed boxes for the dumpster, the garbage to be hauled out into the loading bay for the truck that swings through pretty much daily.

Other times, I get overnight shifts for the big wall-to-wall cleans and the regular weekend Sunday night floor waxing, squiring around the big buffing machine that brings the floor up with a gloss you're never going to get with anything else. The whole store empty and just as well because you can't hear anything anyway, and you don't want to think about what it would be like if someone just came up behind you and tapped you on the shoulder or something. The vibrations from the buffer go spinning right up through my arms and settle there so that even hours later it still feels like I'm guiding the thing around. If I were to go home and fall straight asleep, I know I'd dream about waxing. Flipping the extension cord over at the end of every sweep—if I do it right, I can make a big long loop roll slowly over all the way down the aisle, like a Wild West cowboy completely in control of his rope.

I've always been comfortable in my job. I don't think it's

a dead end or anything—even if that's the way Mary thought about it sometimes.

I got fed up with school early, that's all, even though I still read plenty and they told me all through I was smart enough to keep going. That was back when the schools used to do testing and tell you afterwards that you had "potential." But I wasn't looking for potential. I just found someplace where I like what I do—because I actually do something. You can measure it, even if, just about the time you get everything finished, the whole place clean, it's time to start all over again.

I don't push paper around for someone else. I'm not yakking on the phone about the price of silver, or stomping around in court, trying to keep the next shoplifter from getting a criminal record.

I'm not spending hours convincing anyone they've just got to buy this thing—something it turns out they don't need or want at all. I did that for a while and it was hell.

No, I keep one place clean, and it's got to be clean, so it is. It's hard, heavy work sometimes, but I'm fine with that. Nothing wrong with hard work, with the way it leaves your muscles stretched right out, ropey and tingling at the end of a long shift. I'm fine with going in the front doors of the store and having the place smell exactly like it's supposed to, with coming into the back where my cart is and finding every single thing in its right place, right there at my fingertips, waiting for me. The same, every single time.

I get to go through the day, my day, every day, and then I go home, and the phone never rings and they don't call me back in. If there are extra shifts, they ask me if I want them ahead of time — sometimes I say yes, and sometimes I say no.

I'm fine with all of it.

I wash my hands of everything the very minute I step out the door.

End of story.

CHAPTER 9

Nov. 21 — I walked back from the grocery store, because it was one of those fall days where it's wet but it's all warm, too, like the rain's brought the warm air back into town and just left it lying over the city. The rain had stopped and the sidewalk was all covered with wet maple leaves — a kind of throw-back to earlier in fall, and I had a bag of groceries in each hand, swinging them like I was a kid or something, and I looked back down the street over my shoulder, and there was a guy behind me, way back — like nine or ten houses back — just a round-shouldered little guy in a dark jacket, but it was like I could see his eyes, like they were fixed right on me or something. And I know he caught me looking, because even from that far away I saw him tuck his chin down against his chest, and then he turned up a walk to a house and reached up for the mailbox. Then he walked back to the street and away from me, but I took a laneway in the complete opposite direction from my place and waited right on the corner to see if he turned up, but he didn't. I spent the whole evening thinking about it, wondering if there was anything I could pick out to describe him, anything that I could tell someone about how he looked, and there really wasn't anything. But I think I'd know the shape of him if I saw him again.

CHAPTER 10

Starlae
Potatoes
Milk
Meat
Cat
Beans
Bread
Cheese
Fish
Cake
Candy
Pie

The first grocery list I found and actually kept? July 24, 1961.
Well, it was dated 1961, anyway.

It came out of a book I found on a sale table years ago, and
the list is almost as old as I am. It's actually on the back of the
library card, the dates nice and clear there from someone's effort
with a hand stamp. And, yes, I know that *starlae* isn't a word.

I've looked at it a hundred times if I've looked at it once, and that's the closest I can come to making out what it says. Maybe it's a trade name for something, and if I were old enough, maybe I'd recognize it right away — the right parts of the word in the right places to make it coalesce into meaning something. Klik is still on the shelves, just another luncheon meat in a can with a key — but drop that word with half of St. John's and they can taste that pink potted meat, feel the mealiness of it on their tongue like they've just taken a bite out of their lunch sandwich at school. Chances are, they'll remember wanting to trade it for something else, too.

I still take that list out every once in a while, just to see if the penny will drop, just to see whether or not starlae might finally come to me, as if the letters might come into focus in a way they never have before.

The rest of it just stares me in the face — the same old things, the same things I might even buy. The paper's browning now, but the best part is the handwriting, the way the words stack up right over each other, but every word is so clearly, carefully, exactly the same script as the one above it. Four capital Cs, two Bs, two Ps. And each one the absolute exact mirror of its fellow. Cursive — I don't know for sure if that's the right word, but it sounds right. It sounds old enough.

People don't write like that anymore. They just don't have the skills hammered into them the way they used to — they don't build up that same muscle memory any more, the results of the forced effort of making the same letters over and over again in a handwriting primer with some Christian brother at the end of the aisle, Brother John or Brother Jim with a big ruler to swing at you when you did it wrong or you went too slow. People now probably wouldn't even know what a script book was anymore, even if you put it right there in front of them. They'd look at those strange sets of lines and ask if they were expected to be composing music or something.

That's something that comes over me more often now, a feeling like I'm straddling too much stuff all at once. More to the point, that I'm straddling too many years.

I'll be looking at one single thing, and the next thing you know, I've got it all tied up with a whole bunch of other stuff—memories and experience and the things I don't feel like ever telling anyone—and, all at once, it's just too exhausting to keep thinking about.

The lists are part of it. There are so many now. It's been too many years, with too little of me spread across them really thin, so thin that I'm almost transparent. I'm stretched right out, trying to hang on to everything I can't let go of.

It should all be useful, it should be of value to someone. All that information. All the stuff I know.

Because it's not only my teeth that I've still got—I've got my hearing, too, and it's perfectly good hearing—not that it would have to be for me to hear them.

I mean, I can be standing right next to someone, standing right there, and as long as I'm working, wearing the dark blue overalls with my first name on the patch on the front—an oval with *Walt* in a stupid fancy script I never would have chosen—they'll be completely oblivious.

There's something about being staff that just makes you invisible, at least until they need you. There's something about being cleaning staff that's even worse. Like I'm deaf or maybe stupid. And I can tell you one thing—I'm not stupid.

It's the same with the cashiers; they're not even two feet away from you as they push the groceries across the scanner, but people will still stand right in front of them talking about all kinds of stuff or fighting with whoever's in the store with them. And it's like you're not supposed to hear any of it, much less take it back to the break room so you can share it with each other and have a really good laugh. You wouldn't believe half the things the cashiers know.

And people just spill it out, none the wiser. The conveyor belt between you isn't soundproofed. It's like people chattering away on their cellphones, spilling out all kinds of personal information for anyone who wants to listen. Anyone like me.

I think you should only spread stuff around if you want to share it, if you trust someone with it.

There's not all that much I'm willing to share.

I grew up downtown, right in the centre of St. John's, in one of those row house neighbourhoods where you know all your neighbours' business real well because you share a wall with them and their life is pressed right up tight against yours. I lived on Bond, a long, narrow street that runs parallel with the waterfront, on a block where all of our backyards were framed in by other houses. When I looked down on them from my bedroom up on the second storey at night, it was like a walled courtyard—wooden houses, cheek by jowl with each other, all hoarding those small backyards. Two or three trees down in there, the crowns up higher than the roofs on the downhill side of the block, their branches matte black against the twilight sky. When I was lying there on my back, waiting for sleep, it didn't matter whose yard the trunks actually stood in; it was like the trees belonged to every house on that block.

There are people who spend a lot of time and effort blaming their parents for who they are, and maybe they have a point: "Look how fucked up I am, but it's only because they were so fucked up first."

I don't subscribe to that particular theory. My dad drove truck, my mother was a housewife, I had two brothers and, in age, I was stuck right in the middle.

Robert and Allen. Robert's a linguistics professor in western Ontario and Allen's got a heavy-equipment business in northern Alberta. Dad died first, right at retirement, out in the backyard with a gardening fork stuck into the ground next to the great big spread of his rhubarb, shut down in barely a blink of an eye by a myocardial infarction. Mom died three years later, three lonely, needy years later, and everyone else was off on the tenure track or whatever, except for me.

Walt, well, Walt was a grocery store janitor and of course he was home, even if he was the disappointment of the three. The disappointment, even though I was the one who drove over to shovel the snow. I was the one who kept track of the medical appointments and took Mom in the car to see the doctor. I was the one who had to juggle shifts and bring over groceries and finally clean up all kinds of shit, literal and otherwise. I should have been prepared for that.

I was just a janitor, after all.

And I wasn't even the executor.

Allen was.

CHAPTER 11

(St. John's, NL)—The Royal Newfoundland Constabulary (RNC) is seeking the assistance of the general public in their investigation of a criminal trespass in the west end of St. John's. The RNC is looking for witnesses who may have seen a male suspect in the Cowan Heights area, especially in the area of the linear park, on Saturday, Dec. 14. Anyone with information on the alleged trespasser is asked to contact the RNC at 729-8000 or Crime Stoppers at 1-800-222-TIPS (8477).

"Now they're giving us peeping Toms? What's next? Lost snot-noses from the mall?" Scoville was more upset that Dean had ever seen him, twitching behind his desk near the wall like an angry little bantam chicken.

"This keeps up, and we'll end up with every jumped-up teenaged girl with a job downtown and an attitude, and every single time one of them decides not to come home at night, we'll have her mother on the phone wondering why we haven't found precious little Bethany yet. They're all dumping their shit on us, Dean, and I bet they're having a good laugh about it, too."

Dean didn't disagree. But he also couldn't always find the energy to care. The new job was mostly time in the files with Scoville, and Dean wasn't sure he was ever going to like the guy. Sitting in the office with him, Dean thought, was like sitting particularly close to a small, angry, pot-bellied wood stove. It was hours of flipping through files and hearing the other officer sighing, pushing his chair back, sometimes muttering under his breath.

About three times a day, Scoville said he had liked arson investigation better : "You drive your own bus, and fires are public, so there's always enough pressure to keep you sharp."

"I wouldn't mind so much if the cases were bigger — or if we could take more time with them. I could spend a month just on that Mary Carter file and that Walt guy. Dig into the whole thing, just the way it gets under you skin," Dean said. "A woman missing, enough question marks about her husband and the whole investigation to keep it on the front burner. But it's not like we're ever going to get the chance."

There was no direct pressure in their office, but there was the continuing pile of cases sloughed off from all over the building. After the first press conference, they hadn't heard a single word from upstairs. Scoville had put a sign up over his desk, magic marker on white paper: "The Mushroom Patrol."

"Aren't you afraid of someone seeing it?" Dean asked.

"If someone important were to actually come down here, I'd be afraid already," Scoville said.

Even when they managed to get out of the office it was just to follow old tracks: redoing interviews, hoping that the latest talk with a witness or a family member would jar something loose, something that they hadn't coughed up in all those other interviews. Often, the interviewees were disinterested or downright dismissive. Dean had already heard "it was a long time ago" more times than he could count.

It was hard to even find the energy to come into work.

Some mornings, Dean would lay on his back in bed, look at the ceiling, and believe there really was no good reason to get up. Nothing would be challenging or different—it would all be the same.

Because things would be where they always were. Every piece of the house was still in exactly the same place she had left it. Dishes in the cupboard, pictures on the wall. Same bookcase, same blankets, same wall. Waking up was just falling right back into the same old order—except, at the same time, it wasn't.

Because everything had changed. Subtly, but absolutely undeniably.

Julie had briefly held both sides of his face with her hands when she told him she was leaving, and all he could think about was the feel of those hands.

"This is the part where you do something, Dean," she said. "This is the part where you at least say something. Anything. You just fucking speak."

But he didn't. He could feel every single thing about her hands, the warmth, the familiar touch, where each finger rested. But he couldn't find a single thing to say, couldn't find a way to push the words out.

She'd taken her hands away — cool air on his face — and she was gone.

Dean was full of words, packed tight, but he said nothing.

It wasn't that Julie had caught him with another woman, or that he'd caught her with someone else. It was slower than that, each step more deliberate and somehow harder to avoid — it wasn't a simple big mistake. Part of it had been the way he liked police work, spent more and more time at it. The way she'd ask him to change one thing about his routine — if he could come home earlier for once, if he could take a break so they could share lunch — and how nothing could ever change, not without Dean being out of sorts and almost confused.

It was also the fact they'd bought a place out of town, miles from everywhere, and Julie needed more than just trees outside and one tired cop to talk to in the evening. It was that she had quit her job to work at home, and while the work she was doing was great, it was lonely, too.

Dean thought that, in retrospect, he should have been able to see every one of those things, see how they would pile up and weigh them both down — years analyzing evidence and statistics, building charts — but still he hadn't seen any of it coming, and also couldn't find one single spot where either of them might have taken even one step differently.

Compelled to what was, looking back, an obvious end.

So Dean would drag himself out of bed and get dressed to head downtown to work. And at least that still made sense for a little while, until the quiet of the office felt like it was hemming him in completely.

Then he'd sign out a car, any car, leave Scoville right there at his desk, and drive around the city, sometimes unable to even figure out afterwards exactly where he had been.

Drinking coffee, tucked away along the back edge of a high school parking lot.

On a side road out near the dump.

Sometimes not back to the headquarters building until it was fully dark and Scoville was long gone. Never wanting to drive home to that empty house. Knowing full well that it was only a matter of time until someone higher up noticed and everything else came unstitched, too.

There were times when Dean felt completely outside his own skin—as if the things happening around him had no connection to him at all.

And not sleeping. It was like he didn't know how to sleep any more, listening to the house creak and settle in the cool of the night, sure that she was about to call and willing himself not to answer it. Wondering if he would be able to resist. Then up in the morning, exhausted. For the first time thinking that maybe being an ex-cop wouldn't be a bad thing either.

CHAPTER 12

2 hair dye — Golden Blond
soap
bus pass
diapers

A small white note, short, half open like it was a wrinkled little butterfly trying to skip over the lip and escape from one of the produce displays, pushing its papery wings out into the warmer air so it could fly away.

I didn't see where the note came from. I didn't see her.

I wished I had. As soon as I read it, I wanted to go through the store and track her down, spot that hair, and go straight up to her, if only just to tell her it would be all right. And maybe it wouldn't be all right at all. But I really wanted to tell her that it would be.

Because — this is stupid, but it's true — that's the kind of note that makes you want to be behind her with your arms out, ready to catch, makes you say, "I've got you," right up close into her ear, a note that's almost a cry out loud right there in front of the iceberg and the romaine and the leeks, the kind of cry someone makes just when they realize they can't help falling.

I'm surprised I found it at all, because I always try to move fast in produce — the produce guys are out there in the rows almost full-time. There's broccoli to stack and throw crushed ice onto, and three colours of bell peppers to pull out of those strange heavily waxed cardboard boxes. Apples and pears to arrange in ranks like fruit platoons. Lots of rituals to take care of, and those produce guys guard their turf carefully, like you don't really have any right to be hanging around there, because the produce is for them and the customers only, and "isn't someone calling for a cleanup in aisle eight? Just move along."

Only the meat section is worse — they're the closest thing there is to a grocery cult. Meat is the place where they look straight into your eyes and know you can't ever be counted on to clean anything right, even if cleaning is your full-time job. Because you can never, ever hope to clean well enough to measure up to the standards they set.

The meat guys, they take care of their own stuff. Their own racks, their own knives, their own small acreage of tiled walls and floors that you sometimes catch them washing within an inch of their lives. Lots of soap, disinfectant, and some kind of sanitary religion that involves extremely hot water, big boots, heavy rubber hoses, and the kind of water pressure that makes you want to bend a loop of the hose into your shoulder like you were a firefighter or something.

They're the only ones who wear white, and also the only ones allowed to wear stuff with stains on it, too, like each stain was some kind of badge or something.

It's an almost universal attitude for them, even if the meat comes in pre-cut now and they're just slapping it onto the Styrofoam trays and shrink-wrapping it. Seriously, that's something a monkey could be trained to do. But they call themselves butchers, even if that only means they know what a pork chop looks like without a label on the shrink-wrap plastic to tell them.

Don't believe me? Just look at that stupid spinning metal bucket-cart they always bring the meat in when they're shelving it — nothing like it anywhere else in the store, and the darned thing's probably specially designed, and most likely costs a mint. All to haul pre-packaged meat. To shelves. It could be a fucking wheelbarrow.

But back to that note.

Heartbreaking.

It was just a crumpled little piece of white paper, and you had to imagine that it was pulled out of a deep pocket where it had been stuffed, eight spare words in all, and you could draw the scene up in front of you as solidly as if it had been etched on stone. Down in the bottom of a winter-coat pocket, probably with a damp ball of Kleenex and a half-used tube of ChapStick.

Yes, I would have liked to have been able to find her.

And, yes, it had to be a her — men don't ever have that kind of list, never anything close to that desperate, even if their wives are bringing in a list like that on every single trip.

I picture her with a kid stuck there on one hip and a fold-able stroller out in front with a smaller baby stuffed down in it—no cart, because the list's so short. Or maybe she's with one of those staggering, newly walking toddlers, falsely independent and casting out in front of her, one of those toddlers with the bulky square-diapered butts stuck out behind them and that dazed aura like they're always about to fall down and still can't quite believe it could actually happen.

And when they do fall, they've got a face on them like they've suddenly lost every single scrap of faith they ever had in the whole entire world.

Mom walking behind them in that exhaustion haze that means she absolutely needs a list, even though she really only needs five things—so few she could count them on the fingers of a single hand.

Tired enough that she doesn't even know, isn't really sure, that she even has hands any more.

I've seen them leave kids in those seats in the carts and walk completely away into other aisles, the abandoned youngster shrieking until their mom realizes they've been left behind. Other kids being pushed around the store while they're half-leaning out of the carts with the plastic-clip safety belts not even done up, and you can imagine them going just that little bit too far, the physics already pointing their heads right straight for the floor. Moms with a half-drawn, half-resigned expression that suggests that a fall might not be entirely a bad thing.

Women with their coats half opened or buttoned wrong, maybe a button missed or just plain missing. In a rush to get everything done and to get to the bus stop out front before the Number 2 hauls away without them. If they don't make it, it's another critical fifteen minutes before the next bus pulls up. And that fifteen minutes might be the difference between a calm child and neutron-bomb, ballistically tired, screaming two-year-old.

Every time it happens, I think maybe I could be a help — if nothing more than to try and give her a little smile when the whole thing's starting to come unhitched.

Things come unhitched. You see that if you can see past how annoyed it makes you that someone else's kid is having a meltdown.

I held that note in my hand, right up against the handle of my cart, and I couldn't stop thinking that I could do something if I could find her.

Golden Blond, with at least one kid in tow behind her or out in front.

Mary said she wanted kids, and I guess I did, too. Said it, I mean — I said I wanted kids, because that was one of those questions that just popped up once when we were on an early date, and it had all the immediate gravity of an absolute deal-breaker.

"Do you want kids?"

"Do you want to get married?"

Those definite questions, those imperatives that make the

hair stand up on the back of your neck, make you founder and wonder, even when they come out innocent and sudden-like: "Do you like strawberries?" or "Have you ever had a cat?"

I don't think I stopped to even consider what it was I was saying when I first said it —the whole thing seemed so incredibly foreign. Of course I wanted kids—globally, I meant. Not like next Thursday or something.

But once you've said it—at least, once you've said it to Mary—well, the discussion is over. You don't get a chance to go back.

Sometimes, I think I said I did because she wanted them so much.

Or else because it's the kind of thing that you're supposed to say when you're a couple.

Children are the kind of thing that you are supposed to want, and she did. She wanted them like they had always been a necessary part of that list, that important list that she kept close and that I was never allowed to see. I think she had the number of kids she wanted and the sex and the names and everything else all picked out and stashed away. Thinking back, I'm absolutely sure she did, that she had them all drawn up already, sketched out right through high school and college and all the way to them having her grandkids, and all I had to do was my part.

I've wondered since if it would have made a difference if we had actually had them—if they would have acted like some kind of carbon shield for the impending explosion, if they would have been capable of knocking down those scattering, tumour-causing gamma rays of temper before they managed to do the real deep genetic damage you can never recover from.

It's hard to imagine, that those invisible rays zing right through you, doing nothing until that random moment when they knock some strut or guy-wire off a critical bit of DNA in just one cell — and they're not even there any more, because they're still winging off through the universe without ever being seen or heard or even felt. Uncaring. You should get to feel them, really you should, like some pinprick or shiver or splinter or something — at least you should get to feel the ones that end up changing everything, that end up *mattering*.

Other times, I've wondered if it would have been fair to bring kids into that, to have them caught there between Mary's hammer and my anvil.

Mostly, though, when I look at it square on, I think that maybe we should have tried. Or tried harder. Or I should have tried harder. As if, because we didn't, we ended up missing something, as if there was something worth looking for that we didn't try hard enough to find.

I didn't find Golden Blond in the end, not that time, not in the store or outside — outside, where I even held her note there under my nose like I was a bloodhound or something, like there was some way to catch a scent from it and track her tired footsteps across a hundred yards of rough-grained concrete sidewalk.

But all the note smelled like was damp, the way damp paper smells when you've been clenching it too tightly in your hand; the way you hold on to something you depend on. At least until it fails you completely.

CHAPTER 13

Dec. 17 — Daniel won a trip to a Mexican resort, on raffle tickets he kind of had to buy because his boss was selling them. And the trip's going to be such a relief. It will be nice to be away from here for a while. I can't put my finger on why I'm so creeped out — I keep catching myself looking around, like I'm in a movie, not noticing that someone's following me or something. I spin around and there's next to no one, maybe someone walking in the same direction on the other side of the street. And the curtains? I used to pull them closed, sure, but now I feel like I have to make certain every scrap of glass is covered. Even if I can't see anyone, it's like there's someone back out of sight, watching me. I haven't seen anyone, not for sure — although there was one night when I was convinced I could see someone out near the back fence from my bedroom window, convinced enough to call Daniel. He came over and he said there was no sign of anyone there — and sometimes I feel like maybe it's something that I'm putting together out of nothing. One thing's for sure: I don't like this at all, and Daniel's still making fun of me, asking me if I saw the paparazzi lining up outside the windows for a candid shot of my tits. He thinks it's a joke. I don't. Got in a big fight because the cat food was put back in the wrong cupboard — I must have done it because Daniel says he didn't touch it, but I opened the cupboard where the ironing board was and Bo's food was in it, and I don't know why, but it just sent a chill through me. And then I had it all worked out that Daniel had moved it, until he said he didn't.

CHAPTER 14

Carrots (Organic? Baby)
Cantalopes
Apples (Macintosh)
Cucumbers
Cabbage
Rice Crackers
Granola Bars
Onions
Cheese
Organic Yogurt + Plain
Cereal From Organic Isle
Eggs
Hummous
Bread

The note itself wasn't that important. All of it in pencil letters on the back of a piece of junk mail from her member of Parliament—the envelope not even opened. I held it up to the light, used scissors to clip off the very end of the envelope, a thread of paper so fine that it curved into a curl as I cut it. Like a fingernail, the kind of sliver of something that they'd slip into an evidence bag on a television crime show. Inside the envelope, an NDP pamphlet on "Putting your pension first." On the outside, her name and street address. And I knew exactly where the street was.

I spend a lot of time walking around the city. I always have, even though St. John's isn't really a city that's made for walking. I don't mean because of the hills either—I can handle the hills, I'm used to them, hardly even notice them most of the time. If you're not going up a hill, you're going down one. No, it's the winter, and the drivers, that make the walking hard. If you're out on the street in the winter, you're mostly on your own, a single little hunched soldier moving pretty much unnoticed and low through a sleeping enemy encampment. The cars whizz by and hardly even check their speeds, so you're a momentary headlight silhouette and nothing more—there for a flicker and then gone. I've been walking for years, and no one I know has ever mentioned seeing me.

As soon as there's snow, the streets are all narrowed down—hemmed in by the snowbanks, the sidewalks completely covered—and the weather freezes and thaws so regularly that there's often slush and puddles just waiting for a car to fling them all over you, if you're not slipping on ice as you try to get out of the way. You have to be ready for it, have to be on your guard. For the slush. For the cars themselves. For the occasional car mirror that plucks at your sleeve when

someone cuts by too close. I think that's a good way to live—
to be on your guard. To always be ready.

You hear that all the time now, especially about things
like credit card numbers and the Internet and everything.
Personal information, everything out there spinning around
and eventually falling into the wrong hands. Like there's a
blizzard of information, drifts of it just waiting for people
who are up to no good to come out and shovel through. But
it doesn't matter how many times you hear it: it's really nothing new. People have always gone around shedding private
information like they shed dead skin cells—constantly, and
without even noticing. A piece here, a piece there—if you're
dedicated about it, about collecting things, it really doesn't
take very long to start putting the puzzle of a person's private
life together.

Turn on the radio now and there's bound to be someone
earnest on, talking about the way someone can use the things
you type into your computer.

But people don't listen: that's the fact of it, people don't
listen at all. Never have. They go around in a fog all the time.
Maybe they are worried about typing their credit card numbers into their computers—maybe they are—but they're
just downright sloppy about everything else.

I've got grocery lists that people have written on the backs
of cancelled checks, the other side listing everything from their
home address to their bank account number. Several times, lists
jotted down on bank statements, and you can find out everything from how much the electric bill was to what the bank was

pulling out for the mortgage. Doesn't matter what it's on—you're at the cash and you're thinking about paying for your groceries and whether to put them all into the cart or whether they're light enough that you can carry them, and you're dropping that list right there in the handy wastepaper basket that's right by the cashier, the one with the brand new black plastic bag lining the bottom. Or else you're leaving it in the cart. And out the door without as much as another thought. That garbage bag I just emptied, and that I'm about to empty again.

I try to read between the lines on a list, and sometimes I just want to go and see how close I am to actually getting it right—I mean, I draw them up in my head right down to the colour of their hair, their size, their shape, their mannerisms. What they like to wear. How many people live in the house. It's half game, half hobby. Maybe even a little bit of compulsion. But you'd be surprised how often it turns out that I've gotten it almost exactly right—a few little things off, maybe, but all the broad strokes in the right places.

In summer, you can just follow someone out the door on your break, find out where they call home, come back later. Real simple, just foot leather and patience. But that's not the easiest way to do it: if someone's going to just offer you up an address, you can head out any time.

First time I did that, Mary was safely off with her friends at a downtown darts tournament, and I took the list written on the parliamentary mailer.

On the front, her name and an east-end address up on Signal Hill Road.

In a little row of houses, it was the yellow one, the number on the front in enamelled tiles. I've just got brass numbers from the hardware store screwed tight onto the front of the house, and that's certainly fancy enough for the mailman to find you.

I remember that night was a crisp one in February, bitter cold, the stars you could see against the flat glow of the streetlights as hard and bright as bits of glass. I was bundled up good, insulated boots and a heavy coat, watch cap pulled right down over my ears. It was solidly on the freeze side of the freeze-and-thaw cycle; the snow had been knocked back a few days earlier, but what was left was all frozen over, so that everything had its own new and imposed topography. Hard-ridged plains, rises and falls of white ice, the snow that remained as patterned and hard as the meringues you can buy already made in the baking aisle and fill with your own fruit.

I walked fast, my breath shooting out ahead of me in clouds, my chin tucked down and in away from the cold. I didn't have to bring the envelope, because I had the name and address memorized. I could already picture the neighbourhood. Three streets up from McKay, seven blocks in total, a turn to the left and up the hill, right side of the street, counting up the odd numbers as I went.

I walked right past it the first time on purpose, a steady pace like there was somewhere up the hill that I was supposed to be, trying to mimic the quick sideways glance of the only-slightly-interested as I hurried past her house, trying to hold what I saw on the inside, trying to make it appear like an image rising up on photographic paper.

You could see into the little living room through the front windows, and it was one of those busy little rooms; it looked like she fretted over it a lot—plants on the mantel, a couple of small lamps. A big spider fern in the corner, up on a high table, spilling out all over and about to be large enough to be called messy, a few spider strands already shooting out and away like lifeboats leaving an obviously sinking ship. A square mirror right up over the mantel. I could picture it catching her eye every time she went into the room, her right hand coming up to fix her hair. Curly hair, and that means there's always something, a stray curl or two, to push back in place. That's what I mean: I didn't have anything more than the envelope then, and I already was sure she had curly hair, like that information was hidden in the curve and bend of her script. The whole room full and fussy, but also neat, like every complex place where something sat was both important to her and carefully planned out. All the lights on, like she might be expecting someone. Everything in place. Waiting.

Then I was walking past the glass front door, glimpsing the long hallway heading back to the kitchen, the stairs on the left-hand side, right up against the side wall. Black banister, white balusters, no stair runner, white stair fronts with black tops. Lights on in the hallway, hardwood floor.

I didn't see her from the front of the house at all.

Only one name on the envelope, and the thing about those MP mail-outs is that they fire them like a shotgun—they like to get every single voter, and the NDP always save paper and put all of the names in the household on the same envelope. It's so environmentally conscious that it almost hurts. And whoever gets to the mailbox first gets to be the one who opens it and lets all that righteous intensity pour out on the floor — because "look, it's addressed to me."

I get them now, still addressed to me and to Mary Carter. I burn them.

The fact is that you can only walk by a place a couple of times before you start looking obvious, the neighbours fretting with their curtains at just the right time and deciding that you're looking for a place to rob or something.

People can go from completely oblivious to neighbourhood sentries in the blink of an eye — that's what it is to be in a city with a healthy dose of small town still right there at the core. So I went up the hill and then down again, and then up the hill toward the big hotel. Really works your legs; you can feel the heat in the fronts of your thighs growing with every step.

There's a street that goes right underneath the hotel, a street running out over and down from Signal Hill Road. I don't even know its name, but it curves around for maybe two blocks and joins up with a road back down to the harbour. So short it's hardly worth its own name, although I'm sure it has one.

On the lower corner, anchoring the corner, really, is a big house. It's one of those old St. John's piles that was really nice once — when you had groundskeepers and a housemaid or two — but the kind of place that now always needs more work than the present owners can afford and that still has all the land it started with back when land was pretty much free for the taking.

This one, the yard's the thing they've been trying to save money on, so it's not like the fence is in good shape or the lawn is the kind of manicured grass that stays all lit up with outside lights or anything. That meant a big dark patch of ground up over the back of the yellow house I was interested in, the ground tucked in under a grove of mature trees. And the good thing about that frozen hard ground? Even though it made a bit of noise if you stepped on the wrong place, you could pretty much make your way in under the trees without leaving a mark.

I found a smooth grey maple right in there away from the road and just sort of settled back against it, still on my feet but with my legs folded under and my back square against the trunk, up high and looking down over the back of her house. In a lot of St. John's houses, especially in the older row houses, the layout is exactly the same.

Crouched down there in the snow, my ass inches from the frozen ground, I had an unimpeded view of the back of the house—an even better view of the neighbour's, but I wasn't interested in the neighbours. I'd find out later that the sight-lines weren't the same in summer. The branches that were up out of the way without leaves in February filled right in and dragged down into sight when the maples came out in spring, and it was like a curtain dropped over the backs of the whole row of houses.

Like me, she had the bedroom on the back for herself, maybe for the same reason as me: Signal Hill Road can be pretty busy, too, lots of traffic heading up the hill at all hours — everything from buses hauling daytime sightseers to late-night teenagers revving their way up the hill for impatient and cramped car sex — and the vehicles need the same kind of extra push to get up the incline that your legs do.

I knew the rooms I was looking at right away: kitchen, bathroom, back bedroom. A lot of places in St. John's, the bathroom's out on the front, but for simplicity's sake, it's always on one of the corners. Cheaper to have all of your plumbing aligned vertically. Fewer pipes, fewer pipe chases. About seven o'clock at night, good and dark in February, and she was moving back and forth through the kitchen at first, that sort of distracted fridge-to-stove-to-sink thing that everyone does when they're cooking half-heartedly and not really thinking about what they're doing. Over to the fridge to get one thing, back to where the stove must be, back to the fridge for another. A lot of wasted movement, but a better chance for me to see what she looked like, to see how she moved.

She was a small woman, almost thin, and with curly brown hair (I saw that and felt the way you do when you're watching a game on TV and your hockey team scores a goal). I already knew her name was Joy, Joy Martin. Nicely built from what I could see — with the counter in the way and the height I was at, I could see her from just below the belt buckle up. Black pants that looked like jeans, and a loose sleeveless shirt, fancy for the kitchen unless she was expecting someone. Some people are just like that, expectant, always thinking that someone's about to show up and they have to be ready, the house clean enough to at least be presentable. I wonder if those people go to bed every night disappointed when no one does show up, as if making all that effort was some kind of magic charm that would make people—the right people—just arrive. Whether it was also heartbreaking when they just...didn't.

She was pretty, but in a kind of a small-featured way: small nose, the St. John's chin—round, with her jaw set back, almost stubborn-looking—the kind of face someone might draw if they didn't have much room on the page. Elfin, maybe.

The phone must have been ringing, because she walked out of the window frame and then back in again with a black cordless up against her ear, and my view was so good that I could see she'd taken off a big earring to answer the phone and was holding it in her left hand. So, really expectant, enough to get dolled up with jewellery. With her head tilted, you could see the lines on her neck where the skin folded and bunched—it made her look suddenly older. Made the expectant seem both urgent and forlorn.

And no one came.

She barely left the back of the house: ate in the kitchen—although I could only see her forearms and the plate, her hands carrying bites of food up and out of sight—and then up to the bathroom. Couldn't see her directly in there at all, but mathematics are funny: angles and reflections and declinations. I got a mosaic-corner scrap of her reflection when she was taking off her shirt, just a fragment in the top edge of the bathroom mirror, the angle just right with the medicine cabinet door ajar, the kind of chance thing you see once because the stars literally align and that never repeats itself ever. An older woman, but that's an observation, not a criticism: I'm an older man, and she was in good shape.

That was more obvious when she turned the bathroom light off and the bedroom light on, sweeping in through the room in her underwear—black bra and panties—coming straight over and pulling the curtains closed all at once. Then, the room dark for a moment before it was lit by the flickering blue of the television set rippling through the narrow sliver of room that still showed. I imagined her in there, all wrapped up and warm under the sheets in her nightie or whatever it was she slept in, the television muttering away at her for company, that blind screen completely unaware of how white her skin had looked against the jet-black lace of her underwear.

I wondered about that, all balled up at the base of the cold tree. Nights as cold as that in St. John's, you sometimes hear the trees creaking and cracking, like the ice is working its way inch by inch into the centre of the wood and that it's splitting somehow right into the core. The hairs in my nose all gone stiff, like the cold was busy working its way into me as well.

I stayed even after it was only the light of the television behind the closed curtains, the night air all around me completely still the way only a winter high-pressure system can be, and while I sat there, I wondered about why it is people pick particular sets of clothes, especially when they seem chosen for other people but there aren't any other people around.

Whether it was quiet desperation, or whether it was some kind of transmission of unconscious need. Like those radio signals they used to flick out into space, transmissions that were supposed to tell other civilizations that we were peaceful or that we knew our periodic table or that Beethoven could put a few notes together, and, by the way, here's a symphony or two — try that in your alien earholes, if you've got any. Then I thought about how, if I were in a television show, everything wouldn't just peter out this way, that there would somehow be a much more definite end to the night.

I mean, it's not a sex thing.

I didn't pull it out up there and hold it in my hand when she was walking around her bedroom or anything. It would have frozen off.

But really, I wouldn't have anyway, cold or not: it's nothing like that at all.

I didn't feel any different than I would watching a mystery show on television and seeing the pieces all fall into place, figuring it out in that last few seconds before they actually have to come right out and tell you because you're stupid or something. Saying it's intellectual curiosity is perhaps the wrong way to put it, but that's sort of what I mean.

Every single time, you learn something new.

Keep going back right through the winter and on into summer, and I swear that you keep picking up things you either missed or that you didn't realize were important the first time you saw them.

If I got caught at it, I suppose they'd call me a voyeur.

I don't think of it that way, though: I think of it more like a hobby, like birdwatching. Me, the detached observer, watching the interesting habits of different kinds of people. And there are lots of different kinds of people, and lots of different kinds of habits.

Getting up from there that first time — just standing up — was tough. My knees unbending like rusty stuck hinges, and the first few steps back up the hill to the road I was almost staggering, trying to get my joints to work. Trying not to make too much noise, looking around to see if anyone had noticed me once I started moving. And I was really cold. Out under the lights, the street was completely empty, and I was out and onto it, relieved and elated at the same time.

Joy Martin of Signal Hill Road, I thought, *I know you a lot better now.*

I knew I'd recognize her the next time she was in the store, even if her back was facing me and I could see only her height, her hair, and that simple sweet curve of her neck. And I knew that I'd keep learning more about her.

Files? You don't have to keep files. Not in any kind of detail, not more than a note or two — maybe just a list of your own — to jog your memory in the right direction. If you've got any smarts at all, you can keep it in your head for when you need it.

And Mary at darts? Not one single bit the wiser.

CHAPTER 15

(St. John's, NL)—The Royal Newfoundland Constabulary (RNC) is seeking the assistance of the general public in locating missing person Mary CARTER.

On Sunday, November 22, officers from RNC Patrol Services responded to the report of a missing person. CARTER was last seen in the area of McKay Street in St. John's, NL, at approximately 1:00 p.m.

CARTER is described as 5' 7", 125 lbs, with brown eyes, short black hair, light build. She was last seen wearing a bluish-grey T-shirt, black-and-red sneakers, blue jeans, and a black windbreaker with a reflective stripe.

The RNC is continuing the search and is seeking the assistance of the general public.

If anyone has any information pertaining to the whereabouts of Mary CARTER they are asked to contact the RNC at 729-8000 or Crime Stoppers at 1-800-222-TIPS (8477).

"Whose wife hasn't done a runner? You're an asshole or worse, she's already getting her coat on, halfway out the door to her mother's and she's still shouting at you."

That was Scoville, looking down at his hands as always while he talked, worrying the tip of a pair of scissors in under one of his fingernails, his legs thrown out in front of him under the desk like he'd rather have them propped up on top. Then he looked up and across at Dean, eyes opening wider as he realized who he was talking to.

"Sorry. Didn't mean anything by that," Scoville backpedalled fast. "I guess buddy's wife could just be staying low."

Dean shook his head. That year-old news release was the last activity the case had seen. The last activity in the file at all.

"I don't think so. Not for six months let alone for more than a year," he said. "Not with no sign of her. Not using a credit card, no money out of the bank account, no one using her social insurance number. So she's not spending or working, not unless she's managed to get new ID."

Dean was holding a coffee and not drinking it, sitting at a desk straight across from Jim's. Counting off the reasons on his fingers, one by one. "You've looked at the file, I've looked at the file. There's not one single sign of her from anywhere—not family, not friends, from the very day she was reported missing."

"If she's dead, best bet it's going to be the husband," Scoville said. "Who else?"

"That's the way it usually goes. And there's nothing in the file to say anything different."

"So why are we sending out a new press release, then?"

Dean didn't say the most straightforward reason out loud—that doing something was far better than another day of spinning wheels, doing next to nothing in a windowless office.

"Maybe we're shaking trees. Just to see what falls out. Maybe it's the kind of thing that we're supposed to be doing."

Dean could almost see the way Scoville felt, as if exasperation was radiating off him like a colour. So he took a chance and told him the real reason: "If someone in the media picks this up, even just for a little while, it's going to put the pressure on everyone from the chief on down. This town's too small for people to go missing and stay missing. Some reporter makes this their bread and butter for a while, the brass are just going to tell us to drop everything else until it's sorted out. Then we get to go visit this Walt guy, make him uncomfortable. Uncomfortable people do sudden things. And that would suit me just fine."

He put his coffee down.

"The Carter one's got meat on it," he said, but he said it to empty air. Scoville was already looking down again. Dean thought about the case for a moment, and for some reason suddenly imagined Julie, running away. Turning her face back over her shoulder toward him as she ran. And it struck him that she looked afraid.

He shook his head, shook the thought away. Dean wasn't sure it was the right thing to do, bringing Scoville into what he was thinking about Mary Carter—he didn't know the other officer that well yet.

But then Dean saw that Scoville was looking up at him again, as if he'd suddenly discovered intelligent life on an otherwise-empty planet.

"Beats chasing endless teen runaways gone jittery on ecstasy," Scoville said. "You want to shake it up? Shake away."

CHAPTER 16

juice
meat — T-bones
cat food
receipt book
crackers
juice mix
crackers

On a Post-it note, the sticky top folded over once so that the paper had a kind of top-edge-turned-down, slightly stiffer spine. I remember thinking, right when I found it, "This one's a man."

A man for sure. You could almost see him moving through the store the way men always seem to do, like they're playing at being soldiers on a mission.

Combat shopping. Everything checked off in his head as he went, not a single glance side to side. Alone and in deep, behind enemy lines. It sounds a little melodramatic, but some of them move through the store like it is completely hostile territory, like everyone is singling them out as a stranger. And it helps to be a stranger; strangers can shove their cart into line just ahead of someone with a cartload meant for a whole family, and do it without a moment's regret.

This wasn't a note from the kind of person who would ask for any sort of help, even if he can't find the canned coconut milk to save his life and time's ticking down before the date comes over. (See, sometimes coconut milk's with the ethnic food, around the pad Thai sauce and the curry. Other times, like it was done for a lark, you'll find someone has stocked it in with the bar mix — "Would you like a pina colada, or a nice tall rum and coconut milk?" And if a shelver is really pissed off, try vegetarian food. Or you could ask me — because I know. But he won't ask. Won't even think of asking.)

Male grocery shopping? I've been there. I've certainly seen it, and I've even done it myself. And it's always done with purpose — get in, do the list, get out — like there's some kind of pride in that. Show me a distracted man in a grocery store — a guy who meanders, or who keeps picking things up and putting them down — and I'll show you a man who really doesn't want to get home. That's a man who needs an excuse to be doing something else, anything else.

For the rest of us, the purpose is just too much of a driving force, and a list is the one thing that proves you've gotten everything done. It's there in the man wiring — it's all about the getting through. Here's a problem — solve it. The urge to check each thing off just as quickly as you can. Like you're supposed to run through the checkouts at the end and smack a bell and shout, "Done!" and then hold both your arms in the air, waiting for all the applause.

Tell me there's no difference between men and women, and I'll take you straight to the aisle where the canned tuna is. It's on the left-hand side, heading toward the checkouts, slightly higher than knee level. That's all I have to do.

Women will stop and bend down to look at all sorts of cans, comparing prices between different brands and who knows what else. There's more kinds, more brands, more styles of tuna than there is pasta. Chunk light in oil or water, solid white, skipjack, yellowtail — and that's before you start comparing brands. Men? Grab some chunk light in water, throw it into the cart — "Done!"

You can almost hear them thinking "See? Record time."

As if that somehow makes any kind of difference to anyone.

Watch sometime, and just see if you can actually prove me wrong.

Women have crashed into me with their carts, sure, heads down and running fast. I'm not saying they can't be in a hurry, can't button down with purpose. I've been hit by serious, hard-looking women with shiny tap-tapping hard-soled shoes and mouths drawn so tight that their lips seem to have no colour in them at all. Anyone can be in a hurry.

But men ram their carts into me ten times as often, cutting around the corners at the ends of the aisles as if they were race car drivers on that last desperate curve before the finish.

I don't want to make it look like everyone's typecast, but

the fact is that sometimes they are. Saying "it takes one to know one" sounds trite, but it's true just the same. Set a purpose, get it done. And if you don't get it done, and get it done fast, it'll eat away at you like nothing else. It'll downright consume you. We're wired that way — and it's not the only wiring we've got.

Tom Quinton across the street, he always wanted to fuck Mary.

Sorry, but there's no polite way to say it, because, straight up, it was true.

For years and years, he lived right across the street — and he was married, too, the whole time. It started almost as soon as we bought the place.

We used our marriage money for the down payment, and that very first day — the two of us out looking at the front of the place we'd just bought — that old letch Tom Quinton was across the street, looking Mary up and down like his eyes were right inside her clothes, his hands on her smooth skin. Thinking about cupping her naked ass. I caught him at it then, and more than once after that, and so did she — but Mary just laughed at the whole damn thing. Laughed and did a little pirouette there in the living room as soon as we went inside, like she was showing it all off. Like she was making fun of me for being upset about it.

That just made me more angry. Not at her. Made me want to go across the street and belt Quinton one. Or, more likely, go over all smiles and new-neighbourly to borrow some tools and then return them all broken, the saw blades with teeth missing, a power drill with the bits overheated and snapped off. Screwdrivers bent, if it took me pounding on them with a hammer to do it. Fake a shrug and a smile, and apologize unconvincingly

I was hot-headed, and while I'm a small guy, I was whip-lash strong back then, muscles like wire rope under my skin from part-time stock work, unloading semi-trailers of canned goods one case at a time, bringing them on a hand truck into the back of the store, and then going back for another.

No forklifts or hydraulics then. Not like now. Now the stock guys can be oblivious fourteen-year-olds with no hard muscles at all and just a little fuzz on their upper lips.

Back when I started, it was the kind of job that meant you never had to look inside a gym unless you were a boxer, because when you were done for the day, the only thing you wanted to be lifting was a drink. Talk to me about how easy a job it is when you've unloaded more canned tomato soup than you could eat in an entire year of lunchtimes. And it didn't matter if you had anything going on upstairs or not — it didn't matter if you didn't think about anything ever — because you weren't hired for the thinking, just the lifting, and all that mattered was how much and how fast.

"Strong back, weak mind, get the job done" — I had a manager who said that right to my face, said that was the only kind of employee he wanted.

So I'm sure I could have popped Tom one, easy. And taken him down, too, probably with the first punch. He wound up in a job with the city, but not outside: one of those inside jobs where the closest thing to heavy lifting was making sure that all the filing cabinet drawers were closed at the end of the day.

But I'm more patient than someone who just goes over and pops a guy in the mouth. You probably wouldn't believe it, but I am.

Unless I'm pushed.

Later on, when our wives got to know each other better, the Quintons would ask us over all the time, and I bet that Ev Quinton thought we were the best of friends.

That was back when you could sit around all night playing cards and smoking cigarettes, talking the whole time, just four people and a few drinks and the kinds of snacks you pour straight out of a bag, just chips and pretzels and maybe nuts. Bridge mix, those strange chocolates where it's impossible to know what kind you've got until you put it in your mouth — and then it's impolite to spit the whole darned thing back into your hand when it turns out to be a kind you don't like.

For a while, Tom was teaching in the trade school, and believe it or not, he'd started smoking a pipe around the same time, like he was suddenly a university professor or something. When it wasn't his turn to deal, he'd be turning that pipe upside down and rapping it off the ashtray, poking around inside to clean it out, and then packing it tight with loose pipe tobacco all over again before lighting a match and sucking the flame right straight down into the bowl.

It always looked like a lot of work for very little return — it seemed like he'd hardly get the thing lit and have a couple

93

of puffs before it was time to tap it all out again, and start back up with the scrape, scrape, scrape. Like an old car you spend more time fixing than driving, and what's the use of that?

The pipe smelled better than cigars, but not much. Like a mixture of tobacco and rubber bands. Get him started on it, though, and he'd launch into some great long lecture on how they go about picking and curing tobacco, about the small yellow leaves at the bottom of the stalks that they call suckers, the ones that have to be picked off and thrown away, and about how you can tell when a pipe tobacco is high-quality, even if it smells just like burning cabbage. Truth is, he was packed tight, just like his pipe, but he was stuffed with a whole bunch of useless information that was supposed to make you think he was something special.

They had a small square table for cards, their dining room table, really, but with the centre leaf taken out, and I swear that Tom liked to play cards because his knees were so close to Mary's. His knees poked in there close enough to feel the heat of her, radiating out from her skin.

The worst part was that he thought he could keep it all out of sight. He wasn't the kind of guy who'd give you a nudge with his knee while you were bent down fixing the snow blower and say, "Mary — she must be a hell of a ride, hey?" Nothing like that. Nothing that you could take on, just one time, and straighten up for good. But obvious enough.

With the table shrunk down, it was like their entire dining room was larger somehow, or else it was like we were four kids playing at being adults, the walls too far back and the whole space just wrong. Alice in Wonderland, but with our legs and arms stretched to where they shouldn't rightly be. Ev would be running back and forth, filling the bowls and getting more drinks, and Tom would be doing his best to look down Mary's shirt with me sitting right there, alternating between seething rage and absolute cold.

Of course Mary knew all about it—women always know more about where your eyes are than you think they do—and afterwards, when we were back home, she'd tell me not to get so worked up, that "there's a difference between window shopping and actually buying."

I'd swear I'd never go back there, but then Ev would call Mary, and it always seemed to turn out that there was another Friday night, another hard lungful of pipe smoke, and that same carefully painted dining room with a small wallpaper border pasted around the top edge of the walls, like someone had taken a child's dollhouse dining room and forced it to grow up in a way it was never meant to do.

Ev was the only reason we ever went back.

You know paperwhites? Those bulbs you can buy already forced up and growing for Christmas, small daffodils that come out all expectant and face-up like someone's lied and told them spring's just around the corner? And then they always end up dead once the season's over, never any smarter and having lived their whole lives as someone's instant accessory. But when they burst open, they're fully involved.

Sometimes, you talk to someone, and it's like every word tells you that there's more to them than you ever expected.

They open up and expand somehow, because they're really way more complex than you'd ever expected, petal after layered petal.

With Tom, it was the absolute opposite. It was like every word confirmed your worst fears about how shallow he actually could be, and then he'd go ahead and show you there was even less.

On top of everything else, Tom couldn't stand not having done the most or the largest or the fastest.

Start talking about fishing and he'd have to tell you about a trip he'd taken years ago "up on the Labrador," and he could look at you bald-facedly and say something as stupid as, "The fish we caught were so big that we had to let them all go, because landing them would have meant sinking the canoe — that's how big they were."

Or cars — I had a big-engine Ford for a while, good and fast and always hungry for more gas, but any time I raised the topic of cars, Tom would remember a big-block Chevy that he'd had until the police had ordered him to take it right off the road. "Too much power for a street car," he'd say, claiming to have juiced it up right there in his driveway with nothing more than common sense, copper tubing, and a old handbook on turbocharging a Datsun. "Simple," he'd say, like that was enough to serve as proof.

Get a rose to finally grow in our backyard, despite the St. John's climate, and he'd remember the time he'd had a greenhouse, and kept his roses blooming right into December and beyond and how, that year, they gave bouquets for Christmas all over the neighbourhood, and all the women for blocks around were delighted.

I was supposed to just go along with it, no matter how outlandish it was. Never call him on it.

Because if I did, guaranteed, he'd find a way to turn it around so that he was really talking about something different and just barely possible—and he'd stick his chin out and dare me to call him out again. After the first few times, I realized it just wasn't worth pointing out what a blowhard he really was.

Really, I couldn't be bothered to keep going, but Mary made me.

"We just have to visit for a while," she'd say. "Ev has to put up with it all the time." She called Tom's behaviour "compensating," and then smiled when I pretended I had no idea what she was talking about.

But that didn't mean I had to tolerate him looking at Mary like that all the time. And giving him a good talking-to—or a knock in the head—was obviously out of the question, was obviously the kind of thing that would make Mary look at me that way she did, with that sort of half-crushed, half-hopeless look she must have started practising when she was about six years old.

I call that look "cosmic disappointment" now, now that she's not here to turn it on me.

Tom, with all the things he said he'd seen and done, well, it turned out there was a thing or two he couldn't handle anyone else knowing about. A thing like the single prescription label I found on the floor in the store, right there with his name and the dosage and everything, the name of the drug so familiar I didn't even need to go on the Internet to know exactly what his embarrassing little problem was.

Then it was as simple as letting him know what I knew, without ever letting on how I knew. Just dropped it on him one day, slid it in half-apologetically like Ev had let it slip to Mary or something. Big strong Tom—not strong everywhere. Child's play, really.

And after that, every time I came out the front door and he was outside, all I had to do was give him a little wave, look into his eyes, and wait for him to break it off and turn away.

Ev's invitations to play cards dried up, but I don't think that was her idea.

Eventually, their house sold, but I heard they didn't make much money off it, even though they'd had the place for years and did a fair amount of fixing up in that time, too.

It sat empty over there for a while, everything looking all closed up like it was turned in on itself, and the weeds started pushing up tall through the little strip of garden they'd always had.

Their daffodils keep coming up in the same row every year, though, just the way the bulbs were planted. Stupid damned daffodils, they don't really have a clue about anything, do they?

I feel sorry for Ev. A life sentence she probably didn't deserve. Probably still listening to him banging that stupid pipe in the ashtray, too.

CHAPTER 17

(St. John's, NL)—The Royal Newfoundland Constabulary (RNC) will hold a press conference at 2 p.m. on Wednesday, December 20, to provide media with an update on progress in an ongoing investigation. Media are requested to be at RNC Headquarters and set up no later than 1:45 p.m.

"Should we tell the chief that everything was right there in the files already, or just let him go on thinking we're brilliant?" Scoville said.

"I doubt very much that *brilliant* is the word he's thinking of," Dean answered.

They'd told the chief they were ready to close their first file. They'd decided that he didn't really need to know why, that it could mean trouble for the original investigating officers.

Dean and Scoville knew St. John's—hell, the whole city held barely more than 200,000 people—so when they had three different files in which three different women had been assaulted, and in their witness statements all said that the man who had attacked them smelled like mould, the two detectives just looked at each other across their desks.

"Was Frankie Beaton in jail then?" Dean asked.

"Simple enough to find out." Scoville pulled the computer keyboard over toward his stomach. "Whoever took the statements must have been new if they didn't have Frank in their sights."

Frank Beaton had been a regular at Her Majesty's Penitentiary for almost twenty years: he was there again when the two detectives went to interview him, and it wasn't long before he admitted to all three of the offences, telling them how he'd picked the women and why—the why mostly being that he was drunk and he'd see them walking home at night.

"Not much of a planner, then," Dean said as he and Scoville signed out of the prison.

Scoville made a humphing sound.

"He never was. He's probably told half the guys in here all about it, and was just waiting for the first question from a cop so he could spill it."

Chief Adams spent a long time in front of the microphones explaining how the RNC had finally solved the cases: he was big on diligence and thoroughness and careful police work, not above tossing in the fact that it wasn't only the Mounties who always got their man. Dean was relegated, along with Scoville, to being the chief's stern backdrop, spending the time thinking about how Julie had called to tell him that she had a new boyfriend, a lawyer, and that the lawyer had suggested that maybe Dean should be paying spousal support.

Half the time, he couldn't fathom what she wanted.

The other half, he thought, he couldn't care less about: it didn't matter that Julie was all locked up in the practical side of things, like who should pay for what and who should use which credit card, or whether their credit ratings were going to be affected because he'd left every single one of their bills, still in their envelopes and unopened, in a pile like some kind of shrine at the end of the counter.

He didn't drive down the street where she now lived— he'd managed to come up with a range of careful detours, one of them past the narrow trench of row houses on Cabot Street, a neighbourhood you only drove through because you lived there. It was, he thought, the kind of street where people looked at you as if they already knew whether or not you belonged—and if you didn't, as if they thought you should probably be minding your own business.

He'd gotten stuck there once, waiting for a pickup to squeeze through, and an older man had come close enough that it seemed his face was pressed right up against the driver's side window on Dean's car, looking in as if he was wondering just who the hell Dean was and why the hell he was there.

Parked cars tight along the uphill side, one narrow lane where cars always took turns threading their way forward, Cabot Street's greatest benefit was that it was one full block below LeMarchant Road, where Julie had gotten herself set up in a two-bedroom apartment filled with the best of both their furniture.

Then he started thinking about Scoville instead, and how the new job was actually turning out better than he'd thought it would, that they'd settled into an easy offhandedness that he hadn't had with another detective since he had started upstairs in crime stats. And that it was all right.

With a start, he heard the chief speak his name.

"Inspector Hill and Sergeant Scoville would be happy to answer some questions for you," the chief said. Just like that, the questions began.

CHAPTER 18

Baked beans
Sausages
White bread
Margarine
Tea bags
Milk
Matches

I used to get out into the country a lot—I mean a lot.

In the summertime, I'd take the car down to the North Harbour Road to go fly fishing, my lunch with me in the knapsack, teabags and a bottle with milk and sugar tucked right inside the kettle I'd use to boil the tea I'd have while I was eating.

There are five or six rivers down there where no one else ever fishes. All around them are big wet stretches of impassable barrens with yellow standing threads of marsh grass, the small patches of white-capped sticks of cotton grass—the kind of grasses that tell you exactly what week of summer it is, if you have enough experience to know what you're looking at. The same grasses that leave a clear trail behind if you walk through them, a clearly made path after one single pass. You'd leave a trail, but you'd also be exhausted, because you sink almost knee-deep into the wet black peat that's down underneath that lovely green field, and there's even more effort involved in pulling your foot back out, that great sucking reverse step that leaves a hole ready to fill in with boggy water. You can imagine that there are thousands, millions of trees down there under the surface, all dark strands and acidic brown water. How anything under there must break down fast. Walking, it's hard on the joints, pulls your knees apart into the loose knot of bones and gristle that they actually are, and all the time, being in the place is somehow close to a religious experience.

Of all of those rivers, I like the O'Keefe best — Mary's father told me about it, like he was giving me special permission to fish there. You won't find people where I fish, not two or three miles up a stony, scrabbling stretch where there might be a few pools and steadies every hundred yards or so — and steadies that change, because last year, a tree dropped across one part of the river, and the next, ice froze around the branches and the spring flood carried the whole snag away. All the time I fished on the O'Keefe, I only ever saw moose and caribou. And even they were occasional visitors, nosing slightly out of cover just long enough to realize I was there.

Except once — I did meet a fishing warden down there,

but it turned out he was looking for someone else, for a poacher with a car that looked like mine, so he worked his way through the brush and up on top of me before I had any idea he was even there. And when he stepped out of the trees and I saw it was actually a person, materializing virtually right next to me, I was both relieved and so frightened that I could literally feel my guts turn to water.

He just wanted to see who I was and what I was up to, and then I watched him melt away downstream and disappear, his khaki backpack and dun jacket merging right into the colours of the brush, and the second he was gone, it was like I could imagine that he had never even been there. Funny, though: moments after catching up with me, he knew I wasn't the person he was looking for—at the same time, he managed to keep that official facade, that "Let's see your licence, sir, and could I have a look at your fish," even though he'd already decided that he wouldn't really want anything from me. There's a message there: everyone falls back on the formulaic, the process, the questions they ask by rote. I was glad to see him go: I didn't fish again until he was truly out of sight, as if fishing while he was still in the distant background would damage that spot forever.

With enough water holding in the headlands and draining down, the O'Keefe can be remarkably fast, even at the top, even right below the highway where it's narrow and working its way around the foot of a long draining bog in a deep, gentle curve.

Walk over that bog to reach the river and you can't help

but have the feeling that you're standing on a huge sucking sponge — that there's more water tied up in that living soggy peat than there is in the entire river that's racing by in front of you in little white-water rips and then pooling in great curling steadies.

I know there are plenty of moose down there: I've found their lies in the brush and grass and wild strawberries — great flattened circles where the plants are all crushed down — but I've never found a sleeping moose. I suppose they hear you coming long before you ever get close, and that they're up on those spindly strong legs, alert and quietly on the move while you're still splashing awkwardly through the shallows and noisily toppling the loose rocks along the shore.

That's the only way to travel any of those rivers: right in them. Otherwise, you're just forcing your way straight through scrub, and pitching into bog holes and moss pits you don't even see until you're right in them. It's all wild hedges of stunted spruce and hanging deadman's moss, light-green netted tufts of lichen that grab the moisture they need right out of the air. If you're hiking the river, and you're lucky enough, there's a bit of beach gravel now and then, just a thin shoulder of it, really, and just enough for you to get something of a rest while you walk, because mostly you're knee-deep in water and standing on uneven rocks.

When I'm in the woods, everything around me kind of overloads my brain — the combination of the heat of the sun, the smell of the low brush baking in the heat, the small bright-coloured needles of the dragonflies hovering in the air and then suddenly darting away—on top of the fishing and the walking, too, the sheer complexity of all of it has a way of capturing every single scrap of my attention, so that I couldn't think about anything else even if I wanted to.

You come up the gravel bank to the road completely soaked with sweat, filthy and bug-bitten and ragged, and yet shriven—completely, fantastically, wonderfully whole and clean again.

I don't know anything else like it.

I don't think I ever will.

CHAPTER 19

Whip cream
Kidney beans

Liquor store

Dollar Store
• paint brush

Walmart
• Chandelier bulbs
• Whoppers
• Cedar mulch (4 bags)
• sympathy card

Home Depot
• cedar stain

So much there — I've thought about that note a lot. On note-paper with her name, Lori Neville, right there on the top, the name of her company, too, along with her fax, phone, and email. The paper was all rough and stippled from getting wet and being run over in the parking lot before I found it.

It looked different when it was in the box, when it was just mine, different from when someone was holding on to it and waving it at me.

"Know her, do ya?"

A police officer with the name "Davis" on a piece of fabric tape stuck to the front of his jacket had it between his fingertips, held delicately as if it were contaminated waste or something. One of the shoeboxes was open on the kitchen table and the lists were starting to get spread out all haphazard on the counter; I caught a glimpse as I was being ushered out. "How about this one? This Alisha a friend of yours?" Davis asked, holding another one of the lists. He was the only cop in the room right then.

"An acquaintance," I said. "I've seen her once or twice."

It's smart to be as honest as you can — the best lies are packed full of truth.

The police weren't saying what they're looking for. They rang the doorbell at six in the morning, shoved the papers at me, and told me a judge had signed them, so now they could search the house. The guys in charge weren't in uniform, but they were definitely in charge. The tall one was Inspector Hill; Sergeant Scoville, the other one, was shorter and rounder. Hill told me straight off that I could call my lawyer if I wanted. Scoville said it would be better to just shut up and leave, because "lawyer or not, it's going to turn out the same way."

When I asked, they said no, they weren't charging me with anything.

They had twelve hours to go through the place, they said. I had to go, "but not too far, ha ha," and they sent a cop named Roberts upstairs with me, and he stood there while I hung up my robe and got my pants and shirt out of the closet—and then he checked the pockets on both of them, and even went through my wallet right there in front of me, taking the bills out, fingering his way through the little pockets, taking out all the cards before slipping them back in and handing it to me. Never saying what it was he was looking for.

The wallet's black, real worn, and Mary gave it to me one Christmas six or seven years ago. I can still remember taking everything out of my old wallet and moving it over, the kind of task that gets you thinking about every scrap of paper you've got in there and how long you've been hauling it all around. The two of us, sitting on the couch in the living room, wrapping paper around our feet and Mary still in her nightgown. Christmas was always a kind of low-key affair; we took things pretty slowly, because everything had a way of being over all at once and then we'd be left alone with each other. Do that—get left alone with each other—and Christmas dinner can be wreckage before it's even out of the oven, a couple of bottles of white wine gone before you've gotten around to making the gravy, and someone spoiling for a fight and only keeping it in because of the holidays. At least that's the way it was by the Christmas with the wallet, a Christmas where Mary ended up passed out on the sofa while I, violently drunk and unable to even slow down, threw up over a railing into the ocean, every street in the city empty except for the people who had a place to go and were busy going there.

I stood there in front of the policeman for a minute, stubbornly sorting everything back into the right places, putting the credit cards in upside down the way I like them, so that the ridges of the numbers are above the leather slits and you can pull them out quick with your fingertips. I hate being behind someone who can't get their card out quick at the cash, and I won't ever be that person.

While I was doing that, Roberts was fidgeting like he was supposed to have taken me downstairs long ago. He's just an extra in this film, I knew that. The main characters were downstairs, carefully somewhere else and out of sight.

They can't rush you, though—they're not allowed to. I know the drill. They'll go through the whole house—taking things out of their places, moving them around, putting them where they want, sometimes bagging things they think are important. Eventually, they'll give it all back—at least they do with me—but they can sure as hell make a mess while they're looking. They can even cut open the mattresses and haul out all the drawers to see if you're stupid enough to have taped something incriminating to the bottom, and they can leave all the contents spread right out on the bed. But they can't rush you—they just chivvy you along, using the same official voice they always use to say "nothing to see here, sir" and "move along" at car accidents.

They've got a job to do — that's the way I try to think about it — and I try not to get annoyed with them and the mess they're going to make, even though it will be weeks before everything's sorted out and back to where it's supposed to be. Sometimes they're gentle, taking stuff out and stacking it in order so you can put it back. Other times, though, the search is more like a punishment.

What I mean is that it's like they've already decided you're guilty, that they think it's just a matter of them proving it, and so you deserve the mess they're going to be making, just for the fact that you're not giving up the ghost and confessing or something.

Ask someone who's been on the wrong side: it's amazing what kind of behaviour the police can justify if they think they're in the right. And there's absolutely not one single thing you can do to convince them otherwise.

This time, it meant an unexpected day out for me: late November, and everything dying back into beiges and yellows, sometime beaten down flat by the first of the snow.

I got out to the car, trying not to look around at any of the windows on the street where there were bound to be busybodies back in the shadows having themselves a good look.

They let me pick up my coat near the back door before I left, but not before they went through all those pockets carefully, too, even the inside ones, like I might have known they were coming and slipped something incriminating in there.

You feel like asking them just what it is they're looking for, as if you really should be helping them or something. It's a hard habit to break. I looked at my backpack and decided not to even ask. I already had my long boots in the trunk, and they hadn't said anything about wanting to look through the car. Maybe they're saving that for another day. Maybe the warrant doesn't go that far, some cop inside the house already kicking himself for not getting that extra bit of permission, too, imagining I'm about to trundle off for the distant horizon with every single thing they're looking for.

The whole thing makes me wonder about judges, what their worlds must be like, signing off on warrants for people they don't even know, when what they have is half the story, and only the half the police want to give them: Do they just suspend all disbelief, sign their names, and let the police get on with things?

I don't know how many warrants they've brought to my place; I don't know how many different judges it's been, either. All I know is that judges seem to cough up permission to go through my place pretty darned quick, and pretty darned regularly, too. And then the cops come in like the tide, only one or two of them frequently enough for me to recognize.

I was at the highway and filling up the gas tank before I really even thought about where I wanted to go.

I knew I had twelve hours to kill—by then, I guess, it was maybe only eleven, but I'd have to be out until six in the evening, anyway—so I cut down the Salmonier Line and then pointed the car toward Branch, right at the foot of the peninsula.

I like driving — it lets me think. By then, I wasn't really worrying about the police and the house. They'd leave a mess for sure, give me a list of anything they took, go away without finding whatever it was they were looking for. So I thought about the road instead, going too fast, liking the way the corners felt as the car leaned into them. The way you can feel the weight of the car pulling against the tread of the tires, like the only thing between you and a rollover down the bank was something as simple as that zigzag pattern cut into the rubber. It's astounding how quickly we all trust in patterns. And how, miraculously, those patterns often end up working just fine.

I drove out to the old provincial park at Red Head, five or six rivers past North Harbour. It's a bit eerie now, the pea-gravel campsite pads still laid out there in the river valley, the sharp incline of Red Head rising up steep and somehow ominous behind them. The whole place, the whole floor of the valley, is filling up with alders, tough little interloping trees that inch their way in on the old road and the campsites more and more with every year.

Down at the foot of the road, there was a big stone beach, a wall of loose stone thrown up by the swells and blocking most of the valley, standing maybe twenty-five feet high. Enough force in the waves that you could hear the fist-sized rocks clacking hard together every time the water swept ashore. Climbing up, my feet launched quick little landslides of rolling stones, vees of moving rock that start fast, then widen and slow, everything settling back into its own kind of equilibrium a few moments after you're gone, like you're some kind of passing irritation.

I think of the police that way now, too—a small disturbance, a ripple of motion in the world that leaves a sharp and obvious mark but really doesn't change the whole thing all that much.

I wish they'd get me out of their minds, move on to something else, but I don't really think that's going to happen in a hurry.

I think, because I keep to myself, people think I'm smug, and I know for sure that rubs the cops the wrong way. There are all kinds of stories, all the time, about cops picking out someone just because they seem odd—"This has to be our guy, because who plays the oboe?" or something like that.

They even have a name for it—"tunnel vision." Find a guy who strikes you funny, and look for all reasons that he must have done something.

I hope you're having fun at my house, I thought.

I hope your hands are sweaty inside your rubber gloves, I hope you're being thorough enough to burrow down through the dirty laundry piled up in the basket, I hope you're going through the useless tasks of checking inside the toilet tank and in the basement boxes I haven't opened in years.

I took the papers out of my pocket then and read them, and it said right on the top that the search warrant was about Mary again, and that's no surprise, so I crumpled them up and stuffed them back into my front pocket.

By the time I got home, back to the house the police had borrowed for the day, the paper of the warrant was damp and the letters on the outside were starting to smudge. It didn't matter: the words were still as legible as they needed to be, and I've got a box for the warrants now, too.

I hoped that they'd had the decency to check that the door was locked before they piled into their cars and left. When I tried it, the screen door was closed, but it wasn't locked and my front door wasn't either.

You can tell me it wasn't meant as some kind of message, but I wouldn't believe you. It was a message all right, a message that they'd been and gone. On their own terms.

It was a message that they could, and would, come back any time they wanted to.

CHAPTER 20

Jan. 10—I think I have a stalker. Maybe not a
stalker. Just some guy. An older guy. I just think I
keep seeing the same guy around, but I'm not sure.
I don't want to get caught staring at him or something. I mean, if he is watching me, I don't want to
make eye contact or anything. Daniel thinks I'm
crazy—worse, really. He said he thinks I'm full
of myself, like I'm imagining there's someone following me because it makes me more important or
something. That's exactly what he said. Nice, right?
But I'm sure there's someone following me—it's
not just a feeling. Like that first time in November,
but it's harder to catch him at it now. It's like there's
someone walking back there almost all the time, and
it seems like—I'm sure it looks like—the same guy,
walking far enough behind me that I can't make out
his face or anything, but if I slow down or stop, he
turns around and heads the other way before I really
get any kind of look at him, before I could really
swear that he's following me. It's all so quick. Should

I confront him? Shout at him? I don't think so. If this keeps up, I think maybe I should go to the police or something. It's creeping me out.

CHAPTER 21

Hamburger
Buns
Steaks
Ketchup
Mustard
Hot dogs

Liquor store
Beer
Tequila
More beer

She was almost in the middle of the road when I first saw her, halfway down the Salmonier Line, wearing just a T-shirt and jeans, and it was pounding down rain. I'll tell you, May isn't always the friendliest month here, not even the last week of May when every other province has all the leaves out on the trees already. I was coming around a curve at the bottom of a long hill, coming fast the way you do when it's a little after

7:30 on a dark spring morning, rain, and there's nothing else in sight.

You watch for moose at that hour of the day, not for blond-haired pixies in soaking wet Levi's.

And yet there she was, looking right at my car and waving her arms over her head in that frantic way that can mean anything from "Give me a lift to the store, would ya?" to "My parents' car has gone over the embankment, and they're trapped down there."

So I stopped, and she came around to the driver's side window, a little slip of a thing like a drowned rat, and she struck her hip off the mirror, hard—I could see that in her face, the flash of pain, and then she put her left hand down and rubbed where she'd hit.

"I'm trying to get back to the cabin," she said.

"What cabin?"

"I don't know. The cabin. I haven't been out here before, so I'm not really sure. Can you give me a lift?"

There are cabins not far from there, a fair number of them, and I can tell you just where the side roads go off, because I've driven by them more than a few times. I mean, even if you're going somewhere else, sometimes you like to turn off the main drag and see how the other half lives—you know, the ones with houses and families and cottages and Jet Skis and the cold beer on a big deck next to the barbecue.

But there weren't cabins right where we were, just a few miles above where the road goes across the Salmonier River. We were close to the gas station, and I looked in the mirror before I stopped; there was nothing behind me but empty, wet road.

It was pretty clear she was drunk, or at least had recently been drunk. There was a smell coming off her, a smell like plums or something, the smell that always tells me someone's been drinking. I looked in the mirror again, hoping someone else would be coming, that maybe I could pass the buck, get moving, and let her take her chances with the next car. It was still pretty dark, and the spruce trees come right down to the road there, so it all looked like something out of *Little Riding Hood*. I was just waiting to see the wolf or something, and meanwhile, the girl was cold and wet enough that she had started to shiver.

"Come on," I said, "let's see what we can do." And I reached across and unlocked the door on the passenger side.

She walked around and I watched as she trailed her hand, the tips of her fingers, along the edge of the hood as if her balance depended on that thin, fine contact. She got in, falling into the front seat, really, her hair all stringy and down around her face. I worried for a moment about the seat getting wet, pushed the thought away and looked straight at her. She had a small face, framed in by her hair, a snub nose but pretty, and she was right on that age line where her face was changing into what it would look like for the rest of her life. That spot where you lay down the laugh lines or crease your face into a permanent pout.

Blue eyes that would be prettier if they could focus a little better.

"Walt," I said, and I stuck out my hand like we were

being formally introduced somewhere. She just looked at it for a moment, as if it were a fish she wasn't really interested in touching, and then she grabbed like she didn't really have a choice. Getting it over with quick.

"Lisa."

I'll admit it's not the brightest thing I ever did, telling her my real name or giving her a ride and everything.

Or any of the rest of it—none of it was really bright. I know it's always easier looking backwards, when you can pick any one of a hundred spots that could have made things different, where you could have said, "Well, that's it then, have a nice day," and just walk away.

But that's not the point.

"I've been walking on this damn road for hours, and it hasn't stopped raining once," she said. It looked like she was telling the truth: she was soaked through, enough so that I could see the lines of her bra under her shirt, and on both sides of the road, all of the candles from the spruce trees were turned downward from the weight of the water on the branch tips.

"Where were you going, anyway?" I asked.

"I was up at the cabin, some friend of David's. Over there." She waved her hand over her shoulder. "All guys. All drunk. You can imagine where that was going." She looked confused for a moment, as if she had lost her train of thought, and then her face cleared a bit. "So I started walking back to town. I think back to town."

"Town's an hour's drive away," I said. "I don't know how far it would be walking."

"Whatever. I guess I thought they were supposed to come looking for me, right?" She was looking out the window as rain poured down the glass. "And maybe they were going to apologize for being such dicks."

With her inside the car and the windows rolled up, the smell of booze was much stronger. It was the kind of smell that would get you into the backseat of an RCMP cruiser for a date with the Breathalyzer, if a cop pulled you over for speeding or no turn signal or something.

She leaned against the window then, and rocked her shoulders against the seatback. It made it seem as though just reaching the front seat was the end of a long climb, and she was perfectly happy with staying put and thinking over how hard done by she was. Like she was more concerned about how she got into this jam than she was about how she was going to get out of where she was now.

"I can't run you back into town — I've got plans — but maybe you can go back to the cabin. Maybe they're all sleeping it off by now."

She didn't answer.

"Which way did you come from?"

"Don't know. It was dark. You're right; they should be sleeping by now. We were doing tequila shots at four and Dave had already passed out when I left. I just stumbled out and kept walking.

"I only found the highway 'cause a car went by and I saw the headlights."

She was right about the dark out there. People who stay

all the time in the city, they don't really know about dark. Out on a highway without streetlights, rain clouds covering the stars and any moon there might be, and you're lucky if when you stop for a piss, you can still find your zipper. I tried to picture her making her way along the road, one foot on the pavement, the other on the gravel just to keep moving in a straight line. Lose your way just a bit in the black, and the next thing you know, you're right in the middle of the road.

I had my alternator go once, night-driving on the highway just up from Gambo, and when the battery went dead, it was like I'd gone blind or something. I reached for my cellphone — not to call anyone, not way out there, but to use the light on the display to get my stuff out of the trunk and wait for a car to come along.

"Do you remember coming down a hill," I asked her carefully, "or did you just walk along the flat?"

"Down a hill, I think," she said, and then she smiled a bit for the first time. A little lopsided, but it sure brightened up her face. In a nice way.

"There are a couple of places — back at the Deer Park, or maybe the Colinet Road. Any of that sound familiar?"

"No. The cabin's brown, I think, and there's a white pickup out front. Dave's truck. Big truck."

I told her that we could take a look, that I'd drive her back up the hill and we could see if she recognized the place. By then, the rain was coming down in sheets again, and if anything, the sky was getting darker. Water was rushing downhill at us in the ruts on the pavement, and when we turned in the Deer Park, the trees were whipping around in the wind. We drove past a few cabins, then a few more, sometimes just driveways, and the puddles were hiding bigger and bigger potholes the farther back into the woods we got. I'd point to a place, and she'd look, shake her head, and rest the side of her face against the window—and every time, she seemed more and more resigned.

"I've only been there once," she said thickly. "If I see the truck, I'll know it."

"Are you sure you came downhill?"

"I think so. I dunno."

The air in the car was getting strong, and then the rain was slacking off again, so I opened the window and swung into a driveway to turn around.

"We'll try down on the Colinet Road," I said, but she didn't answer. I thought for a moment that she might have been sleeping.

After that, the conversation got a little bit strained—well, her part of the conversation did. I kept talking, and every now and then she'd grunt or throw a word in somewhere. We had a twenty-minute drive or so in the other direction, and I told her about working at the store, about the lists, the whole thing. Easy enough when she wasn't even answering. How you meet lots of people, but have to make your mind up about them really quickly, because you don't get to spend much time with them before they're gone again. Sometimes she'd rouse herself for a minute or two, enough once to tell me that she had finished school and had been working at everything from landscaping to home care, trying to find something that suited her. About her basement apartment, and how she wanted to get a car of her own.

I think I told her about ten times as much as she told me, and that really wasn't like me at all.

By then she was really drifting—when she looked at me, it was like only one eye was focusing, the other one kind of drifting away as if it had lost the only line between boat and wharf. Not a pretty look for anyone. We passed more cabins, she shook her head, and we got to the end of the road. I got ready to turn around again, and was beginning to wonder if I was ever going to get her out of the car. She hadn't seen anything familiar anywhere, not a landmark or a familiar sign or anything.

Then, all at once, she was sound asleep.

She was right out of it, and with the car stopped to turn, I got my first real chance to have a good look at her, curled up against the door with her two hands, palm to palm, tucked in under her cheek. I reached across and brushed the side of her face, her cheek, with the back of my right hand. And I swear, she nuzzled over, moved toward me and smiled with her eyes still closed, smiled like she liked the feel of it, as if she liked being there, as if she even liked me.

Somehow it seemed as though she belonged there in the car—and sure, she was only in her twenties or so, and I was in my forties, so mathematically she could have been my kid, but you know, it's not impossible.

There's a little shift that happens, and it happens all the

time, in all kinds of circumstances. Like your eyes suddenly are working a different way, and you size everything up differently.

That's the way I felt, looking at her. Like it was the difference between someone you've just met and someone you know. Like I could know what she was thinking, and what she wanted, and maybe it was me. A long shot, but maybe it was me.

Don't get me wrong here.

I mean, I know all about "no means no." But she wasn't saying no.

She wasn't saying anything.

I started driving again but I kept looking over at her, at that little sort of half smile and the way her hair had dried all feathery in around her face. We were just driving back up the road by then, no point to it, really, the cabins going by on one side, and I knew that, soon enough I'd turn around, and the cabins would be going by again on the other side.

Eventually I just turned the car up one of those narrow little forestry roads, the ones where you push through a tight little throat of spruce trees and then pop out on a full-sized logging road back along the edge of some clear-cut, green just starting to come up between the wet-black stumps. I stopped and put the car in park.

The rain had stopped completely. We were up pretty high, the front of the car pointing out over toward the river, and mist was jumping up from the bottom of the valley. Jumping up, rising fast, coming out from under the trees all at once.

It was an older clear-cut, the slash all knocked down by age, the sort of place where, even though it looks like a war zone, enough time has gone by that you know nature's going to go ahead and take right over again, that it's just been biding its time until it's sure you're gone. Fireweed first and quick-covering raspberries, then the opportunistic deciduous trees like alders and impatient birch.

Lisa didn't wake up when I turned the engine off. I could hear her breathing. I could almost feel the long, deep breaths. She was out of it, out cold, probably unconscious.

I got out of the car and looked down the long clear-cut into the valley. It's strange — we spend so much of our time around people that it's almost impossible for our heads to take in a big long sweep of trees and stumps and slash where there's absolutely no people at all. No one in sight. No one who would hear anything. Some old, flattened cardboard beer boxes on the forest road, soaked through and coming apart — so there had been people recently, but not now. The air full of that smell of wet you get after rain, the tinny sharp smell that makes you say, "yeah, I remember that," just before you go ahead and forget about it all over again.

I remember hitching my pants up over my ass. I'm always hitching up my pants, like I'm an old tomcat, the back side of me just melting away. My pants are always heading somewhere south, almost like they have a mind of their own, and they'd like to be somewhere warmer. Like Cuba. But I remember that time, that hitch, like it was some kind of punctuation, as if it meant something particular, as if it were a step forward in the way a gear turns — always forward, never back.

Always done — never undone.

I went around to Lisa's side of the car and looked in through the glass. It struck me that she was a far prettier girl in repose — that talking, or at least talking when she was drunk, made her face move in almost unattractive ways. And I thought that, lying there asleep in the soft light coming down through the mist, she was possibly as pretty as she would ever be in her entire life.

I opened her door. She snored a little, but she didn't move, and I lifted her legs out through the door, her head sliding back against the side of my seat. She shifted a bit, but her eyes didn't open. Her mouth went slack, though, loose almost, and that was jarring.

I was picturing her just like that, exactly in that position, leaning back against the seat — but I was picturing her after I'd taken her pants off, naked from the waist down and her legs spread and her feet hanging out through the door, the balls touching the ground.

Somehow, all at once — even imagining it, even fantasizing — it wasn't the way I thought it would be. It was like a crime scene photo. In my head, it was like someone had switched a light on for a moment, and just as quickly switched it off again.

I don't like to think about that. I still don't like thinking about that. Amazing the emotions that churns up — how fast you rush from embarrassed to furious. Like water rushing in and back out again.

I left her, wide-eyed and alone, looking for all the world

like she was ten years old or something. The rain had stopped completely, and she was pretty much dry again anyway.

I may have said something about keeping an eye open for her on the way back from the river, and that if I saw her, I'd pick her up. I did keep my eyes open, as much as you can when you're driving and trying not to go off the road, but I didn't see her.

She was gone.

CHAPTER 22

ear plugs
travel pillow
ipod + recharge cord
camera + battery charger
toileterres — razor/shave cream/tooth brush face wash
Hair Dryer
slippers?

That one with the Facebook, the one with *banans* and all that. The one with the long legs.

Halfway through March, when it's dirty weather here and the sleet's always waiting and about to come slashing down, she'd put up on her site under one of those daily photographs that she and the Daniel guy were going to Mexico, and that day the picture was her in a bikini, and underneath, she said, "What do you think of this one?" And it all makes her seem disappointingly shallow.

It's not that hard to figure out when a house is going to be empty, not when someone has told you that they're going to be going away already. In March, by the time I'm off work it's closing in on dark, even on the day shift, so I walked over to her neighbourhood like I was doing her a favour, just to make sure the place was locked up tight.

Nothing more in mind than that, just to go and see whether everything was okay at her place. I didn't ever worry that someone would see me, that they would ask questions. Not even once. After a while, you're so used to not being seen that you can slip that over you like clothing.

I was absolutely certain she had already left. You spend enough time reading about someone's movements, watching them closely when you see them, and it's really like you know them, even if some part of you, some grounded, hidden part, warns you constantly that you really don't.

I knew her street and I knew her house, and there were a couple of lights on inside but not on the porch, and it was a squat square little two-storey, detached on both sides with the kind of porch you can walk right up onto, roofed over so you can put down the groceries and get out your keys while you're safely out of the rain.

So I walked straight up the walk and onto the porch and tried the knob, gave it a good twist, shook the door, and waited: there was no sound at all from the other side. And the door was locked, all right, but right near the stairs at the front there was a flowerpot that had been moved, just enough off-centre so that you could see where it had been before, a little dirty fingernail of washed down soil left behind, and I thought, "Wouldn't that be a stupid place to leave a key?"

Sure enough, there was a single key under there, flat and gold-coloured and the same make as the front door lock.

I tried it and it was the door key, all right, so I just kind of inched inside sideways and closed the door behind me, wondering if there was someone coming to check on the place or water the plants or feed the cat or whatever it is you do when someone has gone to the trouble to leave a key out for you.

The house was empty — I took a quick look right through all of it, peering into the rooms where the lights were on and making my way slowly through the dark ones without flipping on any other switches. The cat fled up the stairs in front of me, orange and white, and it made no noise at all with its paws on the carpeted steps, stopping at the top to give me a quick look. I stayed downstairs, went through the room off the living room where she had the computer, the kitchen — a lot brighter and shinier than mine — and then went up to the bedrooms.

One of them obviously hers — well, theirs, because inside the dresser there were men's clothes, too, though not many — and she was not the neatest, because there were clothes all over the bed, shirts and pants and skirts that looked like they'd been selected for the trip and then rejected, left lying where they fell. Like there was going to be absolutely no need to deal with them — to even think about them — until she got back. I had an almost irresistible urge to pick them up, to feel the fabric between my fingertips, maybe even to fold them and try to find where they were supposed to be put away. But I managed not to.

The mess of the bedroom seemed odd, because the kitchen was so clean—knives lined up in the block like they were all in the same order they'd been in coming out of the package, the counters all wiped down. White-framed glass cupboard doors, every door closed, and behind them, dishes and plates all piled neatly. Nothing in the dish rack, nothing in the sinks, even the two baskets down in the drains clean. The cat's dish was off to one side, and it was piled high with food. The cat was still hiding somewhere upstairs, under a bed or in a closet, but that was all right, because I don't really like cats all that much.

There were plants in the house, but not too many. Not like the indoor jungles some people make, where there's stuff hanging down all over so you kind of expect spiders or bats or huge bugs or something to be hiding out in there among the big wet-looking leaves. I put my index finger in the dirt in each one, and they were still damp, damp enough that they wouldn't need watering for at least a few days.

I didn't take anything—I didn't really touch anything besides the soil in the flowerpots and a doorknob or two, but I did look around and save it all up in my head.

I think I was there long enough to get a feel for the place, for where things were, for what was important. Then I put her in the house, too—coming down the stairs in sweatpants, cooking in a T-shirt and jeans in that glossy kitchen, her lips pursed as she tried to make out the ingredients in a recipe. I could see her so clearly I could imagine how she was holding her face slightly pinched around the corners of her eyes, like I was making her nearsighted on purpose. Trying to imagine the sound of her feet when she walked, the pattern of sound under her bare feet. That she was moving around leaving closet doors open, her clothes half out of the hamper, completely comfortable in her own space.

I was careful to lock the door when I left—I even pulled it hard shut and then gave it a little tug, a shake back and forth, to make sure the lock was really locked and that the latch to the doorknob was properly seated, too. We have strong winds in March, and even a small draft can just plain pull the money out of your wallet, just over a day or two, the furnace down there alone in the basement, working hard and trying to keep up.

I imagined that it wouldn't be too long after I closed the door before the cat would come out from wherever it was hiding and make its way back to the endless and moving view out the front window. Cats are cagey things; it would probably be there soon enough to see my back, departing down the sidewalk.

I'll try to remember to look for it, if I come back.

When I come back.

Know what? There are a lot of places that copy a key in an hour.

Know what else?

You can hold a key in your hand until it's as warm as your skin and still have it back in its hiding place before anyone even knows it's gone missing.

CHAPTER 23

January 12
Sexual assault arrest made

(St. John's, NL) — Police say they have solved the case of a trio of year-old metro-area sexual assaults, following analysis of the cases by the department's new cold case squad.

The Royal Newfoundland Constabulary (RNC) announced the arrest of forty-seven-year-old Francis Kevin Beaton for three downtown assaults at a press conference Monday, saying the charges were the result of a re-analysis of case files using new investigative techniques.

"The RNC is always at the forefront of new methods and technology," RNC Chief Winston Adams said. "We take the investigative process seriously. It may not always move as quickly as we would like, but it never stops. Not while I'm chief."

Asked about the investigation, lead investigator Inspector Dean Hill said that he and his partner had used new interrogation methods to help identify Beaton as the alleged assailant, but refused to elaborate.

Beaton is already in custody on other charges. His next court date will be March 15.

"We are surely going to be buried in leftovers now."

That was Scoville, in the passenger seat with the folded newspaper in front of him, talking slowly as the tires hissed on the wet pavement and Dean drove.

It had been a week since Dean had signed out a car from the pool and, on his way out the door, unexpectedly found Scoville waiting for him.

"Heading out?" Scoville said. "I guess I'll come too."

He didn't ask, merely said he was coming and then climbed in the car.

Dean was afraid that Scoville was going to give him some kind of lecture. Or worse, that he was going to ask if Dean wanted to talk about it—and if there was one thing Dean didn't want to do, it was to talk about it. Any of it. Not about work, not about home. The driving wasn't meant to stir things up—it was to tamp them down. To shift things into order. From the station to the east end. Out the big looping ring road, in on the downtown arterial, around the harbour apron, and then back to the station. Backing into the parking spot, leaving the car nose out, ready to go.

But Scoville didn't want to talk about anything either. He just sat in the front seat, staring out the windshield, chewing on a plastic coffee stir stick. They drove, Dean setting the direction, making his usual cycle through the city he knew well. After that, Scoville rode with Dean every time, regardless of where Dean took them. Scoville didn't say anything about the route, didn't ask.

Now, with the newspaper in his lap, Scoville was quiet but obviously seething, sharp little sentences leaking out every mile or two, his face flicking through angry little tics.

"Squad room calls us the recycling team now. It's all a big joke," Scoville said. "Bursey came down and dropped a file on my desk and said, 'Another load ready for pickup.'"

A few minutes later—"Then the shithead walked backwards out the door, beeping like he was a garbage truck in reverse."

Another handful of miles went by.

"We solve one simple thing and we get every little trespassing file and mischief complaint they couldn't bother to deal with in the last couple of weeks."

At Cape Broyle, the waves came in slow and even, the edge taken off their anger by the disinterest of the long, flat bay. Dean had turned off the ring road in an unexpected direction, making Scoville lurch up in his seat for a moment. They wound up parked right by the water. The bay there was a long funnel, closing in, and the ocean swell had been ordered and knocked down. By the time the waves neared the end of the bay, they were little more than a lop on the shore, less a slap than a backhand, their curl a simple echo of the real sea.

They toppled onto the beach resignedly, flatly, limply, with almost a ruled edge of regularity.

Dean saw the black sole of a boot at the tide line, along with one bulb from a string of Christmas lights. The bulb was green, and there was a hint of verdigris on its shiny brass base. Gathering it all up, helpless to do anything but that. While he watched, the waves slowed — so much that they might almost have stopped. He knew they were too far out of town — out there on a shift when they should have been setting up interviews, shifting paper. He hadn't meant to drag Scoville into it, he thought, into this near-circling of the drain.

He didn't say anything to Scoville, and Scoville just sat in the car, somehow managing to look satisfied without ever changing his expression.

Just up the road, there was a "for sale" sign in front of a light blue mobile home, right below a street sign for Kent's Lane.

The trailer had burned — pretty much last night, Dean thought, looking at the wreckage — and its blackened rafters were holding up only the blue sky. Parts of the building looked as if nothing had changed, while others screamed silent catastrophe.

The windows were all broken and blown out — burned, tufted furniture was scattered around the snow-filled yard. There was no sign of where the people who used to live there had gone, or whether they were even there when it had started to burn. A police car sat at the end of the driveway; Dean recognized the officer in the front seat and waved.

"There's something we're missing about Mary Carter," Dean told Scoville. "There's a pattern here we're not seeing yet."

"Arson's easier," Scoville said. "If you find proof it was burned, you run through the easy suspects — business owner who can't pay the bills, overdue mortgage — or if it's an arsonist who isn't connected to the place, you look for opportunity and other fires. They follow a line. Almost always men, and they work their way up from something small. A shed, a car. Later, abandoned buildings — eventually, places with people in them. They move up every time the thrill slips, every time something becomes routine. The more they do, the easier it gets."

Dean realized that Scoville had said something important. Like a coin falling into the right slot, like a mechanism grinding suddenly into motion. New patterns emerging, keys into locks.

"That Walt guy. It still bothers me," Dean said. "It doesn't matter what he says about what happened. There's just not enough going on with him.

"We go and tear his place up and he's never curious about any of it. Just heads out the door, doesn't even bother to get pissed off. Never calls us to ask if there's anything new about Mary. There's just not enough, not enough feeling with him. Nothing coming off him at all. Like nothing has changed."

"Yeah, except his missus."

Dean didn't laugh.

"People are different," Scoville said with a shrug, looking

across at Dean. "And you know that's not how we're supposed to do it. We're not supposed to pick the guy and look for the evidence. We're supposed to let the evidence do all the talking."

"I know it's him," Dean said, even though he hadn't completely figured out why he knew it. "And the more I kick it around, the more I don't think it's just Mary, either. If we start broadening this out, he might fit in other places, too."

"That's actually good enough for me," Scoville said. He was looking straight out the windshield. "Fact is, I don't give a fuck either way. Let's just put him in the sights and get him then."

CHAPTER 24

Mar. 28 — I got an email from Erin — she's one of
the last of my university friends who hasn't moved
away. She's taking care of Bo, and she was supposed
to be staying at the house. Now she says she's making sure he's fine, food and water and cuddles, but
she's not staying over. She says she's uncomfortable,
can't put her finger on why — except she says she
was following the note I'd left on the counter to the
letter, and the plants were already watered, so she
wondered why I even asked her to do it if they were
already fine. I'm a bit pissed off with her not staying there — I don't like the thought of Bo lonely and
wandering around in there by himself. But there's
part of me saying, "Yes! I'm not imagining it." At the
same time, I don't like the idea of her being so afraid
she's not staying.

CHAPTER 25

Jackie
Needs choc milk
2 white
Two of each
Miss Vickies
Apple Juice
Ginger ale
pepsi

I could imagine her in my head—daydreaming, gathering up what a Jackie might look like, imagining her on her side, her back to me, half asleep in my bed. A little chips-and-ginger-ale curvy, but that's just fine, too.

Maybe this is why some guys need pornography, to put them that much closer to women they see on the street and know they'll never even have a chance to get close enough to touch. Not me: I can take a note, especially a new one, and just imagine the woman who wrote it. Imagine her in the store, imagine her in my living room. Take that thought and spend hours driving just like that, not even putting the radio on, barely seeing the scenery through the fantasy.

I remember really well that there had been too much water in the O'Keefe for the fish to be holding there, and not enough in the Big Barachois to stir the weeds and bring them up from down between the sharp rocks. So I went further to the Little Barachois, where there are always fish to catch, even if it's only the pale-fleshed ouaniniche, land-locked, puny salmon that you always see coming up at the last second, strangely olive-coloured through the water and quick like little bullets.

They're so pale and soft inside that they aren't even worth keeping, certainly not worth keeping to eat, so as soon as I caught them, I'd shake them off the hook. The only worthwhile moment they give you is that first hard electric strike you never expect, the one you feel through the line the instant they hit the fly, a strike that always makes them feel like a larger fish. But see the colour of them through the water, and the only thing you're thinking about is letting them go.

And all the time, there's the sheer physical effort of watching the fly, looking to see the fish strike, even keeping your balance. Just standing up is an intense kind of concentration that leaves little room for anything else to make its way around in your head. You don't think other thoughts. You don't work over an argument you had with your wife. You don't get into "what I should have said was . . ." Because there just isn't room.

And I love that.

A couple of hours after I got on the river, I was climbing up and over the big shoulder of one of the two cliffs that leaned in toward each other and made the river suddenly deep. I was farther down the river than I'd ever been: those cliffs had always turned me back before, because it's no fun to scramble up fifty feet of rock just to turn around and struggle back down again.

Besides, someone died down there once: there on that exact piece of cliff, only on the right-hand side, opposite to where I was climbing. I don't know who it was or when they'd fallen; all I know is that they did, and that the body had lain there until a rescue helicopter came in from Gander to airlift it back out.

Once I'd climbed back down, the water was disappointing; between the cliffs, the rock pinched in and made a place deep enough for trout to hold, but on the other side, the river only broadened, with scattered river rocks poking up black and dry through the shallows.

But I was stubborn and angry with myself, not about to just let disappointment win, not after getting myself that far from the road. So I kept pushing forward, making myself work down the current, tired enough that I had stopped watching where the side brooks came in, stopped paying attention to the drifts of moss and the occasional brightly coloured flowers and small orchids.

Then I cut a corner, after about half a mile of flat, shallow river, hardly more than a gentle curve around a stand of juniper, and all at once, I saw a cabin off to the edge on the left-hand side of the river, in under the trees where the river had suddenly gone still and deep. I remember, for a moment, being split between the cabin and the river — the cabin obviously a surprise, but the river curving into a great, deep left-hand cut bank that just shouted big trout.

When you're walking along a river, it's not like you're making your way along a path where you might be expected. You suddenly arrive somewhere, and it's like you've deliberately chosen to sneak up on someone. You're coming in the back way, no one expecting you.

So when I see something new ahead of me on a river, I always go slow.

The cabin was leaning, a corner post so far gone and rotted that one side knelt right down low and I could see up onto an edge of the roof. An old-style roof, the sort of thing that needs an annual tarring with a pail and brush to stop the nail heads from leaking.

The front door was half-open — a white-painted, peeling door, three rectangles of wood — and the inside of the cabin was dark.

It's funny what you do without even thinking.

I pulled my fly line back into my left hand in loops without winding it onto the reel, so that the reel wouldn't make the soft but regular mechanical clicks the ratchet makes when you wind it in. I pulled myself sideways to the edge of the river, the shaded side, and pushed my back into the high ferns so that I was as far out of sight as I could get.

And I waited.

It was a hot day, July, bright with the sun cutting down the way it does around eleven in the morning or so, and I could feel the heat of it on the top of the baseball cap I wore to cut the glare off the water, and there was sweat in the middle of my back and deep down along the backs of my legs inside my boots.

It was quiet enough that I could hear the beating of my heart in my ears, the gentle swoosh of the blood in the small capillaries.

There were big aspens or poplars down in the dip around that cabin — they had to have been brought in, planted there, because they were just too out of place on that river — and the light that was passing through the leaves kept changing, flickering on the surface of the pool, as if the water was moving far more than it actually was.

Even today, I don't know what I kept waiting for.

I waited and I took the tip of my fishing rod and threaded it in through the ferns and brush so that I could lay it down silently and have both my hands free just in case I needed them.

The cabin was aimed so that the front door opened straight out onto the small, deep, sheltered pool in the river, a place where the river had turned along some unseen contour line toward the ocean, the sharp directed edge of the current cutting straight into one bank, carving into the ground and then hanging there, the water curling slowly around as if it couldn't quite decide where to go next. There was a dab of dirty river foam circling gently at the centre, circling like it could spin there endlessly, nothing ever changing, with the brown edges and the peaked tops of the foam looking almost caramelized.

There was probably a trail that came straight in to the cabin from the road somewhere on the other side, maybe even something as wide open as an all-terrain vehicle, the brush cut back and the track etched down to the rock by the passage of knobbed tires. There had to be. Certainly no one would be making their way down the river every single time they wanted to get there.

I sat and waited, and when no one came out, I finally crossed the river and went up the noisy gravelled bank in front of the door, walking that way that says "notice me, notice me, here I am, I am here." Every foot set down deliberately heavy.

As I got closer, I realized that the cabin was abandoned — and that it had been abandoned for a long time. Each piece I was looking at became slightly harder and more distinct as I approached, like the building was taking its time coming into focus. The paint peeling more, the front edge of the porch bending farther toward the ground than I had seen from the other side of the river.

Where I thought there had been window glass, there were only open sockets, the glass long since broken out.

When I reached the front door, I found that the floor inside existed only in small patches, most of it rotten and fallen in. I went in: there was a small oil stove in the corner with an aluminum kettle still sitting on top of it, a sagging jerry can on the floor with fuel. A dirty-looking countertop with one half of a yellow plastic box of rifle ammunition, 30-06 shells, the ones you need to drop good-sized game, caribou or larger, but with not a single one of the twenty-five bullets left in the box. Twenty-five holes, no takers.

The whole place stank of mould and neglect and something foul or rotten; I stuck my head around an inside door into the back and pulled it right back again pretty quickly.

In that one back room, there was a camp bed frame pushed into the corner, up against the wall, the mattress rotten and settled through the frame in tufts. That room had one small window with dark, mildewed curtains, the wind occasionally breathing the fabric back and forth gently, the room brightening and then blinking darker as they moved.

At the foot of the bed, a tangled quilt and blankets in a ball, like someone had just then gotten up out of that soggy bed and thrown the covers over into a fat mound.

The only thing I could think was that there had been people there, that it had to have been some kind of special place for someone and that at some point they had stopped coming, that there might not be one single clue left that could even begin to tell me why.

Part of me wanted to keep looking, to turn the place over and pick through every scrap of the remains to try and find some kind of sign, to discover who had felt it necessary to board up one broken window at the very back but leave the rest of the glass scattered across the remains of the floor in great sharp spears. To pick up the white enamelled bowl with the bottom rusted right out, just to see if there was something out of sight beneath it.

I remember thinking that even the empty tin cans in the ragged trash bag could tell me what those people ate or maybe when they had been there last, if I dug them out and had a good look.

At the same time, there was a part of me that wanted to get out of the place as quickly as I could.

I can collect the whole outside of that cabin in my head any time at all from the first time I saw it — the long, swinging curve in the river, the dark corner of the building protruding from the shelter of the trees. The sharp, brisk, deliberate destruction of it all.

And everything else — the heavy, constant smell of the mould on the walls in the front room, the long curls of the wallboard pulled away from the anchoring nails and bending toward the floor like gravity working on heavy, drooping leaves.

Then I was heading back up the river, the sun cutting bright down through the trees and reflecting off the water, making me blink as I tried to work my fly across the surface, fishing just to keep my arm and my mind moving, more than anything else.

It was like the things around me caught my attention but fled immediately, fractured and insignificant: I remember a stand of birch, white-barked and unusually straight, all together in a huddle on one small piece of flat land. Shadows that I saw out of the corner of my eyes that looked like people standing back in the shelter of the woods until I broke my attention from the river and actually looked — then realized it was nothing like that at all. All of it caught up in my head in fleeting little pieces, all broken apart and loose as if they couldn't find clear traction in memory.

It was only a little past noon, but I got off the river and climbed through the alders up the gravel embankment to the car, threw my boots in the trunk and drove the half hour on the looping Cataracts road to Placentia, the rocks kicking up from the tires and rattling against the bottom of the car in an uneven rhythm.

I drove the long way back around on the highway, thinking I'd find another place where a river crossed the road and I might feel like heading up or down on the water to fish, and that it might all run clear and cold and pure again. But there wasn't the right kind of river, or, more to the point, there wasn't any place I felt like stopping, so I burned up a tank of gas for virtually no reason at all.

I got home cranky, the release I normally get from a day on a river completely gone, and that night, doing the dishes in the kitchen, I broke a wineglass on the edge of the sink, a wineglass Mary had bought, and cut my hand badly. Strange the way single events can anchor themselves so clearly in your memory, down to the exact day itself, even the exact time of day.

For almost a minute I stood there and stared down at my hand in the water, at the foam clinging to the edges of the metal sink and the water slowly staining red. Standing there and staring at it like the blood wasn't coming from me at all, as if it was just blossoming in the water all of its own accord.

A month later, in the middle of the night, I sat up straight in bed next to Mary. She was snoring slightly, the covers thrown off her so I could see that she was wearing only panties and that the lines of moonlight were threading in through the blinds and landing on her skin in an even pattern, like she was wearing an elaborate dress made out of strips of skin-tight black fabric. There was the wind, knocking up against the house in regular, familiar thumps the way it does when it's an eager night-time northwesterly, rattling in the maples. Everything was exactly, precisely familiar, yet not quite right — everything jarred sideways by what was going on in my head.

And I realized that I was covered with sweat, the bed soaked under me and cold, and I also realized then what it was that had been bothering me about the cabin on the river.

It hadn't caught me when I was there, hadn't even occurred to me, and I think it's because there was something I was trying hard not to see.

Sometimes the whole picture is too much — your head doesn't want you to have it, because you can't deal with it yet, because you aren't equipped to deal with the rush of sounds and sensations and sights all over again.

When that happens, I think your mind rips it all into shreds and stores it that way, and you can somehow deal with a handful of individual scraps until it's time to start weaving them back together. Like there will be a time later on to consider the whole thing, so that you can assemble it in some place a little safer.

Awake in that night, I could suddenly see much more.

The cabin was all right there again, like a movie running through my eyes, with me walking into that back room, feeling the flex of the rotting floorboards under my fishing boots and seeing the way the light came through the broken glass in the window.

And there was something about the way the camp bed was pushed up against the back wall, about the tangle of wet bedclothes at the foot. Sitting up in bed, I could feel my breath rushing, blood thumping in my ears.

You can look at things and have them not make any sense to your head and your eyes.

It might take a day or a week or a year before something lets the pin drop and everything starts to make sense, but when it does, the bits all click together so tightly that there's no other possible explanation. You don't escape it then, because then you just know. And once you do, there's no undoing it—no unknowing it.

Safe in our bed and our bedroom, with stripped, striped Mary right there beside me and the wind safely locked outside, I was suddenly acutely aware that I had been in a cabin where someone had gotten up and left a bed in a hurry, and that bundled up against the wall of the cabin, they'd left what looked an awful lot like someone else's dead body.

CHAPTER 26

Mar. 29 — Apparently the people at the resort are
far more spooked about Mexico than they have to
be. I mean, it's bad and all, because lots of people
go missing and plenty are killed — journalists and
police especially — but it's not like if you step outside
the resort, you're instantly whisked away in a van or
something and held for ransom. It sure doesn't feel
menacing. I think I know menacing. I guess a lot of
it is where you are and how well you know the place.
I met a couple of girls on the beach — Daniel was
sleeping; about the only thing he's doing down here
that's close to Mexican is a siesta — and they were
saying that they have been beating around the interior for almost six months, that they stick together
and have fun and once in a while, they book a resort
room for a day or two to get cleaned up. One of
them, Anne, said, "The front desk takes one look at
us and the backpacks and, every time, you can see
them trying to decide if they should have us marched
right back out the front door." Her friend's Liz.

She's smaller and darker, with a mouthful of white teeth: "We just whip out our credit cards real fast, and always speak English." They're from Oshawa, and they say that most of the country's nothing like this—that a lot of it is really old and the country-side's beautiful, that you've just got to get away from the sand and the high-rise hotels to see what the place is really like. I like the idea of that—just get-ting away. "You can fall in love with it in an instant," Liz says. "And we know lots of people who have just stayed down here, teaching English in small schools and living completely different lives. The visas can be a bit hinky, but nothing's impossible." It struck me then that, even with the strangeness of the place and everyone going on about how dangerous it is and everything else, I actually feel safer here than I do at home. Like a weight has lifted. And I don't know what to do about that.

CHAPTER 27

Flowers — hall, sitting room x 2, dining table
Imperial cheddar
Prosseco
Grand Marnier
Madeira
Calvados
Armagnac
3 red
3 white
Plum Tomatoes
Hot Sausages 1 lb
2 lb regular sausages
Frozen bread dough - dinner rolls
Persimmons?
Pomegranates
Grated cheddar
Fruit for salad
Cream
2 Cups pecans
Butterscotch pudding

Pistachios
Dark Choc
Lady fingers

Organized. You look at a list like that, and it just screams organization, yells out into the darkness that this is someone, goddamn it, who has it all under control, every single piece of life firmly pressed into place, right from when they were an infant and had their hands and feet pressed down in those old-fashioned plaster of Paris casts, old writing on the back, "Elizabeth at eight days." Set firmly, almost from day one.

Hard not to envy someone who can live like that, who can hold on simply by pure force of will and self-possession. Because will isn't easy, especially when you look around and find out it's fled.

Every now and then, I wish that the years could spin backwards, and that I could suddenly find a way to fit in somewhere in that coil of past time, step back onto that carefully ordered track that Mary and I stepped off of somewhere. And that Mary stepped off far further than I ever did.

I wouldn't want to forget everything—I think I'd want all the knowledge I have now even if I wanted to turn around and do things differently. Otherwise I'd just live that same exact pattern all over again—make the same choices, step the same steps. Dance the same dance.

But I wish sometimes that I could be one of those people with blind, unquestioning belief. Someone who could keep living a life, however dreadful, because it was the right thing to do, and the right thing is what people are supposed to do. Always.

Because that kind of belief would be such a gift. A real comfort.

I've never been good at belief, and I think I've gotten worse and worse with every passing year.

Think of it this way: Einstein might have been real pleased about figuring out relativity, about tracing it right there in front of his face with a pencil or chalk or whatever, but when he went outside, do you suppose it ever made him feel like he was in the least little bit closer to the stars?

I imagine it actually made him feel like he was farther away from them — and maybe sometimes he felt bad about that, too.

Nothing quite like seeing the world the way you want it to be, right there yet always out of reach.

When things didn't work out just the way she had planned, it was like Mary began to fly apart. Maybe that's not the right description. Pull away, for sure. Parts of her certainly flew apart. Flew out from her — left her orbit altogether. She had belief — some kind of belief. And then she lost it and came undone.

Not obviously at first — it wasn't like she woke up one morning and was different. She wasn't speaking Hungarian or licking the sheets, not adopting fleets of feral street cats. No, it was like small pieces started to break off of her, at first like moons that had all at once lost confidence in her gravity, moons spinning out and away from the security of their usual, regular orbital field.

Then it began to be bits of Planet Mary herself.

There was nothing wrong with her rotation—she still spun, all right. I think it was just that, suddenly, there was too much spin for all of the bits along the edges to bear.

I don't mean she woke up all crazy and strung out and screaming, that she forgot the meanings of words or began winding sticks in her hair like birds were nesting there and the eggs might hatch out any day, little beaks and bright eyes poking out from their hiding spots near her scalp and singing their little plaintive "we're hungry" notes into the room every time they laid eyes on you.

That would almost have been simpler.

I don't mean any offence to anyone this is happening to, but it's like living with someone whose stomach is always out of sorts. Someone who constantly has a non-defined, non-specific problem dogging both them and, in the process, everyone they live with.

When there's suddenly a real diagnosis—even if it's a stark and final one—you know how you're supposed to set your face about it. You know how you're supposed to look to the world, what you're supposed to do. There are things to be dealt with, even if those things are truly horrible. There are things to be done and there are things you can safely not give even the slightest fuck about. But until then, you don't know whether to be honestly worried or justifiably annoyed.

With Mary, everything was in that horrible land of the not-quite-specific. All that happened was that things that had been crucially important even just a few days before suddenly didn't matter. They faded all at once—and that didn't make any sense to me.

I mean, if you want to retire to British Columbia and grow hybrid roses and banks of forced asparagus or whatever, or if you want to buy an Airstream and head to the deserts of the southwestern United States, spending every other week in a Walmart parking lot so that you're never more than a hundred yards from someone else's clean toilets, you're not supposed to suddenly stop, wake up one morning, and decide it would be just fine to spend every single day wrapped in fog in a two-storey saltbox house out in Flatrock instead.

You either want things or you don't—and the things you want badly shouldn't just wash right out of you, or wash right off of you, with one single tick of the clock.

But that's exactly what seemed to happen with Mary.

I couldn't decide if I was exactly, precisely to blame, or if it was just another way that her list was supposed to work—like there were entries on it that were categorized as "either/ or," and since the "either" hadn't happened, there was nothing left to do except settle for the unattractive "or."

When I started thinking that way, I also thought the "or" might be every bit as predetermined as everything else.

I came home from the store one afternoon to find that she had painted the entire front room. Tied her hair inside a plastic shopping bag, put on her painting pants—the pants that had smears of paint from every room in every house she'd ever lived in — and worked like a dervish.

She had wanted a certain number of rooms when we bought the house, and, of course, we'd found a house with every single one she needed. She didn't say anything concrete, but I knew she had ideas for them all. Mary liked painting. Often, she didn't so much paint the rooms for the things she wanted them to be as she painted them in a way that wouldn't exclude what she thought they could become.

The front room upstairs, I know she thought it would be a nursery, despite the noise. So it had always been pale colours — not obvious nursery colours, but a beige that could be repainted in one simple coat to something she thought was suitable. After a while, it became a mild café au lait — nothing definitely "baby" about it, but also nothing that would immediately rule out baby, either.

I came home from the store that day and it was dark blue — the kind of dark blue that would take three or four coats to ever come close to being a light colour again, and it wasn't like anyone was going to put a crib in a room painted the colour of ten o'clock in the evening on a late summer night. "Hey baby, here's a nightmare for you: it's getting dark now, it's actually dark all the time, so maybe no one's ever coming back. Sleep tight."

Beautiful, it was. Carefully, precisely done? Absolutely.

Welcoming? Not one single bit.

It was the kind of solution that's more like a dare than anything else — a dare that says, "Let's go."

That's sort of what I thought Mary's dark blue paint in the upstairs front room was supposed to be, too — a sign that she was spoiling for a fight.

Just waiting for someone to say it out loud — "What the fuck were you thinking about?" — and start the whole thing up.

The room's still that colour now, and the funny thing is that I like it — or at least I've gotten so used to it that it just seems right.

Dignified, more than a little standoffish — and maybe just exactly the way a study is supposed to be. I go in there often enough — I just don't often stay.

After the painting of the room, the next thing was the basement — or the things she would take out of the basement and simply leave on the curb for the garbage men.

I'm sure that the garbage men thought they had struck the jackpot.

You wonder sometimes if there's a ton of stuff that just doesn't make it all the way to the dump — and if, somewhere at home in garbage-man-ville, there are spouses who roll their eyes as yet another pile of curb-side treasures shows up at the front door.

Are their garages packed to the roof? Do they rent weekend flea market tables and set stuff out for sale?

It must be tough to just take perfectly good things and toss them in the back of the truck, then press the button and watch the hydraulic ram crush them, turning absolutely everything into garbage.

I didn't even realize what was gone for several weeks, not until I went down to the basement and saw the empty room off the laundry. A big rocking chair went, along with a bunch of boxes from her mother. I'm not even sure what was in some of them, just that the room had been full before and now it wasn't.

Turned out later that the Christmas decorations had been in some of those boxes, too, so Christmas came and we started all over again from scratch with brand new stuff. Other stuff went as well: Raggedy Ann dolls that Mary had kept for so long their faces had changed and shrunk in the sunlight, developing a look that was more mental than freckle-faced happy.

All she was willing to say about it was that "there isn't a point anymore," and she said it, every time, with her hands thrown out in front of her, her palms down and her fingers somehow arcing upwards. I can still see it — a combination of dismissiveness and the motion you'd make shaking water off your fingertips.

It looks kind of fatalistic, seeing it written down like this, like she was shaking the dust off of a set of biblical sandals or something, and maybe she was. But those were her exact words, and she offered up the same exact motion every time. And I have to say that it didn't seem fatalistic at all, then. It just seemed resigned.

When she did it, I could also see that there was plenty more in there behind her face just waiting to come out. Sometimes, the sides of someone's face work like they're chewing a kind of particularly wordy gum, like they've decided they're going to force themselves not to say even one single word, but their jaw can't help going through the motions. I remember thinking once that, if she were there, Helen Keller could just place her hands on both sides of Mary's face and know absolutely for a fact every single thing that was going through Mary's head.

I think that it was all an opening gambit — the painting, the cleaning out. I think it was her way of trying to get me to hook into and haul out those words hidden behind her face.

If only I had been willing to pull that line.

I was pretty sure I knew what she was going to be talking about.

You don't have to be Einstein to realize what it means when the room you've always tacitly agreed would be the nursery has been painted over. What you have to be is completely, absolutely, magnificently stunned.

Because there's a time when it's just better to play dumb. And be smart. And manage, against near-impossible odds, to pull it all off convincingly.

Einstein probably would have just started thinking about stars.

CHAPTER 28

Kitty litter
Coffee cream
1 Fresh Milk
1 bag oranges

Sometimes, it's more than what's on the list. I mean, it's still the list, but there's something else that makes it valuable. One I found in the parking lot in the rain, almost a perfect square, a torn piece of white bond paper stuck down with the water so that it looked like a big postage stamp glued to an oversized envelope of asphalt.

People were pushing their carts right past it, right over it, like it didn't even exist.

Not surprising that the note didn't gather any interest. It was washed-out blue ink on the front, open handwriting with each lower-case *f* boasting a semi-circle to the left on the top, the capital *F* like a backwards number seven with a line drawn back through it.

I had watched it flutter down to the pavement from inside

the store, staring out through the big thermal-glass windows as a woman got into her car. It fell as she turned and settled herself into the driver's seat, and I watched it fall all the way. It was a little bright green car, and I knew her. She was a regular, in her mid-twenties maybe, and she lived on Gower Street, I was pretty sure with a couple of other young women. They sometimes shopped together, and I'd noticed that, when they did, the groceries were rung in all at once.

The things people use to write their notes: this one was obviously torn from a piece of regular typing paper, and it dried out unevenly on my counter, with the grocery list side face down on a sheet of paper towel, because the real message was on the back with a different pen, this one in black ink.

The same handwriting, except it was the top right corner of another, much larger, note, with the words left behind in something that was almost like a poem.

Like this:

have

to loan me

on Friday

back pay

and an

Written fast, the spaces between the letters much larger, just the end of each line left there and spelling out a clear message, but the same handwriting, the *f*'s and *e*'s and *a*'s all exactly the same.

You get short lists, and sometimes you wonder if the people are just disorganized and in a rush, whether they can't plan their way out of a simple corner, or whether the amount of money they have to spend on groceries has just made them cut their purchases back to the absolute necessities. And if that's the case, it's amazing how often cat food or dog food or kitty litter always makes its way onto the page — "Sure, I'll starve, but there'd better be Kibbles 'n Bits for Tigger."

This corner of paper, it was maybe one-sixth of the whole sheet, but the message was there in the words I had. All there, if you know how to read it. Everyone knows there's a huge part of the population that lives paycheque to paycheque. Most people, if they were to miss just one payday, wouldn't even be able to buy food. Nothing saved up — no rainy day fund. If they needed money all at once, they'd have to resort to all sorts of things you'd never expect.

It was pretty obvious: a message left out for one of the roommates, asking for a little help, just a little loan until her pay came in. And it gets you thinking — at least, it got me thinking.

It got me thinking about money and the way it can just pile up when you make your way from store to home with nothing more on your mind than a six-pack of beer for the fridge and another steak, not bothering to spend it on anything else. At the same time, it got me thinking about just what it is some people will do because they're desperate for cash.

It's about intersecting lines, really. Intersecting lines and the gamma rays pulsing straight through things and creating their unplanned little consequences. And it's about trying to figure out the clearest way to nudge things slightly sideways so everything collides and everything seems accidental.

Leave your car up on Gower Street without the right parking permit and maybe the parking enforcement guys are going to look close enough at the tag hanging from your mirror to see if you're in the right zone and then slip a ticket under the wiper. And maybe they're not.

They're certainly not going to do it while you're sitting in that car, waiting. When the parking guys see the shape of you bulked up in the front seat in the dark, they shy away in a hurry, like they're used to always being the target of the brute force of confrontation, and perhaps they are.

But you can see them taking stock of you in there, can see their brains working along the lines of "I'll come back later and check that white Toyota again." And you can be sure that they will. Maybe you'll get a ticket in the end — not much you can do about that.

I was sitting on the uphill side of the street, looking west, watching, a straight-line view across to the front door of her house — it was one with a public laneway right next to it, those slim little laneways that are asphalt-paved straight up to the next cross street but without any streetlights, right-of-ways that every single drunk in the city seems to know about, so that, on their way home and bladders filled to bursting, they can lean their foreheads up against your outside wall to keep their balance and piss on your siding.

I was watching the cats in the laneway — there were two of them right out at the end of the alley, like they were supposed to be the start of some kind of homemade Disney movie or something, one of them all smooth fur and a bright red collar, the other a ragged, skinny, high-assed tom.

The tom was thin the way tomcats always are—slinky-thin right through the ribs and sides, and then with their butts stuck up higher than the rest of their bodies, like every bit of strength was packed into their hindquarters, all hard purpose and blunt design. The well-kept one was bigger, heavier, and more tentative—someone's house pet out for a night on the rough—and it was easy to see what was going to happen when they finally got close enough to fight.

Because it's not like they're going to make friends and have a hundred kittens and catch evil robbers and make their own movie.

No, there's going to be ragged torn ears and a claw-raked face, deep bites that do what cat bites always do: get infected and weep thick pus and lead to big vet bills. You don't have to be a genius to see that coming.

I think people forget how much we're like animals, because most of us are too busy trying to force a square peg in a round hole and make it seem that, really, the animals are more like us.

I was watching television, maybe a couple of months ago now, and I saw this piece about the bushmen, about how they catch animals, and not by hiding or sneaking up on them either. They catch them because people don't have fur. That's the simplest way to describe it. We're supposed to make the most of what we've got, right? Well, people have the ability to sweat.

The bushmen just chase the animal until the ibex or the antelope or whatever it is overheats and can't run any more. Three, four hours of running, until finally the thing just stands there panting, too hot to keep running away, and the bushmen are all long and ropy there under their sweaty skin.

The animal stands there, helpless, and the bushmen practically walk right up and stick in their spears.

It's all about patience and doggedness, and that's worth remembering. You don't have to be the fastest or the smartest. You just have to be the most willing to keep going. The most persistent.

I saw her coming out of the house, her and two friends, and they were all done up. By then, the cats were almost nose to nose: when the door opened, the tomcat fled, but I'm sure he didn't go far.

Friday night and you almost need to have night vision, because it's so late when people finally decide that it's time to go downtown and pay bar prices. They stay at home and get warmed up with their own liquor-store-priced booze, heading downtown when they're already well lit and when the bands have finally decided to start playing.

I didn't know where she was going for sure, but I had a good idea, and anyway, if it turned out she was going to a house party or something, I could always head back up and try to get the car and get home before I really did have a ticket.

But they were headed downtown after all.

I was afraid one of them would turn around and spot the shape of me behind them, but it turned out I didn't really have to worry. Not one of them turned around, not even once.

The three of them clearly together and overflowing—that's the easiest way to describe it. Laughing and absolutely involved in themselves. And what a wonderful thing that would be, just to be inside that feeling. Walking down the narrow street with the close-ranked downtown buildings on both sides, their words echoing back and forth off the concrete, the high corners of their voices rattling off the pavement and the windows. I'd hear the peaks of every sentence, but not the valleys.

They ended up at a small bar off a laneway running down to the harbour. It was a small place I already knew pretty well, with a pool table and a few scattered televisions high on the walls for the boyfriends who get distracted too quick and need to keep an eye on one game or another when their conversation skills flag.

A pint of beer for me, and I was doing my best to nurse it, to not drink too much too fast, while watching her and trying not to get caught doing it. Looking right over and drinking her in, but ready to throw my eyes sideways if she looked up. Once in a while I'd get caught, that was okay, but I couldn't let it happen too often, or suddenly I'd become "that creepy guy."

I pretended to watch one of the hockey games in a television off to the side, but really I was looking back in the mirror at her reflection, and it wasn't hard to see that I was right about her, absolutely right about the note.

There's a way people behave when they're short of

cash — it's like they hold it closer to themselves, like making sure that they have the right change is suddenly a necessity.

They study the inside of their wallet as if counting what's inside two or three times over will make the cash magically multiply into more. I've been there: it never does.

Not lately, though. I'd been to the banking machine, and I could feel a fat wad of twenties bulked up in my pocket, and I knew my whole plan depended on timing — making just the right call, just the right judgement about what I could ask for and how much I would have to offer. The right amount to make the whole thing almost tragically irresistible, the right amount to make everything possible.

It still might all go south. I knew that. She still might walk away before I even got the first part of it out, before I even managed to cast the fly out there on the surface of the water.

Here's something about that bar. Down near the washrooms, down the two tight switchback flights of wooden-treaded stairs, when someone takes a shot on the pool table upstairs and misses, you can hear the *thunk* of the butt end of the pool cue on the floor as they let it slide through their hands and the end bounces down hard. One hard thud, clear punctuation at the end of someone's turn.

The missed shot, the scratch. You can't hear anything when they make a shot, but you sure can tell when they fail.

What I was going to say is, "I have a business proposition for you."

I'd say it to her right as she came out of the bathroom, me

standing there, her still in that last little bit of disorganization that everyone has when they're coming out of the washroom, that quick pat-down with the palms of your hands, making sure that everything is zipped or buttoned or at least close to in the right place.

She'd give me that half-disconcerted look, that look that says, "I think I should know you but I can't place why," and the truth is, she'd be right.

I'd say: "I know how much you need the money. And you know it, too."

There are plenty of sharp little marks in your memory: those "turned-corner" things, inked real heavy so you can pick out, with barely a moment's notice, the instant something happened. The spots you can honestly look back at and say, afterwards, that a whole bunch of things changed, even if you can't clearly say why. The places where you can draw up memories as being before or after.

It would have been quick and quiet, tucked in a doorway by the cigarette machine, fast enough that it would have all been over before the next person upstairs felt that their bladder was too full.

And I know absolutely that it would have worked, just the way I had planned it — there's no doubt in my mind at all.

Instead, I left the bar right away, left my beer: straight up the stairs and out the door without looking either way.

I felt great, knew I was in charge of the whole thing. My plan — my decision.

With Mary, you were never in charge. You were along

for the ride, no matter how hard you tried to grab the wheel and drive.

And I have to say it's addictive, that being in charge, even if the sheer rush of it passes quickly.

I saw that girl again at the store — saw her coming in, dark blue jacket like a sailor's pea coat, big round buttons up the front in two even rows, blue jeans.

It was cold out, and her eyes were in the process of sweeping over me when she stopped and straightened up and locked right onto me, and then just looked away as if I wasn't even there. She was carrying one of those green baskets that you get when you just need a few things, and she had it loose on the inside of her elbow. I followed her with the cart, watched her ass, the shape of her mouth, the way it curved slightly downwards as she turned and looked at things on the shelves. Knew for a fact I could have owned every inch of it.

I can hardly describe the feeling that went through me, the rush of it, right down to my toes. Exquisite. As easy to touch as the fruit laid out in front of you in the produce section, ripe and full and round.

CHAPTER 29

(St. John's, NL)—The Royal Newfoundland Constabulary (RNC) is
seeking the assistance of the general public in two missing persons
investigations, Mary CARTER, 48, and Lisa TAPPER. CARTER was
last seen in the area of McKay Street in St. John's. TAPPER, 21, was
last seen leaving a cabin on the Salmonier Line. The RNC is seeking
the assistance of the general public in both cases.

If anyone has any information pertaining to the whereabouts of Mary
CARTER or Lisa TAPPER, they are asked to contact the RNC at 729-
8000 or Crime Stoppers at 1-800-222-TIPS (8477).

"Why do we keep sending them out?" Scoville said. "We
didn't hear anything back last time, and we're not going to
hear anything now."

"You know why—for scraps. What we're looking for is
scraps, something someone's half forgotten seeing, and it's
like we're looking at a guy who doesn't leave any. He's someone who knows just how important scraps are. But there's
always the chance. We just need one."

Dean didn't say that the order he saw emerging wasn't a collection of things, but an absence of things. A lot of things just plain missing, with Walt the constant.

Scoville snorted. "What are you going to want to do next? Start trailing him around? You and me put a tail on him for another month or so, when all he does is fish and walk back and forth from the grocery store? Sooner or later we'll have to find something, or we're just going to have to let it go."

"There's nothing at his house — at least nothing we've been able to find — but now maybe he hears about this and figures that we know something. That we're thinking Mary's part of something bigger. And maybe he'll get sloppy," Dean said.

"Think the two are connected?"

"I don't know," Dean said. "But it is two missing women, and he's in the right place for both. Mary's right in his house, Lisa Tapper was last seen down where he goes fishing the most. So maybe. And maybe he gets nervous enough to slip."

"I don't think so," Scoville said. "How many times have we been there now — three, four? He just gets cockier every time. I'd like to haul off and belt him one, just to see how cocky that makes him."

"I don't know. Maybe eventually we'll have enough to bring him in. Maybe we bring him in anyway, just to try and make him crack."

Sometimes you're furious, Dean thought. Seething, boiling with rage, and you can look out through the red mist of it and understand why it is that wives get beaten — why reasoning flies out the window and you're screaming at someone you love, your fists in hard, ready balls, and how doing real damage to someone else is the only option left. Dean had heard it from men for years when he was still in Patrol, had them sitting in the back of his squad car, banging their faces off the Plexiglas divider between the front and back seats, the red and blue roof lights battering around off the walls and fronts of houses in that staccato that seems designed to push everything to the next, even-more-explosive level.

He was sitting in his own car, parked on LeMarchant Road, in the dark and just a few doors down from the second-floor apartment Julie was renting, thinking that, if she saw him, he might be considered a stalker. He could see slivers of the two front rooms through the curtains, enough to catch the colours and a slice or two of things on the walls. In one, a corner of a dresser that was all too familiar, a dresser she couldn't have lifted by herself but that had left their house silently while he was on shift one afternoon, leaving only four dimpled dents in the carpet and a few loose skeins of dust.

He didn't know why he was parked there. It was not on his route; it was definitely out of character. He realized that — but he was doing it anyway. It wasn't the only rule he was breaking. He was pretty sure he'd had too much to drink to be driving, but he'd taken the keys out of the ignition so the running lights would go off, and then dropped the whole bunch into his lap.

He knew he could talk his way out of it, if someone from Patrol pulled in behind him. Argue there was no "care and control," lean on "the brotherhood." He looked up at Julie's windows, wondered what it was like inside. Wondered who was inside, what she was wearing, whether she still needed to wear heavy socks to keep her feet warm from drafts. He thought about her feet. The wind was up and the bare black tree branches were whipping around over the car, and he could hear the sound of it around the door handles, the wing mirrors, as if the car was still moving.

Pretend the car is still moving, Dean thought. Pretend and don't open the door, don't open the door and don't go up to the front of the house and don't make her talk to you and don't push your way in, demanding explanations until you see some guy on the couch in there, some guy that needs hitting.

Would that be so bad? he wondered. Wouldn't it show her? Wouldn't it make the point? It's not like other cops would show up and arrest him, not any more than they were going to pick him up for impaired. They'd hustle him out of the place once they recognized him and then explain to everybody why it would just be better all around if it got dealt with quietly, saying things like, "You gotta know the guy's hurting," even though Dean wasn't hurting. Not so much. Not any more. He was just trying to find an anchor, to find any sense at all.

Dean could already imagine what it would sound like to

be in the middle of a late-night, booze-filled racket, could remember hustling Stick Davidge out of a bad situation in an apartment on Prospect Street four or five years before, the guy Constable Davidge didn't like with four stumps left for front teeth, Dean explaining that someone would pick up the dental bill and "you don't want to see a good cop losing his job and his pension . . ." Remembering how hard it was to cross that line when you were supposed to be protecting the public, not each other.

Except Stick had developed a real taste for hitting after that, finding a niche on the weekend bar patrol where drunks kept getting their hands caught in closing doors until the regularity of the injuries was too much for the brass to ignore. Stick got a job working for the police association afterwards — he still worked bar at the Christmas party. And Stick still occasionally hit people, but usually it was other cops, so that at least made it closer to fair.

The worst part is that you're not always mad, he thought.

That would be too simple, too explainable. And so much easier to deal with.

Sometimes, you're just working a problem around like a sore in your mouth, poking it with your tongue, feeling the sharp metal taste of it and still poking it again, impossible to resist. Going through the cycles in your head: What if I'd done this differently? What if I'd spoken up? What if I'd shut up? What if I hadn't gone back and raised it that one last time?

Everything like tracks in his head, like some huge switch-yard with heavy purposeful trains going off in every direction, everything right there if he could only decide which route was the right one to take at the right time.

Dean sat in the car and stared out the windshield at the dark, watched two pedestrians scurrying along the block against the wind. Looked up again at Julie's window, watched to see if he could catch even a shadow of her against the wall.

Stopped and wondered how he would feel about that shadow, about whether it would be familiar or foreign.

He knew that there had been a time when he could see the back of her neck in a crowd at the mall and know exactly, precisely that it was her. At the same time, he remembered it like punctuation, like the full stop of a period.

All at once, Dean realized that the one thing he was certain of was that he wouldn't feel nothing. You never feel nothing.

Not unless everybody's spent years moving away from each other. Not unless it's a mutual decision. Not unless absolutely no one is surprised.

That wasn't where he saw Walt living. Not when he saw Walt in the front hall of his own house. Walt wouldn't settle for it—wouldn't settle for anything. What they were still missing was what Walt did instead of settling, Dean thought. He wished that Scoville was in the car with him then, just so he could tell him about it, just so he could say, "This is what's wrong. This is the magic thing."

He ran it around and around in his head, thinking about the way Walt moved, the things he'd said, about the inside of Walt's house. And as he did, Julie's apartment, and whoever was in it, slipped further and further away.

Outside the car, the tree branches were hissing in the wind, the night packed up hard like something was supposed to happen, a lone plastic shopping bag skittering fast down the street. Inside, Dean was writing notes, caught in a pool of streetlight that turned his notebook orange and the ink far blacker than it actually was.

CHAPTER 30

- *Plain yogurt*
- *Dijon mustard*
- *Thyme (dried leaves)*
- *Bread crumbs?*

Small, round writing, black ink in nice tight loops on a piece of paper from the kind of notepads they hand out at conferences. Exactly the kind of scratch pad they hand out at conferences, because this one says CDA-ACB up in the top corner, and it's the Canadian Dam Association of all things, and the other corner says "CDA 2011 Annual Conference, Fredericton, N.B. Oct 15–20."

Wouldn't it be nice to get away, even just for a weekend, even to some place like Fredericton? To go to a conference, see a bunch of people who do the same things you do, share the same complaints and frustrations, and know for sure that there were other people just like you?

Sometimes I think I'd like to get away like that, because staying in the same place sure doesn't seem to be doing anything for me.

I get up in the mornings on the weekend now and I smell sour.

That's the only real word for it—sour. Like something's gone off, some part of me has gone past that "best before" date you always have a look at before you take a swig of milk right from the carton. And I'm boxed in by this house: sometimes the walls are like the walls of a fortress, keeping everything out, the wind hauling hard fingers of snow along the clapboard outside, random branches tapping.

Other times, it's like a cell, and I'm sentenced to be locked in here with myself. Unable to leave.

For years. Forever.

I prowl around the ground floor, leave the upstairs alone, make coffee, drink a couple of cups, but there's nothing really satisfying in that. Think about taking a shower, but I'm suddenly afraid that even the feeling of hot water on my skin will be a letdown. You've got to know that you're in trouble when even the simple things aren't good any more—I'd like to tell that to someone. I'd like to have someone to tell it to, because actually saying it out loud—out loud and to someone else, some other living person—gives it more weight. The feel of hot water on the back of your neck, the taste of fresh coffee, the unreasonable optimism of hearing the lid slap down on the mailbox on the front of the house. All of those things, all gone flat.

I swear I'm not going to become one of those people who goes around talking to myself, dazzling my own constantly appreciative audience of one. I may do strange things, but I do them deliberately.

The first thing I did after she left was let the plants die. Her plants, all of them. She watered them, she talked to them. When the police were here the first time, I could tell they were bothered by that, by the fact that not only were all the plants dead, but that they were still dotted around the shelves, on the fireplace mantel, on window ledges. The cops kept looking at the flowerpots with the dead stalks waterfalling down over the edges, the puddles of curled up leaves all around them on the floor like everything had happened fast, like it was a reaction to some kind of shock. I didn't bother to explain, but if they had asked me, I would have had an answer ready.

They were her plants, I would have told them, and she was the only one that knew what the schedule was. She was the one who cared for them, and, quite simply, they were her responsibility.

So if she wanted to just up and leave, well, that was her decision, too. And decisions always have repercussions. She could come back and water them any time she liked; she was welcome to that.

That's what I would have said. I thought it would have been a good answer, but they never asked, so I kept it to myself. They never got off the same page, those first police officers, just kept to the same bunch of questions that I'd get to know real well over the next few months: Had I heard anything about where she was? Did I know anyone else who had heard anything? And my favourite: "Is there anything else you'd like to tell us, sir?"

Do they teach that one in police school? And did it work on a single person ever?

"Oh yes, I've just been waiting to spill it all out for you..."

One of them was always taking notes, like they were going to go away and compare what I said that day with whatever it was I had said last time. Is there anything I'd like to tell you? No. Nothing at all.

I kept thinking about it after they left. They were the first two guys—I could probably dig up their names somewhere, I'm pretty sure they gave me their cards. Later, those other two, Hill and Scoville, they certainly did.

Mary? People should have seen it coming. That's what I felt like saying.

People should probably have asked her about it ahead of time, about whether anything was wrong or whether she was making plans to take off. Whether there was anything they could do to help.

Maybe they did.

Looking back, there were signs that she was getting ready to fly the coop.

You hear about men who keep their women on a short leash—don't let them have their own bank cards, hold on to their driver's licences, their passports. Make them explain every single place they go, who they see, what they're up to. Men who are jealous, all the time.

Thing is, it's just going to happen anyway, that's what I'd tell them. So start hardening yourself off, get ready for it. Decide what you're going to do.

Things change. All kinds of things. It doesn't make any difference how hard you try to hang on to the things that brought you together. Even dams only hold the water back for so long.

The year before she left, Mary was doing more and more things on her own. Casting out little runners like she was her own kind of wild strawberry plant, each skipping step taking root somewhere new, somewhere a little farther away. Busy all the time with different groups, things I couldn't figure out how she'd even found out about, let alone gotten involved in.

You hear people saying all the time that there's a point — some definable instant in time — when they suddenly knew there were problems in their marriage. Like B.C. and A.D. or something, a single fine and clearly drawn line in time.

I think things just grow slowly, and the reality is that there's a point where you suddenly look back at all of it, see how the points should have lined up, and you just say, "of course."

It's exactly like B.C. and A.D., but you see it retrospectively, only when the writing's already firmly on the wall.

By then, there's so much of everything that's already happened that it's built up over itself again and again like layers on a pearl, so much and so thick that you can't really come close to scraping it all apart again. *Nacre*, that's the exact word for it, the word it would be if resentment grew the way a pearl did, in hard, heavy layers, all laid over and glued down and stacked on top of one another. And all the stronger for it.

By then, it's over anyway.

It's becoming the fossil record, angry volcanic ash falling down around you everywhere and the stupid-ass dinosaurs already well on their way to dying out completely.

Mary had her garden club and darts night on Fridays, and even though she didn't go to church, she had a church group thing that met on Wednesdays and did something with the poor or the underprivileged in some South American country. She told me about it at first, but I've got to say it sure didn't stick in my head. A couple of other things that met late in the afternoons and sometimes went on long enough into the evenings that I'd find myself eating alone, picking away at whatever leftovers were in the fridge.

And friends—a whole bunch of friends that suddenly I didn't know, hadn't even met, and that were all people who didn't ever come to our house, people she'd talk about but that were just about as real in my head as a collection of cut-out paper dolls named Barb and Andrea and Linda.

Just names with no faces, and in my head, it was like they were all a group of similar and interchangeable silhouettes. Mary would come home and be talking away about it, and I couldn't even really keep any of them straight.

I should have been paying more attention, I'll admit that.

I really should have been interested and involved, but I guess I was too lazy. I'd feign a bit of interest and let the whole flood of it just wash over me like a big wall of water—who'd said what and who was pregnant and who was moving away and wasn't that a shame? I'd try and stick in a few bits of "uh-huh" and "really?" and "why would they do that?" but to be honest, I cared less about the answers than about whether I managed to tuck my own words into the right place in the flow so that they didn't sound completely out of place. Just another night discussing cut-out people who lived in a cut-out world I didn't either know or care about and never would.

But I should have.

Because eventually, Mary caught on, and she just stopped talking about it.

Then she started checking off the remaining nights.

Mondays, she went to watch movies with a group of friends — they rotated from house to house, but for some reason, they never came to ours.

Tuesdays, she started volunteering at St. Clare's. Then it was other nights at St. Clare's, too.

It's a big hospital, one of two in the city and the only one that's actually in a downtown neighbourhood. The other one's newer, out on the edge of town so that it could have plenty of parking. St. Clare's, though, is like any other downtown hospital — go visit someone there and you're almost guaranteed to get a parking ticket, even if you're able to find a parking meter open. I swear the meter guys circle around like blackflies, ears on them like bats so that they can hear the moment when the little red flag clicks up and your time has expired. I never had much time for the place — my father was dead before he even got through the doors, and my mother died on the seventh floor after three solid weeks of blaming me for taking her from her house and periodically announcing that neither of my brothers would have "been so awful to me."

There were plenty of red flags for me to see, too, clicking up one after another. Makes me laugh a little now. Maybe if I'd gone to the right Fredericton convention or something, maybe if I had the right kind of notepaper tucked away in a briefcase, I would have had some idea what it looks like when a dam is ready to burst.

St. Clare's looms; it's a big slab-sided place, heavy vinyl-covered floors, and the paint in the hallways beige and so thick it looks like it was put on with a mop. Doesn't matter how heavy it was put on, though; the walls, especially down in Emergency, were scarred from being hit by equipment, by gurneys and monitors and hospital beds. By the janitors' carts, too: I felt I should be able to recognize that kind of mark, being part of the fraternity and all.

I don't remember which police visit it was when I finally told the cops they should be talking to an emergency room doctor named Patterson.

Youngish guy, married, ran a family general practice in the daytime, a handful of emergency room shifts every month. Just enough to keep his hand in. Smug little mouth on him, always half a smile on it.

And Mary? I think after a while, she was volunteering on just about every shift he came in for.

CHAPTER 31

April 5

RNC release year-end statistics

(St. John's, NL) — The Royal Newfoundland Constabulary (RNC) issued its annual report on criminal activity in its area Friday, saying that there has been a 2 percent increase in violent crime, particularly aggravated assault, over the past year.

Rates of other crimes in the region have primarily stayed the same. There has been a 2 percent increase in drug-related offences.

"I know you're not going to be fond of this idea," Dean said, "but let's start pulling in some open files on peeping Toms. Stalking complaints, that kind of thing. New ones, old ones, even nine or ten years ago. Unresolved ones, not the ones where someone's looked out their back window and seen an oversexed teenaged boy fingering the bras on their clothesline."

"How come?" Scoville didn't look convinced.

"Because of geography. And because maybe what you were saying about arsonists could be taken a little more broadly — remember? About moving up the scale, bit by bit. Maybe that would work for other cases where people are driven to do things."

"Why do I think this has to do with Walt?"

"Because maybe it does. But we don't know that yet. So we'll do a little math, starting in his neighbourhood and working out from there. And we'll see what we get."

"There might be hundreds of them. Could be a real needle-in-a-haystack thing."

"Well, we won't know until we do it."

Dean pinned a city map to the wall, white paper with a bright red dot at a McKay Street address, a blue one on a downtown grocery store. Then he sat down in his chair, leaning back, his fingers tented. He remembered, fleetingly, that he'd had a series of voicemails from Julie. Whatever it is, he thought, it can wait. He looked at the dots again, imagined they were bull's eyes, circles radiating out around them.

CHAPTER 32

Bacon
White bread
Hash Brown's

Cherry Blossoms
Diet Pepsi

Simple enough. Another list on a piece of recycled junk mail, this one a small square brochure from a psychic healer: "I can help you in health, happiness, love, marriage, and business. I specialize in home blessings, removing bad luck, and evil spirits, jadoo, obeah, black magic, bad carma, and bad energies. Life has enough disappointments. All is private & confidential. Also available for house parties. I will reunite the separated and heal the sick."

Some nights, I feel like I could use both of those last two, and wonder which of the psychic's "ancient roots, herbs, talismans, spiritual baths, and God-given powers" would be doing the healing and the reuniting.

Eleven at night is the time when the emergency room really gets interesting. People are starting to get drunk, and in a downtown hospital, the walk-ins — and the carry-ins — are beginning to fill the place up. Doctors' offices have been closed for hours by then, and the earaches, sprains, and flus that those doctors usually catch are in trying to cadge painkillers or antibiotics. On top of that, the real crazies are making themselves at home — you can see all of that in a hurry.

St. Clare's has a small emergency room — the bigger one's at the city's main hospital, so St. Clare's catches the handful of downtown patients who can't make their way to the larger one. It's a slice of the city: a core sample, drilled down deep and taking in a bit of every strata as it goes. You can see just about every kind of person there is to see in downtown St. John's, and see them all in a room small enough for a close look.

I'd told Mary I was working a night shift — told her twice, because it hadn't seemed to sink in the first time — and then I walked up to St. Clare's and told the nurse on the front desk that I had a crushing headache I just couldn't shake.

She was only a young thing, wearing a flowered top and green pants, both scrubs, but she still managed to give me a going-over with a weary stare, an experienced inspection to see if I was shabby enough or shaky enough to be trying to wheedle a prescription for painkillers from a harried doctor. Then she nodded me over to the waiting room.

"Just have a seat in there and a doctor will be with you."

She left "eventually" off the end of the sentence, but you

could hear the shape of it in her words, and I could imagine her writing down on the chart that I wasn't any kind of rush case. Or else she was sliding my nice new file to the very back of the bunch of similar files that were all corralled in a metal rack on the corner of her desk. I didn't mind the attitude — didn't mind any of it. I wasn't in a rush to be seen anyway.

The waiting room was ringed with hard blue plastic chairs shaped like buckets, the kind of seats that start to make your back sweat five minutes after you're in them. I sat in the uncomfortable, identical row that ran all along the wall under the opaque windows, because given the chance, I'll always sit with my back to the wall. I don't like people behind me.

I looked around, took the place in: a few low tables, a handful of battered magazines probably coated with a dozen different kinds of bacteria, enough room for about twenty-five people waiting. The room only a quarter full that early in the night, some people rigid in their seats and as upright as if they were at church, others tilted over to one side like they'd permanently lost their balance. Two public telephones in the very centre of the room on a post and one woman crying. Slowly.

The chairs in the centre of the room, the ones away from the walls, were different, less institutional. They were like a collection of odds and ends that nobody had a use for in other parts of the building — soft seats, vinyl, some black, some brown, some with chromed legs: pretty much a sampler, just like the patients.

Every now and then, a nurse would come out with a

file folder, read the name on top out loud, and take another patient into the back. Early on, an ambulance rumbled up to the doors, lights flashing, and the paramedics rushed a guy on a stretcher right straight past the waiting room to one of the examining rooms. After that, no one had their name called for a long time.

The thing about the emergency room is that everyone's already focused inwards: they've got enough going on that they're not really worried about you. No one except me was looking around.

They hurt, or they're afraid, or something bad is happening to someone they're with. Sometimes it's big, sometimes it's small, but one thing's for sure: it's always big for the person it's happening to. And because they're caught up in something big, you don't get caught watching them much—and when you do, you can always bend your face into something a little like concern.

When I first sat down, I was one of only eight other people there—one of them a woman who kept going to the payphone, plugging in coins like it was an old-fashioned slot machine, and then shouting "I'm just smoking too goddamn much, so I came in here. They've got to help me stop" into the phone at whoever was listening, before angrily hanging up. She had hard, staring eyes sunk right back into a narrow, drawn face, and she kept stomping back to the nurses' station, demanding more change for the phone. The nurses were abrupt with her, which made me think she was a regular.

There was a young couple, sitting together, and he had his

arm thrown up over her shoulders, and every now and then her face would crumple slightly and she would emit—that's really the right word for it—she'd emit a soft, deep little moan, her mouth not even seeming to move, so at first it was hard to be certain exactly where the sound was coming from.

Two older men were sitting only a couple of seats apart in a back corner, both small and leathery-looking, as if they had been distilled, shrunken down into their essential selves. Neither of them spoke, but I thought of them as Smoky and Liver: one had the nicotine-stained fingers and wizened face of a heavy smoker, and he kept going out through the doors and coming back five or ten minutes later, trailing the smell of harsh, half-burnt, roll-your-own tobacco.

Liver's fingers were yellow, too, but they weren't the only thing—he was all-over-yellow, every bit of exposed skin an unhealthy mustard like he'd been dipped in some kind of permanent stain, and any time he looked at you, what should have been the whites of his eyes were downright disturbing. Not just the yellowish colour of them, although that was unnerving enough. It was the way his eyes managed to convey something close to abject resignation—like waiting didn't matter, like bad weather didn't matter, like the pain didn't matter, like nothing would ever matter again.

Last, a mother and an impossibly small baby, the baby red in the face like an angry little radish, a baby who screeched and wailed and then fell sound asleep like it had exhausted itself. I wasn't sure which of the two was there to see the doctor, or if maybe it was both.

They took Liver first, and he stood up slowly and shuffled toward the examining room when they called him, his body actually tilted and moving through the room at an angle, as though his compass was permanently askew.

Then it was the moaner and her boyfriend. I still hadn't caught even a glimpse of the good doctor, although I'd heard a nurse mention his name.

Then another ambulance wheeled up, followed by a walk-in with a bleeding gash on his arm that looked a good six inches long, and two quarrelling drunks with some complaint that led to blows, the arrival of hospital security, and finally a pair of no-nonsense police officers who just bundled the pair up and took them away. I sat against the wall and watched it all, keeping an eye open for the white coat I wanted to see, the elusive Dr. Patterson, working one of only a few night shifts that Mary wasn't also volunteering. And how did I know that? Well, Mary's loud on the phone, and I'm used to walking quietly enough that I can come right up behind you and you wouldn't even notice.

I didn't see anyone who looked like him in the first couple of hours, but I wasn't afraid they were going to bring me into the examining room or anything like that: the place was steadily filling up, and the symptoms I'd given them were just mild enough, just nondescript enough, to guarantee I'd be sitting in my little blue chair until every single other patient in the place was checked out. The phone lady was getting fidgety, fidgety in a way that included keeping those sunken little eyes fixed on me like she was staring from the inside of a closet, peering out through the gap between door and jamb. Like she thought those hard little eyes were the only part of her I could see. And I just knew that, if any two patients were going to be left to the very end, were going to be left together in the same completely empty emergency room, it was going to be me and it was going to be her.

Around midnight, when the room was really full, I saw a guy I was pretty sure was Patterson come out of one examining room and flit into the one right next door — younger than me, with a big square face, white medical jacket, and a brightly coloured shirt underneath, like he wanted people to believe he was really a lot more fun than he otherwise seemed. Months earlier, I had dropped Mary off for a volunteer shift and she'd pointed the guy out to me, but it had been all the way across the parking lot, so it was just a far-away guy getting out of his car at a time when it was almost dark anyway.

That was back before she stopped mentioning Dr. Patterson at all, and before I started getting curious.

A half hour after that, two more ambulances came ripping up to the door and unloaded a couple of guys from a car accident or something, and the good doctor got called out from the examining rooms and was going over them right there in the hall, checking to see if they were still breathing and looking at where all that blood was coming from, and I took the time to get a real good look at him then. A real good, steady look, breaking my own rules about not being too obvious, and just when I was doing that, he turned and looked straight at me, his face changing like he was confused or something, like he thought I looked familiar and he should really know me, but then he had to go back to what he was doing.

He seemed like a capable guy, businesslike, and every time he said something to one of the nurses that maybe sounded a little sharp, he had a way of following it up with a rueful little smile, as if trying to admit he'd been too harsh without ever really admitting anything. It was, frankly, easy to see why people would like the guy. Under different circumstances, I might even like the guy.

Then they wheeled one of the accident guys back into the examining rooms and sent the other scooting off to X-ray. A doctor and a few more nurses came down from upstairs, and when another nurse came beetling around the corner with an armful of IV bags destined for the examining room, I knew the doctors would be tied up and everyone would be sitting in the waiting room for a really good long time.

I waited ten more minutes before I went back up to the front desk and told them I thought my headache was getting better and I probably didn't need to see a doctor after all. I got that "thanks for wasting everybody's time" look and headed for the big automatic glass doors, the clouded glass swooshing back to let me out. Two ambulances were still sitting out there, lights flashing, like they were waiting to make a pickup instead of a delivery.

Outside, it was a nice cool summer night, the kind that touches the side of your face with a combination of the fading heat of the day and a gentle humidity. I walked all the way home, face up and occasionally catching sight of the moon through the trees, and there must have been something about my pace or my shape or just the way I looked: four times, people walking toward me looked up all at once, saw me coming, and then crossed the road to the sidewalk on the other side of the street long before they reached me. Like I was giving off an air that said it would be better for everybody to keep their distance. And would that psychic cross the street, too, seeing the great dark shape of my aura coming? Or would that looming personal thundercloud just seem like a challenge to her? There was a lot of bravado in that short advertisement: "There is no problem too big or small. I will succeed where others have failed. All readings and help is 100 percent guaranteed."

Good luck with that.

When I got home and up to our room, Mary was sound asleep—or else pretending to be sound asleep—and I eased quietly into my side of the bed, pulled the covers up, and lay there still, watching the ceiling hanging down over me until I could finally fall asleep.

It took a long time.

That night I had a dream that I was in an examining room, wearing one of those hospital-issue johnny coats and nothing else, my skinny old arse hanging right out in the breeze. And then Dr. Patterson came in the way doctors always seem to, shoving the door open hard so that it banged against the wall. He looked right at the bed I was sitting on like he was looking through me, and then looked at the file folder in his hand. And he opened the door and called out to someone, a nurse

I guess, "Where's this Walter guy? There's no one in here."

Then he just left. And I had no clothes and no wallet and no car keys, and a helpless feeling that if I ever somehow found the energy to get up, go over, and pull open the big door, there would not be one single person left in the hospital who could help me.

When I woke up, Mary had already gotten up, gotten dressed, and left the house.

Once, not even that many years before, I would have told her all about that dream; then, I didn't dare, afraid that she'd just cock her head to one side, inscrutable, and drop the subject without saying anything else about it.

CHAPTER 33

April 8—I called the police right away. Not because
I've seen the guy again, but because I got home and
I'm sure someone has been in my house. I mean,
you can start worrying about things, start second-
guessing everything, forgetting where you left your
coffee cup. Except that's not the kind of thing I'm
talking about. Daniel hasn't been around in over
three weeks—we broke up after Mexico—and
things just aren't right. Little things that aren't where
they usually are: I have a set of stacking coasters,
and they're not on the right table. The can of Comet
isn't tucked out of sight behind the toilet like it
should be. Things like that. I called my parents, but
they said they hadn't been over. The creepiest thing
is that my underwear drawer is all wrong, things
I don't even wear moved up near the top, like my
most uncomfortable bra. My place can be a bit of a
mess sometimes, but I know where things are. So I
called the police and they said, "Is anything stolen?"
and I said I didn't know. And they said, "Is there

anyone in the house right now?" and that gave me the shakes, because for some reason I hadn't thought of that, and then I didn't know. I mean, I'm never in the basement, except to put the shovel down there once the winter's over, and the whole idea is like a bad movie or something. And they said they'd come out and have a look, but that it wouldn't be right away because they had "a lot of other stuff on the go." Just like that—a lot of other stuff on the go. It just sounded so weird. When they did come, they had a look at the doors and went around to all the ground floor windows and talked about "no sign of forced entry." Then they asked me if anyone else had a key, and I said no, but it got me to thinking that it had taken two or three days to get Daniel to drop his key off—I think, really, we broke up on the plane coming home—and when he did, he just left it in the mailbox in a white envelope, no note or name on the outside or anything. Just a cold, impersonal key. I didn't tell them about Daniel and me at first though. It would be like getting him in trouble for something I don't even know for sure he's doing—too much like a bitter ex-girlfriend, and I was in no way the bitter one. And, I mean, there are other keys around anyway: Heather and Sue gave me their keys when they left, but I'm not really sure if they had made more than one each. Still, it's unnerving. I guess this is what it must be like after a robbery: you go around your house for ages, comfortable that it's your own space, and then something happens and you're wondering about every noise, wondering if you'd hear someone coming in the back when you have the television on. Turning the sound down, second-guessing whether you really heard something or whether the cat just knocked something over. It's losing confidence in some crucial kind of way. Losing trust. The kind of thing I would never have worried about even two years ago. More and more, I can't stand staying here, but nobody seems to want to help. I could stay with Mom and Dad, make up some excuse, but I'm embarrassed just thinking about it. So I stay awake long after I've gone to bed, listening for noises, trying to convince myself they're all Bo messing around. And angry, too, that someone could get such a hold on me. I wake up at the very beginning of when it's getting light, and after that is the only time I sleep deeply at all, I think.

CHAPTER 34

Starrigans Place
Leave the stadium
Turn right onto the bridge
After Mount Pearl
Leave the Conception Bay South bypass at Fowlers Road
Then Sparrow Drive

It was directions, I'm pretty sure, on the back of a bank deposit slip. I don't speak French, and it wasn't the clearest writing I'd ever seen — neat enough, just not clear. Still, directions are good, because they don't only say where someone is going to be, they say where someone's not going to be.

Cats, they're more trusting than dogs. Distant, but more trusting. They say dogs are smarter, that there's science to back that up. I mean, you come into a house and the dog doesn't know you, it doesn't matter what size it is. It's going to go nuts every time you turn up, and it's going to follow you all over the place, angry. It might never get used to you in there, moving away from you every single time you put out a hand to say hello.

Dogs don't like me. And I don't like them. I know I said I don't like cats much, but they do grow on you.

Cats, it's more like a self-preservation thing. They'll run away and hide at first, but once they're sure they're not in danger, they'll follow you around the house even if you're pulling open drawers and emptying them into a sack or something. "Guard cat" is not a concept that makes much sense. After a while, cats just get used to you when you're there and don't question when you arrive or when you're gone. You put out a hand and they curve up toward you for a scratch.

I went back to Alisha's house — it's strange how you often end up going ahead and doing things even though some part of your brain is clearly pointing out how stupid you are to be doing it. But I did go back.

First I walked by, and the cat was there on the windowsill. And I still had a key.

So I took a guess about how long it would take for Alisha to get back from CBS, even though I wasn't absolutely sure that I had the right day. Sometimes you have to guess about things: the other side of the directions had a list of the kind of things you're asked to bring to a party, a veggie tray and dip, crackers and cheese, and I thought those weren't the kind of things you go to the store for way in advance. You pick them up when you need them, and as soon as you've got them, you go.

So I looked at the cat, and around the street to make sure that no one was paying particularly close attention, and then I crossed the porch and unlocked the door.

The cat fled for a moment, but after I sat down, it came and sat on the couch near me, staring at me with its big full-moon eyes for a while. Then it came over and walked right square across my lap, kneading my legs with its paws and purring like I'd always been there.

I wanted to know what the cat's name was. I thought that I could probably find it somewhere in the pictures on Alisha's Facebook.

Before I left, I checked the kitchen and nosed around until I found the cat food bag. There wasn't really very much in it, but I poured some into the cat's bowl anyway, so it wouldn't be hungry or anything.

Going back toward the front of the house, I'd turned all at once, and there, with the living room spread out all behind him, was a strange man who wasn't me, but only just for a second or two until I recognized myself in a great big mirror on the wall right below the stairs. After I realized it was a mirror, I thought it was surprising how well I fit into the room — the couch out behind me to the left through the glass door, the curtained windows, the dark colour of the paint. I straightened my shirt then, because the point on one side of my collar had somehow gotten itself rolled back underneath, and then I smoothed down my hair where it always sticks up at the crown and headed for the door. Locked it, like always.

I went back to the cabin on the Little Barachois, too. Not right away, but I did go back.

I thought about it for a while first, but all the time, I think I kind of knew that I was going to go back. Maybe to prove to myself that I was wrong—maybe just to be sure of what I thought I'd seen.

Because there was absolutely nothing, not one single thing, that would make you think there might actually be a body in that abandoned cabin. It was the kind of thing that flits into your head and, if you're half sensible, flits right out again as soon as the sun's up and the ghosts are gone. But for me it was a thought that just wouldn't go away, and when you start worrying at stuff in your head, you start wondering if there's actually something wrong with you just for thinking it. In the end, you either have to prove that you're right or prove that you're wrong.

I took the same route as I had the first time, like I was following a set of directions hardwired right into me. Stopped at the same gas station, got the same kind of coffee—I don't know why, perhaps because there was some need not to have any variables in the equation.

I parked my car, put my long boots on, and took my fishing rod with me, even though I didn't tie a fly to the leader.

I went without my backpack, looking over my shoulder to see if there were cars coming before heading out into the bush. I tried to make it look like any other fishing trip.

I couldn't help wondering if, at any time, there might be a car nosing up over the nearest hill, the kind of car that might have a slow-driving, thoughtful old man behind the wheel. The kind of old man who recites every single thing he sees to the police in perfect detail because he's got not one single thing in his entire life left to be paying attention to. White Toyota, all six numbers and letters on the licence plate, what day he saw it, what time it was, and that when he was driving home again, he'd noticed that the car had left.

By then, it was mid-August, and in the woods, the black-flies were gone because the big dragonflies were out, long, shining green and blue needles that hover over you and then dart away faster than anything else their size.

They say that dragonflies can eat their weight in black-flies in a single day. I don't know if that's true, but I do know the blackflies drop right off as soon as the dragonfly larvae haul themselves up out of the brooks onto the warm rocks and split out of their skins before taking to the air.

One moment, they're living underwater, catching under-water bugs, and the next, they're completely changed, taking to the air like metallic fighter jets, flying so neat and clean and direct that it's like they've spent their whole lives train-ing to do it. Only they haven't — all they've done is take that one step that nature has always meant them to take, even if it means permanently exchanging water for air in a single hot summer afternoon. That hot afternoon when everything changes.

It was hot. The air was steady and humid, no wind but plenty of damp heat, full of the smells of summer: the brush of the barrens was just falling out of the real summer full bloom, but the heat was drying the peat and bringing the complex smell up into the moist air.

It's hard to make your way down a river when you're doing it fast, as if you were using the water as a road. It's much easier when it's something you meander along, looking for spots to fish. When it's a straight, deliberate route, it's hard, jarring work, your feet moving too quickly, so quickly that the rocks turn underfoot and tumble sideways and you splash too much—you're never moving with the river. Always against it. No rhythm to your gait at all, and your balance flees.

It all slows you down, and heats you up, too.

There was plenty of water in over the tops of my boots before I got there, good soakings, mostly from big moon-man strides when I'd stepped into deep holes or simply overstepped my balance. I was out of breath and wet and sweating, too, by the time I spotted the cabin again.

It was just like the first time I'd seen the place: still the sense that someone else clearly owned it. I saw the side of it first, barely noticeable around the corner of the river, and I found myself pulling back again, my back pressed into the underbrush, as if it was still important not to be seen. The door was still half open, the roof still tilted downwards. And I still couldn't shake the feeling that someone was just about to appear in front of me.

I waited several minutes before I crossed the river. Like the first time, plenty of bright sun—the windows of the cabin looking out like empty black eyes. Every few steps I stopped, listening. But there was only the occasional ripple of water along the edge of the riverbank, and back behind the cabin, the dry crackle of a torn blue plastic tarpaulin that had been thrown over the remains of the woodpile, shifting and rippling in what little wind there was.

Inside, in the front room, not one single thing was different from what I remembered.

There was no sign of anyone or anything having been there since I had, and the air held that same heavy mildewed smell that was instantly familiar, the way it caught in my nose and stayed. I stood there for a moment, apprehensive, making sure my eyes had adjusted as much as they could to the darkness inside before I moved again.

The smell in the back room was something else again, and I wondered why I hadn't noticed how completely it permeated the place the first time I had been there. Had it been too early in the year, the nights and the shadows in the back of the cabin still cool enough?

Because there was clearly the smell of old meat—leave a fridge closed and unplugged for long enough and you'll get a hint of what I'm talking about the moment you crack open the door.

It's the kind of smell that seems to stick to your clothes, and certainly sticks right there inside your nose like it's never going to leave.

I almost understood why I didn't see her the first time— because I was sure it was a her: a small-framed women wrapped up tight in that mound of bedsheets and more visible as a human shape than as a human being. It was like someone had carefully rolled her in the sheets, like they were meant to be a shroud. I could see one hank of her hair against the bed, light-coloured and fine, and I could see the sunken skin of what I imagined was the side of her cheek, like she had been shrunk or freeze-dried or something. I could also see that she had been in the cabin for a while.

There were patches on the sheet that were darker, almost black, and when I saw that, I turned around without thinking and pushed my way back out the front door of the cabin. I knelt down by the river, splashing the cool water into my own face, breathing hard.

I sat down, watching the light on the water. That's the other part of dealing with horrible things: the way your head, when it's faced with the completely unacceptable, hones right in on something else instead, something that makes clear and absolute sense, something that distracts and holds your attention.

You find your anchors where you can, throw the lines and hooks out and hope that, somewhere out of sight, something will hold.

As soon as I stopped shaking, I gathered up my unstrung fishing rod and hurried back up the river to the car, certain then that I would never be back to that cabin, to that corpse in its back room.

If anything, I went upstream faster than I'd come down.

When I got back to the car, I kept driving in the same direction, away from St. John's, taking the big loop down around the foot of the peninsula while I tried to get my head in order.

Every time I thought about it, I kept seeing the body

pressed up against the wall, and I also kept hearing the dry plastic rattle of the tarpaulin on the woodpile out back, like it was the dry rattle of air being dragged into someone's lungs. I kept telling myself that I could just walk away and never look back, that I could just forget about the whole thing as if it had never happened. Never tell anyone. Never fish that river again.

That's what I told myself.

Stupid me.

Part of me that already knew that, as far as my head was concerned, she'd be right there in front of my eyes any time my brain took it upon itself to go back, daytime or night.

CHAPTER 35

Steak
Fries
Steak
Fries

That list is my own. I kept it anyway, even though it seems a bit like cheating. I think what I meant was that I could put anything that I liked on a list then. A post-Mary list that was its own little joke, the sort of thing I might have shared with her if she was actually still here, if she had simply gone out of town for a while and then decided to come back.

The steak-and-fries list was exactly what I was doing in the world. I was doing what I told myself I wanted to be doing—but it was like a record skipping, over and over and over again, with me living safe right there buckled into the most regular routine I could find. A routine that was less and less satisfying with every passing day.

The dreams were still there—the ones where I'm walking toward someone, and she turns around to face me and it's

Mary. Not someone who looks a bit like Mary, not someone I could confuse with Mary, but Mary herself. That same less-than-symmetrical smile, the same broad shoulders, and even though I haven't reached her yet, I can feel that smooth skin of those shoulders under my hands.

Sometimes, suddenly, it's not Mary at all—instead, it's her blond sister, her blond, slight, much-younger sister, and there's something that I am supposed to explain to her, except I have no idea what it's supposed to be.

Sometimes her sister is wrapped up tight in a sheet in a cabin fifty miles away, and the thing is, Mary doesn't even have a blond sister.

Mary has never had a blond sister.

That's the worst dream of them all, the one I wake up from with every single muscle stretched absolutely taut, as if I'm trying to burst right out of the bed or right out of my body, and I just can't figure out what to do.

I'd wake up and wonder what it was all about, what it was all supposed to mean. Whether it meant something I hadn't been able to put my finger on yet, but something that might come crashing into me at almost any time.

I went back to the cabin on the Little Barachois again, even though I'd told myself I wouldn't. Even before Mary left.

I went back again, and again, and again.

It's not the kind of thing I could get away from easily.

It got so I brought a chair into the back room, just a green, battered, hard vinyl chair with rust-bubbled rough chrome legs from the front room, and I'd sit with my back up against the thin wall between the two rooms and watch, and wonder how everything could change so slowly.

I imagined that every time I went there, a little bit more of me was left behind in the cabin, just little physical traces like hair or skin weaving their way into the fabric of the place. And at the same time, that my brain was slowly etching thin lines of memory, like the fine tracks on a record, into my head in such a way that they would always be there, impermeable. Thin grooves, connected without ever touching.

Each time, I knew that there was less and less of a chance that I could ever explain it in a way that would make sense to anyone else. Each and every time, I knew I was digging a hole for myself, and at the same time, I was dead set on digging deeper. Even though I should have known better. I really did know better.

You don't just sit in a room with a dead woman.

You call the police.

You tell them what you've found, and they ask difficult, probing questions until everything is settled and you're dismissed, never really getting to hear the end of it all. Without all the answers, but with the clear-cut satisfaction that the police know the exact and whole extent of your part. They only need you to give them your pieces of the puzzle, and then they go out and get the other ones, the ones that belong to someone else. The someone who's to blame.

Because that's their job, finding whoever it was who

picked up some hitchhiker and killed her, or whatever.

The truth was that I found it strangely comforting to sit back there in the near-dark, in that familiar room where nothing ever changed.

Even with the smell, which I noticed less and less.

Safe in a spot where everything was always exactly what I was expecting, where everything just behaved.

Sure, there might be a new place in the cabin where water found its way in or something, and occasionally there were signs of mice that hadn't been there before, but I found that one of the things I could count on was the constancy.

I could tell you that I gave her a name, that body huddled up against the wall, but that would be particularly creepy. I can tell you for certain that I didn't, not even somewhere in the back recesses of my own mind. She wasn't a Lisa or a Heather or anyone else.

She was just someone to listen.

And what I did was talk.

Not so much to her as at her. That was the best part—at her, because there was no chance of it ever being anything more than that.

I would sit back there and talk about anything, about the garden and about what Mary had been doing with it, even about things as simple as how I'd meant to tell Mary how much I liked it out there in the space in back of the house, how she'd made it into a small, quiet haven hidden away in a noisy city.

The fact was I had forgotten to get those words out to Mary herself for so long that, when I did remember them, they just didn't feel like they'd be right coming out of my mouth any more. It was as though the words would sound particularly flat and forced, as if there was some part of it that I was actually trying very hard not to tell her.

In that cabin, I'd talk about the weather and about work, about the people I liked and the ones I didn't—and I even talked to her about the lists.

I really didn't talk to anyone else about the lists.

After Mary was gone, I brought them upstairs to the study. I'd been looking at them for years. I'd go down to where the workbench was, haul a box or two out of the narrow space that always had its share of spiders and those armoured little sow beetles that look like leftover trilobites waiting for eventual, overdue fossilization.

I'd been collecting lists for as long as I had been working in the front end of the store—as soon as I got out of shelf-stocking and into cleaning. First, a few screwed-up balls of paper, twisted tight as if they were hiding secrets or something, so I began picking them up and unrolling them, trying to make sense out of the code of "coffee, coffee filters, deodorant, and bagels."

The more of them I had, and the more I looked at them, the more intriguing they were. Different kinds of ink, different kinds of paper, and all those different kinds of handwriting. Completely unconnected to one another, and completely connected as well—because everyone writes them.

I was finding messages, messages that were in my control, enough in my control that I might be able to solve them.

Everyone jotting stuff down so they wouldn't forget, making memory solid and measurable so the cat wouldn't run out of kitty litter and there would always be dog treats to get the dog back inside when he was running around with his eyes almost rolled up into his head, barking frantic at the entire neighbourhood and not listening to a single word.

Enough bread and baggies to make a small fleet of school lunches.

Something for dinner, whether you were going to eat it while having a conversation or while you sat there with your wife, not even speaking, pushing your fork around like a small piece of heavy equipment focused on its own minor construction project.

I had it all in my hands, if I could find the way to make sense of it, if there was a kind of Rosetta stone that could unfold those mysteries.

I explained that to the woman in the sheet on the cabin bed. I explained all about how I had a couple of banker's boxes full of them by then and never threw any away, no matter how trivial, and about how that had grown into trying to figure out what the list-writers were all about.

What made them — what made anyone — tick.

No one in the cabin told me how stupid it was to be doing that, and no one laughed.

When Mary laughed at you, you knew all about it. Mary laughed and you knew where you fit in the world — and you didn't feel very high up in the scheme of things, let me tell you — because you knew exactly what she thought about whatever it was you were doing.

I don't hold that against her — really I don't — because it's not like she could help it or anything. It would be like blaming someone for having a snort at the end of their laugh — everyone knows someone like that, someone who has a little air-backwards kind of hurking snort, and that's just the way it is. Pointing it out would hurt, and, at the same time, would end up changing nothing.

It's just that Mary's laugh, well — it was a laugh that could hurt.

In the cabin, I didn't have to worry about laughing. Laying it all out may not have made the whole thing make sense, but it made it make sense to me.

I must have had fifty or more notes saying "don't forget milk."

Another fifty or so that could prove there was a segment of society that actually liked boxed croutons. Rows upon rows of lists smoothed out and grouped together, evidence of patterns and routes as plain and distinctive as the whorls in fingerprints.

Then, every once in a while, I'd sit back and think about what someone else would make about that little slice of my own life — if they were to take the part where I was sitting in a crumbling cabin, what kind of person would they decide I was?

Then one day I came up out of the river valley, up over the gravel shoulder and across the empty road, and looked back toward the gravel pit. I saw just the blunt nose of one of those plain-looking black Dodge Chargers, the kind that can belong to anyone at all, but also the kind that the police use for their unmarked cars. Just sitting there, jutting out of the trees a little, no hubcap on the front wheel that was facing me. They'd always been more interested in going through the house than they had been in seeing where I was going. But sometimes even the police must get it into their heads to try something new.

I took my time getting my stuff into the trunk, listening to the broken-up birdsong that starts up just before the light begins to fade. When I finally did get in the car, I rolled the window down so I could smell that particular heavy river smell, did a sweet, sudden little signal-less U-turn, and headed right back up the road toward that Charger.

You can keep your eyes looking straight ahead, and your peripheral vision can still let you know if there's someone sitting there in the driver's seat. There wasn't. Maybe it was someone just heading down across the road to the pond—I'd been down there myself before; it was a spot where the beavers had dammed all the outlet brooks and brought the water way back into the trees, killing them off, the pond now edged almost all the way around with greyed dead spruce. Not bad for trout—beaver ponds can be pretty good—but I'd been chewed up ferociously by flies when I'd been in there last, and I hadn't gone back.

Probably just someone fishing, I told myself.

But you can't be too sure. Or too careful.

CHAPTER 36

Can. Tire
$20 gift card
Plunger
photos
Painting sheet
eggs
ham
potato salad
Sheer curtains

Another note from Joy Martin of Signal Hill Road. I knew the handwriting right away, especially with the ornate, stylized *M* on the top of the notepaper. Green and gold around the letter, and, besides, I watched her leave it on the stainless steel backspill of the checkout, back where the bags are, in the ten-items-or-less lane. She had just three: ham, eggs, and potato salad, the only things off that list that she was going to get in my store. But I didn't care about them: they weren't the ones that mattered.

The paper came from the kind of notepad that someone gets you for a present when they don't know you well enough to think of anything more complicated, more involved than something that uses the first letter of your last name. Not really the kind of thing you could ever imagine buying for yourself.

My heart sank at the end of that list, with the curtains. For more than a year, I'd been taking the short hike up and around to the back of her house — on and off, at least once a week, anyway — and I wondered if it was something that I'd done, if she'd seen anything, if those curtains were the result of something she'd glimpsed out her back window.

I remember thinking that it certainly wouldn't be the same — not if the curtains went where I thought they were going. Too little of the real world shows through the gentle scrim of sheers; it's too much like romantic movies from the 1950s and not enough on the hard edge of things.

I imagine by then that I knew every single pair of underwear she owned, better than if I'd been going in and making my way through the dryer in her basement. Each time, the same — just a glimpse or two before she closed the curtains upstairs, almost always the last part of the evening. I knew by then that she liked her underwear to match, and I knew that, more often than not, she spent most nights working her way through the kitchen, waiting for things that didn't happen.

I don't know if that had more to do with her imagination, with an idea that someone just might arrive, or whether she'd actually been led to believe that someone was going to be at her door any moment. I think it was a combination of the two: watching her try on a bra-and-panties set in purple, and then take them off for far-more-familiar black, I wondered if the underwear she put on was a crucial part of finding her confidence, or a crucial part of losing it. It was summer by then, and I was still leaning on a maple tree up above her backyard, feeling the rough ridges of the bark through the back of my shirt against my spine, the dark coming later, the leaves reaching down.

You think stupid thoughts, sometimes. Like you should be coming to the rescue and arriving at her front door with a bunch of flowers. Like trying to bullshit your way through an evening pretending to be a friend of a friend who someone had tried to fix up with her. Things that have no chance of ever working, but that seem like a noble, movie-star kind of thing to do.

Knowing it was stupid the whole time, but imagining it anyway, so that when she changed from purple to black, there was some small extra possibility rattling around in my head that I could actually feel the warm close weight of her breasts in my hands.

Everything crucial is always about the possibilities, not about the realities. If I hadn't realized that by then, I would have been an absolute idiot. You have to be pragmatic: when one possibility changes, when it shuts down, well, you have to find another.

This sounds even stupider: it was hard to believe how terrible I felt about the fact I didn't have a chance to say goodbye.

That I didn't ever know that the last night I'd watched her really was the last night.

Twenty-twenty hindsight is everything, but when I went back up Signal Hill after finding that note and saw the new curtains and the way her bedroom looked like it had sunk into a kind of shapeless fog, I wished I'd had one last look at the familiar slope of her naked shoulders — just so that I could have carefully saved that image, locked the necessity of it into my head.

I wish I'd had that instead of trying hopelessly to imagine it weeks later while I was standing under the searing heat of the shower, the water on full, the tap on hot as much as I could stand, a hard-on out in front of me in the sluicing water, and me trying anything, anything at all to gather up a clear, sharp memory of her face, of her arms lifted above her head, elbows out, turning away from me and toward her bedroom door.

I couldn't make it slide back into my head.

I remember almost every part of her house perfectly. I remember every time I glanced through her front windows: the plants, the white mantel, the sharp order of it. The mirror I used to picture her in. Except now, I could only picture it empty.

She flits away, indistinct, like someone I was introduced to once at a party and then never got to see again. Losing the thing that was at the centre of your attention, in the middle of your vision, seems particularly unfair. Like that eye disease — macular degeneration. The things that you're looking straight at vanish into a morass of grey, because of something to do with your rods and cones or something. At the edges of your vision, you still can see things—can even make your way around, accommodate that overworked, dead spot that's there in the middle. And what a joke that is: in order to look at something, you have to also look away.

It's a lifetime of rules changing.

To be honest, I know things in the world are always going to change, and there's nothing you can do about that. There are other places, with other curtains. And in those places, other issues to occupy myself with.

Like a place on the Little Barachois with its own sets of curtains, as ratty as they were.

There had been, I don't know, four or five women who had gone missing in the province over the years. I knew about them, knew about them in the kind of way you'd know if you followed the newspapers sporadically, but no one would imagine that any of them had found their way into a cabin on the Little Barachois.

It could have been someone who had found the place and passed away in their sleep or something—someone no one would miss, and that no one really needed to be told about.

But I still didn't want to go to the police—I wasn't sure what I would say to them, or even if I wanted them to know that I'd found her. Because people who are different at all, who respond to things differently, they get misunderstood. You keep to yourself and the police kind of target you, just because you're not like everyone else—that's happened before in this country, to people who might seem a lot less peculiar than me.

You hear about that all the time, how the police find the best suspect they can right away, and then pick the evidence that makes them suspect, and just wash the rest away. They don't even really do it deliberately: they are just looking for the best and quickest solution they can find.

I could honestly say I wouldn't want to find myself standing there.

But there was more to it than that.

To me, a big part was that I didn't feel they belonged in that cabin, as if they'd descend with all their equipment and cameras, wearing the white spacesuits you see the forensic guys wearing on television, and everything I knew would change immediately. As if the order that had been there so long would simply crumble.

You always, always make exceptions for yourself when you're judging what's right or wrong. You fudge the lines because you believe you're different, when really, you're not.

CHAPTER 37

June 5—"I wish you weren't going. Mexico is too dangerous" is what my mother said. "I'd feel better about it if Daniel was going with you again" is what my dad came up with, even though I'd already told them that Daniel and I were done. And I told them that Mexico wasn't going to be any more dangerous than anywhere else—I didn't say that at least in Mexico I wouldn't feel like there's always someone following me around, that Mexico might well be safer than here. I've already found a job with a private school looking for someone to teach English, and they even have a place lined up for me to live. I didn't tell them about how someone had been in my house, about the police not finding anything, about all of that—because that was a big part of the decision, too. Being away was such a relief—not being dogged by someone I could never really see clearly, but someone I'm sure is there, and that I know is watching.

CHAPTER 38

Garbage bags
Paper towels
Barbecue starter

They burn illegal cabins.

Burning cabins doesn't sound anything like conservation, but that's what they call it.

That's what the wildlife department calls it, anyway.

A lot of the province is Crown land, and you need permits for wilderness cabins. You need to be registered for land title and you need to build a proper septic field and a real road and if the property's on a lease, you've got to make annual lease payments, too. It's a lot of rules and a fair bit of money, just for the privilege of staying on the right side of the law.

But because the province is so goddamned huge and empty, there's a lot of ground out there that no one's really keeping much of an eye on, and there are a lot of places where someone can haul in materials and put a cabin, so, if you do it right, you can go unnoticed for a heck of a long time.

Doing it that way, you don't need lease fees or septic plans—just a bit of hard work and a lot of nerve. And unlike the legal cabins, the illegals aren't on a square of land with all the trees cut down and grass planted—the illegals are built in tight under the tree cover, with as much of the bottom branches of a big tree out over the roof as you can manage, just so that the square of its shape doesn't jump out at you like you're looking down from the sky at a big floor tile tossed onto the beach and left there.

The illegal cabins lurk invisible in the landscape.

One of my uncles, Pete, had a place like that, out on the very edge of the Salmonier wilderness area. Not much more than four walls, a roof, one window, and a door—but big enough for three of those old cot beds and a stove and stove-pipe. A way station when you were going in deep fishing, just one kerosene lamp for light. My uncle spent years—*years*—making every bit of his place just right. Hauling in one of those old cast-iron stoves with the grates showing like teeth against the flames on the front, bringing in windows, digging a well and pouring concrete footings, and then, for no reason at all, a random helicopter drifts overhead, someone on their foolish way to somewhere else, and all at once it changes.

He'd brought in sand—bags and bags of washed-white sandbox sand—to make a little arc of beach out there on the side of a pond next to his cabin, walking back and forth over and over again, up to his knees in the cold water with each plastic sandbag on his shoulders, letting the sand trickle out of the bags and sink down to the peaty gravel on the bottom.

And the very next summer, maybe it was exactly that little fingernail of white along the side of the pond that caught the wildlife department's attention and the whole darned thing was gone.

My uncle and my father and one of my brothers, we hiked in one summer, knapsacks heavy. We were just waiting to put them down, and when we got there, we found nothing but char.

My uncle sat right down on the ground. I think he was crying. We didn't even have a tent, so it was a long hike back out again.

He never forgot.

I imagine the helicopters going overhead like something out of a Vietnam movie, everybody on the ground inside their places hunkered down and holding absolutely still until the *whump-whump* of the blades fades away over the nearest hill. And those cabins, the well-hidden ones, can be there for years, passed down from parents to children, and they can be in such regular use that there are ATV trails ground into the barrens right up to the front doors.

But you've got to be careful about that, too.

Sometimes, the wildlife guys find illegal cabins from something as simple as being on a helicopter trip, angling overhead on the way to a caribou count, a simple straight line from there to somewhere else when they happen to bee-line straight over you and notice something that shouldn't be there.

When that happens, they usually land nearby, the officers

231

zipping up their brown nylon wildlife-and-conservation jackets to the top before formally filling out and posting a notice on your front door that you've got exactly sixty days to clear your stuff out. They take another copy with them, and the countdown starts.

Doesn't matter that it might be weeks before you turn up there again and actually find the notice.

Sixty days from when they tack it on the door — that's what you get.

Your personal stuff — tables and chairs, maybe dishes. Clothes and fishing rods and pots and pans. Windows, if you want to keep 'em. Even though you may have been humping bits and pieces in there for the last twenty years by snowmobile or all-terrain vehicle, even though you hammered every single nail into place.

You move it all out, cutlery and gas cans, outboard motor and even the pillows, or up it all goes. Fast.

And it can break your heart.

All at once, there's nothing left.

That's the way it was on the Little Barachois.

A fire is pretty complete, especially when it's done and cold and there's nothing left but wet ashes and cold metal.

After the fires?

When a wilderness cabin burns, there's a postage stamp of charcoal that never, ever seems to change, year after year after year, not even when the fireweed and raspberries cluster in close by the sides, running riot, lipping in over and at least softening the edges. Burnt cabins aren't rebuilt — they're just

232

left, and what they become is absolutely permanent messages, an absence.

My river cabin was no different.

I was free.

There was nothing left of her beyond my memory — and absolutely nothing left that I would have to explain to anyone, even if there had been cops sitting in a black Dodge Charger tucked back into the trees not too many days before.

It was a long walk back up to the car, my legs making heavy, dragging strides the way they do when your muscles know it's the last time you'll ever go that way, when they're setting into their own particular groove of a time that's now clearly past.

The car was where the car always sat, tucked into a slightly wider part of the shoulder where a highway sign gave the river's name, as familiar to me as if it had been a numbered parking spot.

Just the way I had left it.

If I held my eyes just right, it was like I could just choose to believe that nothing had changed at all. Like the car, my clapped-out white Toyota with the rust climbing in from all the edges at once, four worn tires and the windows rolled up tight. Like the sky, still holding blue with just a few tendrils of high, fingering cloud stretching in from the west. Like lungs and legs and heart, still breathing, walking, beating.

Every plant and tree and river rock still in exactly the same place, nothing moved or altered or in any way different.

By the next morning, when the rain had come in heavy

overnight from the west (and it would have rained even more down on the southern end of the peninsula, down there where the land sticks out into the water like a crippled fist, all knots and angles), every trace of me would be washed away. From the river, from the roadside.

It was all gone. Like it had never really been there, even though there must have been some way to prove it had. Forensics, or something like that. Men sifting away at shovelfuls of ground until they found something they could hold up and shout, "bone fragment," the words somehow muffled and indistinct through their masks.

There's a spot in the bog just before that river where someone shot a moose, or else clipped it with their car or something, and the animal just staggered in, toppled over, and was left. Maybe someone took the quarters, I don't know. Maybe poachers panicked, seeing headlights. I first saw the carcass a year in, and the brown camouflage of the hide had slipped away off the rib cage, leaving a row of bright ribs against the surface of the bog, a perfect little cathedral of bone.

It stood that way for another year, an even row of white bones sharp against the ground, but by the next year it was gone, and at the end of the summer, I crossed over the bog where I remembered it being and found an unexpected mound of sedge grass, right there in the middle of the bog where, by rights, that kind of grass shouldn't have been. When I kicked away down into the roots, the moose's spine was right there, the zippered column of bone yellowing away in the peaty brown water of the bog.

It's not a matter of whether there are traces left—it's really more a matter of getting enough information to know just exactly where to look.

Or maybe something even more complex: how to find the right way to arrange the information that you already have.

And how to know that, once it is properly arranged, it's as fixed as time itself.

CHAPTER 39

June 30—The police told me they have wrapped up
their "investigation." Said there was no evidence of
anything. No evidence of anyone ever having been in
my house, no evidence that anyone has been following me. Nothing. I think they have me down as some
kind of chronic complainer now. As if I've got nothing better to do but to call them and have them come
over—like I'm looking for attention or something.
I know they went to talk to Daniel about whether he
had another key—I also know that the officer han-
dling the complaint, Constable Peddle, was different
after he came back from talking to Daniel. Different,
like distant. Standoffish. Makes me wonder what
Daniel said to him, but there's no way I'm going to
try to find out. I don't imagine he would tell me anything anyway. You know how it is when every single
thing you do just seems to solidify someone's opinion
about you, even when they're wrong? That's where
I am now. I mean, I know what Daniel thought
when I first wondered if I was being followed. Well,

that's the feeling that Constable Rick Peddle is giving off now. Early on, he gave me his card, wrote a cell number on the back, and told me I could call any time I needed anything, told me I could just call him Rick. I bet he's regretting that now, regretting giving another crazy, panicky twenty-five-year-old the least little bit of extra conviction. Bet he's already trying to figure out how to respond if I do call some night — and wondering if there's a chance that when I convince him to come over because of the mystery man, he'll show up and I'll be standing there at my front door in a bathrobe with nothing on underneath, all part of my evil-lonely-needy-girl plan all along. But I know I'm right about this: someone is watching me and someone has been in my house. It makes me furious that the cops are brushing me off. I mean, this is why people buy guns, right?

CHAPTER 40

(St. John's, NL)—The Royal Newfoundland Constabulary (RNC) is seeking the assistance of the general public with an investigation into a fire in the general area of Route 100 between the communities of North Harbour and Branch in the days surrounding July 15. The RNC is seeking information from anyone who may have observed the make and model of vehicles left on the roadside, particularly in the area of the bridge at Little Barachois River during that time.

If anyone has any information pertaining to this investigation, they are asked to contact the RNC at 729-8000 or anonymously at Crime Stoppers at 1-800-222-TIPS (8477).

Dean couldn't help but notice how much bigger the windows were on the fourth floor, where the chief's office was—heck, Dean couldn't help but notice that there were windows.

The chief was sitting behind his desk, chair pushed all the way back, and he wasn't talking. Dean looked out the window, watching the seagulls coiling against the sky. Scoville was next to him, motionless in his chair.

Dean knew that if the chief had anything nice to say, he'd start by offering them coffee from the machine at the back of the room. Chief Adams loved that coffee machine, loved being able to make different kinds of coffee by the cup. He seemed delighted every time by the gurgle and hiss, by the immediate appearance of the hot liquid. Other officers joked he knew more about the coffee machine than he did about most of the cases in active investigation.

He wasn't offering, though, and Dean knew that meant it was not a pleasure call. Chief Adams didn't know it, but the trick of withholding coffee was recognized all over the building. "If he's not handing out hot coffee, then he's handing out hot water." Dean had heard that too many times to count, especially from the lifers in patrol, the old-school guys who still hadn't figured out the world could change whether they wanted it to or not, guys who had been hauled up to try to explain the latest George Street nose they had flattened to make a particular point.

The chief was looking out the window as well. Dean had known the chief when Adams had been an inspector, a hard-headed cop from off the beat who would never have dreamed of being chief—a solid third choice who had wound up with the job in his lap when two more-senior police officers had flamed out spectacularly after a spate of wrongful convictions, all thanks to a Criminal Investigation Division given too much opportunity to make their own decisions on charges.

Chief Adams had learned from other peoples' mistakes and he wasn't going there. Dean knew the chief had a career of playing everything exactly by the book. So he sat, waiting for the chief to speak.

"Arson's not in your area, and neither is the Cape Shore. That's the RCMP's jurisdiction."

The chief was long enough in the tooth to sometimes call the RCMP the horsemen, but that didn't mean that a phone call from high in B Division, the Newfoundland RCMP section, couldn't rattle him.

"It's related to a file here in the city, Chief. A couple of files," Dean said. Scoville sank down lower in the chair on Dean's right. He'd brought his own paper cup of coffee from downstairs. The chief waved his hand dismissively.

"Just following stuff up," Scoville said.

"Nothing from you, Scoville," the chief said. "You've been nosing into another fire investigation in Cape Broyle — yeah, I know about that, there's not much I don't hear about, and that was none of your concern. Not your jurisdiction, not your fire. Not your business.

"And you," he said, turning back to Dean, "you're going to have to come up here and convince me first before we go traipsing out into their turf. You should know that, Inspector. You should know that real well, and you should have talked to me before sending that release out. Got your own little team and you're getting too big for your britches, don't you think?"

Dean didn't say anything — didn't say, even though it was right there ready to burst out, that his "little team" had been the chief's own idea, not his.

"I think I'm making myself pretty clear," the chief said. "Aren't I?"

Dean and Scoville both nodded.

"There might be good fishing down there, but we don't do fishing missions." The chief stood up, smiling coldly at his dry little joke. "It's time to start getting some measurable results, something I can take to the media. Something a little more than the fact that my team — not the minister's any more, no, they've got it stitched to me now — really likes to be on the road.

"You've put a lot of mileage on the unmarked cars you've signed out, Inspector Hill." His voice was almost conversational, but threatening, too. "A lot of mileage for not much in the way of results."

By then, he'd walked around the desk and over to where Dean was sitting, slapping an oversized hand down on Dean's shoulder like he was making a friendly point. Dean couldn't help but turn slightly, his eyes falling on the broad expanse of the back of the chief's hand, the tufts of ginger hair springing up next to the rough skin of occasional scars. There was, Dean thought, nothing friendly about it.

The chief put his face down close enough to Dean's ear that Dean could feel the warmth radiating off of the other man's skin.

"Fuck with me and I will be the last person you ever fuck with," the chief said quietly, his tone light but the meaning obvious. "Keep that in mind the next time you're tooling around out on the highway."

Dean and Scoville didn't talk until they were back on the elevator and the big silver doors had pulled shut.

"You lost him twice?" Dean said.

"First time, I was taking a piss. Five hours in the car, a whole Thermos of coffee, sometimes you gotta take a piss."

"The second time?"

"Fog to the floor. But Walt had a place down there—and I think he burned it."

Dean looked at Scoville. Scoville put his hands out.

"I've been doing this for years. I know fires. And I smelled it—I know that smell. If it hadn't been so damned foggy, I would have seen it, too. All I've got to do is find it. If we can find the place, I'll find what we need. You know he was down there—I know he was down there. We just didn't see where he went in. And he's left something somewhere. If I have to spend every single day off I have left this year stomping around that godforsaken bog, I'll do it."

Dean smiled.

"Didn't you already have this conversation with me? The evidence leads us to the criminal, not the other way around? Playing by the rules?"

Scoville scowled.

"You could just shut the fuck up now," Scoville said. "Sometimes I think I liked it better when you were pining for Julie and taking off without me, all by yourself."

"That's over and done with," Dean said. "And if you decide to take off anywhere, you'd better not let the chief find you."

CHAPTER 41

Elsie Tucker — #234
Clear liquids
Chicken broth
Jello

Apple Juice
PRE-OP

That was on a rectangular card, the paper slightly heavier than ordinary bond paper. Perforated edges, top and bottom, where it had been torn off a roll of hundreds of similar cards. Something that looked like it had come out of a solid old computer printer with a bunch of cards just like it, each one waiting to be split apart and matched up with the right meal, the right patient. *PRE-OP* was typed in red as well as in caps, the rest in black.

It was from St. Clare's, and I picked it up on the fourth floor, where it had dropped from one of those rolling meal racks. An orderly comes in with a plastic tray, those heat-trapping heavy trays from the central kitchen that all look the same, slides it in front of you on a bed-table, whips the top off, and you have a look and decide if it's something you feel like eating. Maybe you don't. Maybe you do. No other choice, though. Dinner is dinner. Dinner is served.

I could imagine the one small piece of tape coming loose, the note catching the air as the orderly picked up the tray, that same orderly — exasperated, overworked, both hands full — watching the paper float down, already knowing whose meal it was anyway. So why stop to pick it up?

Too many meals left to hand out, and besides, there's someone whose job it is to pick stuff like that up.

Someone like me.

If there's one thing I know how to do, it's how to look like a janitor. I've been rehearsing for years. Being inconspicuous. Focusing on the job. I took a trip to the hospital on a weekday afternoon, just to see what colour clothes the cleaning staff wore.

Went back a week later, wearing the right colour. The important thing is to walk and keep your eyes purposefully low. Carry a cloth and a spray bottle for marks on the walls, and just keep doing stuff with it, even if you're the only one who sees anything like a mark.

The most important thing of all? That official-looking plastic ID card, the one almost everyone in the hospital keeps clipped to their pants pocket, so low down on their hips that it's hard to make out whose face is on the card unless you practically bend down to stare at their crotch or make a big thing about asking someone to show it to you. Half the time, it's flipped around backwards anyway. And everyone's busy, everyone's moving.

Hospitals are big, anonymous places. Just like grocery stores. A regular tide of customers, of patients, moving through, ebb and flow.

Come in the front door of the hospital, after hours, when there are people milling in and out with flowers and food for visiting hours, and you can make your way downstairs and hardly be noticed. Down in Diagnostics, where there's nothing to steal anyway, the hallways are pretty much empty, and if you walk with enough purpose, the few people you do run into leave you alone.

Down in the basement, in a hallway with half the lights turned off for the night and at least four of the remaining sets flickering in that abandoned-mental-hospital-scary-movie way that the back corners of institutional buildings always seem to have, I found a utility room. Easy to find, really, because it was the only door on the hall with the familiar yellow glow of an incandescent light bulb lipping out from underneath it.

It's a dead giveaway, even in newer buildings.

Whatever kind of lights everyone else has, the janitors always get that single harsh 100-watt bulb sticking out of the most basic kind of screw-in socket. Sometimes there's a wire cage around the bulb, protecting it from attacking mop handles. Sometimes there isn't.

It's always a bare-bones cramped little box of a space,

cinder block or concrete walls, sometimes painted but often not. A big stained stand-up sink, stacks of cleaning supplies on real basic metal shelving. Sometimes, a single wooden chair that's clearly been brought in from home or liberated from storage. To me, those spaces, the ones with the chairs, always feel like they actually belong to someone, despite the official starkness. Pin-ups, but not so often any more: people go out of their way to crane their heads inside and have a look, just so they can be officially offended and you can get a letter put in your file. They used to be expected, pin-ups, proof that you were one of the good guys, because honest libidos need a great set of cans arced right out toward the camera. But like I said, not so much any more.

Sometimes the rooms are locked: it depends more on the temperament of the cleaner than it does on anything else. If you're the kind of person who doesn't mind people coming in and helping themselves to more toilet paper when they need it or to those big brown rolls of paper towels when they run short, you leave it open.

If you want to have the absolute last word on whether or not people are going to have to dry their hands on the front of their pants, then you lock it, play everything by the rules, and check and reload the paper towel dispenser when you're downright good and ready.

The basement room at St. Clare's wasn't locked, and there was a cart in it, packed right in tight between the sink and the door, hardly a scrap of extra room. There was a jacket hanging on the back of the door—which probably meant someone on break and not all that far away. And there was another bonus as well. The janitor had his ID clipped right to the big garbage bag holder on the front, probably left it there full-time and didn't even think about it any more, so I had a quick look around, unclipped the tag, and took it with me.

I closed the door, went back upstairs and went home, because I wanted to get there before Mary got back.

I didn't go up to Emergency at all that night, didn't go searching to see what she and Dr. Patterson were up to.

You have to take your time: if you rush things, they are always going to go wrong. You'll leave something behind, you'll make yourself too obvious, you'll generate too much attention. And when you do, if you do, suddenly you're not invisible any more.

You've got to scope things out, step back from your emotions, and have a good, clean objective look at the circumstances. I saw an armed robber, a guy who held up a convenience store, interviewed on television once, and the reporter was asking him, "What were you guys planning?"

And the guy said, "Well, I'd taken twelve Valium, and we'd run out of beer."

See, that's not a plan.

That's just a circumstance. And when you let your circumstances make your plans for you, you're going to fall into whatever hole they leave behind.

CHAPTER 42

August 1

Cold case squad goes cold?

(St. John's, NL) — The Royal Newfoundland Constabulary's new cold case squad has gotten a chill: case statistics obtained under access to information legislation show the squad, an offshoot of the Criminal Investigation Division, has closed only a handful of cases in the last six months.

But RNC Chief Winston Adams says he's satisfied with the team's work: "This is complex investigation, involving the review of files that are in some cases over a decade old. We're not going to put it on the clock."

Adams was not willing to talk about whether the section's results are going to be reviewed.

"We monitor all our investigative divisions on a regular basis, and ensure they meet our internal standards."

Adams would not discuss what those standards include.

"**There are several** in his area. Joy Martin on Signal Hill Road might be one. There's another nearby, an Alisha Monaghan, both stalking complaints. And Monaghan also thought someone had been in her house. Investigating officer left a note on that one: 'disgruntled ex-boyfriend—interviewed, not cooperative.' That sounds like a domestic," Scoville said.

"Well, pitch it for now. Keep Signal Hill Road. We've got enough already."

"Surprising how many there are."

"Sure is. We've got a lot of footwork to do. We've either got a nest of peepers or just one particular guy. I think we know which guy."

"Think so," Scoville said. He squinted, looking across at Dean. "Everything okay?"

"Never better," Dean said, and meant it. It was all the case now, whirling around in his head when he was driving, when he was on the edge of falling asleep. He'd put the house on the market, paid off the pile of bills, was looking for an apartment. Close to downtown: close to the station.

CHAPTER 43

From the desk of Julia Peyton
Spinach
Coconut
Pears
Sour cream
Cream cheese
Bread Stix
Feta
Rosemary

All of it in light blue ink, on unlined paper—every first letter lined up exactly in place with the one below and above. Precise, every *o* and *a* with its belly perfectly round.

Across the road from my house, Ms. Peyton never seems to come outside. Or at least she never seems to be outside for long, as if the outside air is somehow dangerous or corrosive and she needs to protect herself from it. She lives in the house next to Tom and Ev's old place. She has a small green car, a four-door, although the driver's door is the only one that is ever used, and she has a front light on her porch that never, ever goes out, whether she is in town or not. She is out of town a lot.

And every time I look at the front of her house, the curtains are exactly, precisely the same. Perfectly spaced, every round fold of them even, as if they'd been measured with a ruler and nudged just so.

It makes me unreasonably angry, the formality of all of it. And I know it's unreasonable — see, I get that. I'm not just boiling all the time like some pot left on the stove, the dial turned up to high and the burner glowing orange under there. But she can make me boil, just the same.

I don't know why: perhaps because her poise is something most people never achieve. There is some particular frustration in the fact that I could be upstairs in the front room, looking out and across the road but standing well back in the shadows where I couldn't be seen, yet I could never even catch so much as a hint of someone looking out of her house. And I can't help but think that if she had any humanity at all, I would have been able to catch her at least once. Just to prove there's some small shred of human curiosity in there. That's all I really need.

Just her looking out of her house, me looking out of mine: all I really need is that one little sideways look, that one little captured-moment catch of the eye that would let me know that, deep down, she and I and everyone else are just the same.

It's not some kind of one-upmanship, that she's over there pretending to have something on me — the fact is, it actually feels like she's somehow better. As though, every day, nothing outside her own house even matters—and, well, every single day that bothers me.

That power to simply never put a foot wrong, to never get caught out—I can't tell you how much that makes me want to reach in and mess it all up.

It's like that kid you knew in grade nine with the perfect hair and that kind of smile people used to describe as "winning," the simple in-your-face perfection that grade-nine you absolutely had to find a way to damage, with a hand pushed into that hair to mess it up or a timely shove in the back from the top step. That kid who didn't ever do anything but exist and hold their head at that irritating upwards angle when they were talking to you, like they were looking at you, all right, but at the same time, somehow deeply and intimately connected to heaven or something. To more important things. So they don't really have to pay attention to anything you're saying. And God help them if they happened to absentmindedly smile then, too.

Meet someone like that and you'll understand immediately what I mean, that whether they mean to or not, they have a way of lording things over you.

I mean, people shouldn't be able to do that.

I find myself wanting to settle with them once and for all.

She comes out and gets in the car, and sometimes Tom used to come out first and shovel her driveway in that big-chested, I'm-a-man, look-at-me kind of way that was meant to say how great he was.

It didn't matter. It still doesn't matter.

She comes out, slides the key in the door, and then the brake lights and the white reverse lights come on, both of them exactly the way they are supposed to. If it's snowing, she makes sure every single flake of snow is brushed off the roof and away from the lights first, the brushing done in short, precise motions, each one the same economical length, the same effort every damn time. I watch her from upstairs, and I know what every single brush stroke will look like, how much snow it will push off the car, how carefully and precisely the next arc of the brush will curve through the flakes.

If she came outside while hapless shovelling Tom was digging away, her car keys already in her right hand, if she stopped next to him, and put the palm of her cool left hand on his shoulder for just a moment and then drew it away — not took it away, no, that would be too crass, but *drew* it away — that motion would capture every inch of her. Lady and servant. But usually, he would have already left, and she would climb into her car like, well, like royalty, like she absolutely expects the driveway to have been cleared and doesn't have to give it another thought. Tom never got it at all. Just one more thing he didn't seem to be equipped to comprehend.

Her name is Elizabeth, and she has a particular way of talking to you, every word distinct and placed down sharply with a click like Scrabble tiles, her hair piled up grey and precise, and she always looks at your chest, high up toward your shoulder and slightly off to one side, the left side, as if she'd been told that this was exactly the spot where your heart was, and if she looked at it hard enough, she'd be able to divine your true intentions right through the wall of your chest, right inside that lub-dubbing lump of muscle in there. Eyes staring straight through flesh and bone and muscle. Or something like that.

I had to think that there was some reason why she found it impossible to hold your eyes — as if there were some secret rule that, if she did, she might be caught cold in a way that she couldn't ever tolerate being caught.

I've spoken to her maybe nine or ten times in fifteen years — never about anything important, always something faux-neighbourly like "terrible weather this spring," or a short discussion about the latest person on the street who's decided to renovate their place and put it on the market. The price of lettuce — the fact that the green beans at the store are always in such bad shape that "they shouldn't even be sold," and the fact is that she says that right to me, as if it were somehow my fault. As if I were responsible, by simple association.

We've talked appraisals, and where the city taxes are going to be when all the bills come out in March. She calls me "Walter," and I bet she called Tom "Thomas," although nobody else ever did.

A conversation with her is like dancing, not like at the gym when you're in grade school, each of you in your own space, but formal dancing. Your foot goes here, and mine goes there, and there are always conventions that have to be followed, lines drawn in helpful dashes that you're not meant to ever cross over or step outside of.

Always. It's a kind of dancing that's much more about the linear organization of math and geometry, and much less about the vibrating practicalities of touch.

Her hair piled up there on the back of her head in that perfect dome, pinned in place or sprayed or something, and I have to tell you it's like even the very captured order of that hair is telling me bluntly that there's something else at her core — that there has to be.

That's the part I imagine, over and over again.

I can't shake it — I don't remember when it started, just that it's now an almost overwhelming physical urge.

Disorder.

It might not be all that unusual to say that sometimes you stare at someone and imagine what they'd be like, naked and curving up and under and against you. If you were just looking at Elizabeth for one passing moment, it might seem unlikely, maybe even impossible. She just doesn't seem to vibrate at that frequency. But I've been imagining exactly that for years, and I imagine it almost every time I see her now.

Not because I want it all that much, but more because the thought just constantly nudges into my head and won't go away.

And every time, I imagine she swears.

I haven't said that to anyone. Ever.

I imagine she lies there still at first, not even willing to moan, resolutely formal, until it's all just too much for her to take any more. That she's still looking at my left shoulder, or off into the corner, or up at the ceiling. Her lips a perfectly tightly sealed straight line, neither happy nor unhappy. Neutral.

Then she starts to swear. She starts quiet, but all at once, and the words come out in bunched little fistfuls of filthy language. Not a simple couple of words, either. She swears in full sentences, using a whole bunch of words that, normally, her mouth couldn't even find the right shape to say. Words that are otherwise alien to her, like the sort of messy mildewed-clothing problem from the basement, the old clothes you bundle up in garbage bags and keep locked away in a shed way up at the end of your yard, away from the house, until you finally just make the necessary anonymous run to the dump.

Then she pounds on my shoulders and my back with her fists and scratches the skin, and she coils there under me — completely, uncontrollable angry and involved, heaving up against me like a wild thing, because that's exactly, precisely who she really is underneath all of it. Because that's what she really is — just like everybody else. Like all of us are inside. And she hates it.

Afterwards, I imagine she would straighten her hair where it has come loose and call me "Walter" all over again, two fat, full syllables like I'm someone who had come over to do something absolutely essentially to the plumbing, the kind of work that will later result in a cheque with perfectly balanced and even handwriting, not one single loop out of place or even marked by the slightest shake of her hand.

I can't help but think that's what she's really like.

Even if she has the black and white cat with a red collar and a bell.

Even if her cat has that always perfectly placed collar and bell.

Even if there is not one single thing out of place in her house or in her yard or in her car. Even if she is absolutely as perfectly poised as anyone could be, every single thing thought out and deliberate. Believe me, there's a subtle fire coming off her, if you know what fire feels like — and there's plenty of fire there.

So I'd like to catch her eye squarely just once, catch her eye in that shared visual equivalent of a whisper — just to be clear, just to let her know what I know and that, at the same time, her secret is completely safe with me.

Or that it's anything but safe with me.

But she's more skilled than that, smarter, and she never, ever makes eye contact.

Deliberately.

I like to think that she knows the game better than anyone, knows the value of the bets, knows the potential losses.

I can feel the heat of her eyes on my chest like the skin is about to burn, and she never looks up, because if she were to, there'd be no way to even think of stopping.

And Tom?

Smart as a plank, he was. He could have shovelled her snow for fifteen hundred years and never had a single clue about her at all.

Tom had no idea.

He didn't even know to look.

Sometimes, a couple of beers in and reckless, I start

thinking that I'll just go over and knock on her door—just knock on her door, wait for her to open it, and look straight into her eyes, even if it means I have to reach out and hold her chin in my hand, the soft skin of her neck between my thumb and forefinger, and pull her face up so that she has no choice but to look back.

Make her look straight at me, right there, where the hard truth can't help but flicker back at her. Positive to negative, one great blue-white flashing spark.

Then just wait to see what happens.

I went to Alisha's again right after I knew she'd come back from that vacation.

I'd gotten to know the cat, or it had gotten to know me, and I'd found from her pictures that its name was Bo. I mean, there wasn't really a reason to be there, no reason at all to go in and sit on the couch and pet Bo, but I'd did it anyway, more than once.

I'd try to choose times when I was sure she wouldn't be there. Stand on the other side of the street, in under the big trees, and try to work out from the patterns of the lights in the windows whether anyone was home or not. When I figured no one was there, I'd be up onto the veranda to ring the doorbell and see if anyone came before trying the door and slipping in the key.

This city is still small enough that there's a family grocery store that will deliver your groceries and put them away right there in your own cupboards—the delivery guy has a big fat ring of keys for all of the houses on his route, and he will just come in and leave the groceries on the counter, the meats and milk and ice cream in the fridge, or else he'll put it all away if that's what you want.

I often wonder what that guy sees, what he walks into and walks around and looks at.

Whether he ever takes a few extra steps away from his appointed rounds, whether he opens the odd cupboard or a drawer he isn't supposed to, just too curious about what might be inside. The houses empty and waiting, all around him.

There aren't many feelings like that, not many feelings that are as charged sharp with risk as sliding open a drawer when you know that, if you're ever caught, the whole world changes, and not in a good way, either.

That's the sharp line for sure: one moment trusted, the next a pariah. No more slipping packages of cream crackers or bags of egg noodles behind the knotty-pine varnished doors for you. No more job, no more cheque, and all for having a peek behind a half-opened door off the hall or something, having a door open behind you and the homeowner staring at your back, all nicely kitted out in your jacket from the store. Not the kind of thing you can turn around and just deny.

I would have loved having all those keys. I'm also pretty sure it wouldn't have been very long before I would have gotten caught being somewhere I wasn't supposed to be.

I have my own key ring, though. I suppose I might have three or four different keys now, like Alisha's, that I'm not supposed to have. But I don't make a big thing about it. That grocery guy, I can't imagine how he could go around and never be accused of picking something up and walking off with it, something someone had actually misplaced. You know what people are like: if they found whatever it was they accused him of taking, would they ever come back and clear his name? The odds are probably less than fifty-fifty on that.

The possibilities, though. I mean, just like at Alisha's, up in her makeup stuff, for example, or looking through the medicine cabinet in the bathroom. The cabinet packed so full it was hard to imagine what everything was really for.

The dresser? The smell of fabric, how it feels when it's right pressed up against the little crease there under your nose: it's like lust but without the sex, and I know that's not an easy thing to understand.

It made me wonder about him, about the guy Alisha had gone south with in the first place, because there was nothing of his in the place any more. I wondered if that meant that he had left, or whether he just didn't warrant the space. Maybe she had just settled into the house and spread out gently, continuously, smothering the place with her clothes, her stuff, herself. Because she was in every room.

Sometimes, I'd see her coming out or glimpse her through the window from the outside. There were a couple of places where I could get high enough to see in windows and stay out of sight from the neighbours. But I didn't see him any more.

CHAPTER 44

Peanut Butter	*Bleach*
Coffee Cream	*Coffee Cream*
Milk	*Dish Soap*
Beans in Molasses	*Sausages*
Sausages	*Whole Wheat Bread*
Belgium Bread	*Coffee Beans*
Coffee Beans	*Dog Meat*
Dog Meat	*Ginger Ale*
Ginger Ale	*Potatoes*
Scalloped Potatoes	*Bananas*
Green Pepper	*Gravy Mix*

Two different lists — exactly the same person. Going through the same things, running out of the same things. Same handwriting, same black pen, same weight where the capital *C* in cream runs right into the lower case *r*. Always making the same lists, with some things different, but all of the anchors exactly the same. Coffee with cream, sausages, ginger ale, meat for the dog.

You get addicted to the things you do really well. That's just the way it is. Addicted to the things that have become second nature.

Addicted to doing them in the same order, addicted to doing them right, especially if it just happens that you can do them easily, too. If you play pool well, and someone at the bar challenges you to a game, you don't play worse just so the game will seem competitive once you see that they're not as good as you.

Sure, you might take a few of the lower-percentage shots — you might try things you wouldn't if you were playing in a tighter, closer game, someplace where every shot really counts, but it's not because you're giving a really bad player a chance. Fact is, you almost start competing with yourself, but you'll always fall back on your regular game eventually, and if they're not as good as you, they'll probably lose. The point is that once you have a skill, using it to the best of your ability is part of having it. Even if it's wrong — you can't just sell yourself short and feel good about it. That's not charity — it's just being condescending. Some people might like to do that — not me. Better to be fair and straight up about the whole thing. Put the balls in the pockets, clear the table, and you both walk away knowing something about each other that you didn't know before, win or lose.

I got good at the cold shoulder. It started a couple of years before she left, and it was completely deliberate. I just started shutting down, making myself look as if I just didn't care. Calculated, meant to hurt—and it was absolutely the best defence in a fight with Mary, because there was no one like her for sinking her teeth into the big, noisy, "fuck you" kind of fighting. She was an expert at full tilt—and smart as a tack, able to remember every single word said by everyone, when it was said, and what it sounded like, the tone ascending, the tone descending. Pitch perfect every time.

I'm not sure I could say that she liked fighting.

What I can certainly say is that she liked winning, and she could always play better than I could. Harder than me.

Until I learned to cheat.

I'm not proud of it. But I don't think anyone in my shoes would really blame me.

I just got tired.

More than that: tired of the fact that we always ended up fighting about the same old unsolvable things. There's the little stuff, the markers, like leaving a glass in the living room when I went to bed, or leaving it next to the sink, the last of the ice cubes melting away so that, when you pick it up the morning, thinking that it's empty, water ends up going everywhere. Water, perfumed with just enough scotch to really be a pain.

The truth is that fighting about those things is really about the much bigger issues, the ones you are afraid to even get near. You worry the little ones half to death instead, batting them back and forth in a way that would make absolutely no sense to anyone outside your marriage, when you're really talking in a special kind of hurtful code.

Talk about who left the bath mat out on the clothesline in the rain overnight, because you can't say something as blunt as "I feel abandoned. By you."

You argue about who's fault it is that the bathroom garbage didn't go out to the curb with everything else, but you're really talking about something else entirely, about the fact that some things get your wife's full, complete attention—and the things that matter to you don't seem to matter to her at all.

They matter so little that she can't even keep them straight in her head, even though she knows the precise date of every single one of her volunteer hospital shifts until well into next November.

Watch people on strike on the news, and the strikers and managers are always telling each other to be reasonable. The bosses are saying the union guys are unrealistic, the union says management's a bunch of heartless, greedy bastards, and it often jumps up to pushing and shoving and blocked entrances and picket line violence.

Ever notice how the violence is almost always caught on television, how it always seems to happen exactly when the cameras are on?

Then there's the deal, and everyone's talking about being friends together, and "we're so glad we were able to work this out," and blah, blah, blah.

Ever see anyone go back to work and have the union say, "We just signed this contract because our members are broke and tired and it's too damned cold to stay on the picket line against these stubborn assholes"?

No. I didn't think so.

I think that the real unrest comes earlier. When the workers decide to stop doing anything extra and still get paid — when they're working to rule, taking the paycheque but not really living up to their side of the bargain. That's not theatre. That's the real deal. And nobody sees it outside the company: the boss is wondering why no one's filling the shelves, the customers are screaming blue murder, and the employees are just circling the place like zombies, their eyes dead, doing precisely what they're told to do and nothing else. Used tissue scattered loose in the aisles, and no one picking it up.

I started to work to rule with Mary.

I decided not to fight.

In the beginning, she was just lost with that — she was a small plane with no clear route to the airport, just circling and circling, looking down through gaps in the clouds for anything with the familiar look of a runway.

The trick is not to let anything get away from you — this was especially important later, when she started looking at me with her eyes narrowed, trying to figure out just how much of what I was doing was deliberate.

Keep your eyes open wide, surprised, maybe a trace of being offended that the suggestion is even being made, even if you feel almost like laughing inside.

I saw a nature special that explains it really well — sharks have this extra eyelid, see, this thing they call the nictitating membrane. It flicks down when the shark is biting its prey, a clear membrane that protects the eyes. An invisible lid. That's exactly what I'd do: when things seemed like they were about to start, I'd just blink and carefully cover up whatever I was really thinking. So that cover-up could protect me the same way the eyelid protected the shark. So it could short-circuit things before there was ever a chance of injury.

Mary was the emotional one, the one who sensed things long before I figured out that they were real. She could always make the right guess, based simply on the way she felt. She was more intuitive than intelligent; I remember thinking that plenty of times, although it probably wasn't fair.

Prescient—whole bunches of things, expressions, body movements, and part of her brain would sort it all into an order, see things that the people doing it didn't even realize. Sometimes, it was spectacular—we would come home from seeing friends and she would tell me that they were going to get divorced, and months later, they would.

I'd ask her if someone had told her something, but it would always be something she had seen or a scrap that she had heard. It was the strangest of answers—"because her arm was hanging down beside the couch," or "he was emptying her glass in the sink when she wasn't looking."

I mean, it's one thing if you hear that someone's having an affair with someone at the office—it's something else if you're basing it on the way his arm looked over her shoulders when you were leaving.

Mary had a touch for it, that's for sure. If she said it was terminal, it was. It might not be today or tomorrow, but the die was cast. I remember thinking once, "I hope she doesn't ever decide to look at us that way."

Eventually, I realized she must have done exactly that.

I don't believe that you can change someone else deliberately—you can't take a person and make them into somebody else. They are who they are, and I sometimes think that who we are is more hard-wired than anyone imagines.

What you can do, almost without thinking, almost without blaming yourself for anything, is to turn them toward the crash—turn them toward it, just the tiniest of turns, and let the inevitability of their momentum do the rest all by itself.

Momentum is powerful and cruel, and there's not one single thing that can change it.

I dug a hole right there in front of her and waited for her to fall in. Waited, ready to cover her over completely.

CHAPTER 45

August 15

Missing linked

This weekend, the first installment in a three-part series examines missing women on the Northeast Avalon: who they were, where they went missing, and what the police are saying about the cases. And what they're saying is very little.

See Part One in the Saturday edition.

"I don't need this kind of heat," the chief said. "So you don't need this kind of heat either. And you two started it: you and your damned press release putting one and one together, and now they've started adding and they've got three or six or nine instead and they're howling about it. And you can't tell me that you didn't give them the idea."

Dean was alone in the chief's office because Scoville was on the road teaching an arson investigation course to volunteer firefighters. "The real basics," Scoville had said when

Dean asked him about it. "If you see an empty gas can in the snow outside a burning building, call the arson investigators. That kind of thing." Dean had a feeling the other detective had been looking forward to the break — and he'd probably be enjoying himself even more if he knew what he was missing back at the station. Scoville read the paper every day, throwing it down and muttering sometimes, but buying it again the next day religiously. Dean wondered if he had seen the ads for the weekend series before he headed out.

"So here's what you're going to do," the chief said. "You're going to find some new leads on something, on at least one of the cases they're talking about, and Monday or Tuesday, whenever their series is done, we'll put something out saying we're making progress. And that will at least get the politicians away from my door."

"What if we don't have anything? That's only four days."

"If you don't have anything, you'd better be planning to start making something up. Because if there isn't anything new to put out there, it'll be a slow roast for me, and that means it'll be a slow roast for you and Scoville, too. Except I think that in the end, I'll be better off than either of you. Catch my drift?"

Alone in the office, Dean worked through the Mary Carter case yet again. Tried to find something clear to hang his convictions on. And no matter how often he thought about it, the thing that stuck with him the most was what Walt had done with the houseplants.

When someone leaves, he thought, the first thing you do is try to keep everything the same, in case you can turn it all around.

The second thing you do is try to erase them completely: when you're sure they're not coming back, you pack up their stuff, even if it's pretty clear they don't want it. Because you don't want it there either, surrounding you every day and pointing out how things have gone wrong.

Give the plants away?

Sure.

Dump them in the yard behind the house?

No problem.

But just stop watering them and leave them in their pots like gravestones?

That's not what you do when you hope someone might come back.

That's making the point that there's no way they are coming back. And Dean was sure he knew what that meant.

Waiting almost a week to call the police and say she'd left?

He'd done that, too: Dean had looked back at all the case notes, and the police file hadn't been opened until Mary had been gone for at least six days. Walt had had little to say about that beyond the basics: when she left, what she might have been wearing. Maybe that didn't mean anything by itself, and, like Scoville had said, people are different. But if Julie had disappeared while he was at work and hadn't told him she was going, well, Dean was pretty sure he wouldn't have reacted the way Walt had.

The problem was that it wasn't like Julie, Dean thought. Walt had already know what Mary was going to do. He wasn't expecting any sort of surprise. And that really could only mean one thing.

Then Scoville came back, looking like Dean had never seen him looking before. Soaking wet from the knees down, hands covered with charcoal, a small silver digital camera in his hand. Smiling.

"Bingo," Scoville said.

CHAPTER 46

Elizabeth ?
Kathy and Sam — salmon
Diana — jewellery
Helen — card
Judy — $25 in gift cards
Art — $25 in gift cards

Some people plan out everything. That's just part of a long Christmas note I found, small handwriting balancing out gifts for more than twenty people, including a parish priest. I don't think I plan that well — I try, but somehow I can't pull everything together, not when there are more than a few pieces involved.

My last trip inside St. Clare's was on a night when Mary was actually there. Because the fact is that you can suspect a lot of stuff, even imagine it vividly and run it through your head in full colour and everything, but it doesn't count for anything unless you've got the good clear facts laying out right there in front of you.

I figured I could take the hospital badge I'd swiped and just stay on the edges of everything, just to watch what was going on from a distance. Push a mop around the far end of an emergency room hallway for a while and keep my eyes open, that sort of thing. Do what I'd spent a lifetime doing: being invisible, in no way memorable, my ears and eyes open and taking everything in, marking it carefully in my memory.

It worked out all right, at least in the beginning.

I went in the front door, on the side away from Emergency where most of the traffic is families, and I went straight downstairs to see if the utility room was still unlocked.

It was, but the lights were out and the cart was inside — the coat hook was empty, so I thought there was a pretty good chance the missing cart wouldn't be noticed. I put soap and water in the bucket, and I rolled the whole thing out and shuffled it down the hall and onto the elevator. There's a formal step to it, a pattern you have to use, a careful combination of bored and resigned and just plain looking at the wall. Think bovine or unfocused. I know that doesn't sound very complimentary for whoever's in the coveralls, but the truth is that no one's thinking complimentary thoughts about us anyway.

When the elevator door opened and I was getting ready to get off on the first floor, there were two nurses waiting to get on, just back from a smoke break from the smell, and they made me jump a little. One of them held the door back while I wrestled the cart over the elevator lip and out into the hall, but neither of them really looked at me, and I'm absolutely certain they forgot I was even there as soon as the elevator started up again.

Some things just don't change.

I pushed the cart around the last corner, to a spot where I could look straight down the hall from one end of the emergency room to the other. I couldn't see into the waiting room. It was on the right-hand side of the hall, the examining rooms on the left, but looking down the hall, I could spot any traffic going in or out. There was a gurney about halfway down, parts of a frail-looking guy poking out of the sheets and blankets on it—a foot at the bottom end, an elbow and the bald patch on his head up at the top. And you can't help but wonder what the guy was seeing—what he's thinking about. Whether he's doing the math on precisely how many little teeny pinholes there are in every single ceiling tile, or whether he's conducting some kind of whole-body inventory—thinking about what parts he can feel and what parts he can't, what still works and what doesn't. It's worth being in the hospital for a minute or two just to think about that— to think about having two arms and two legs that still work, and how that makes so many other things seem a hell of a lot smaller.

You get a good idea of how beat up the hospital is from that end of the hall: you can see the gouges that gurneys have knocked out of the walls, and where the screws that hold the bulletin boards up are pulling right out of the concrete, despite the plastic anchors. Because you can see the anchors, too. Bulletin boards with the same old public health messages:

"Wash your hands"; "STDs are everywhere — cover up"; "Wash your hands again." There are places in that hall where the linoleum is literally worn right down through the pattern on top, and it's the thick institutional stuff, too. But it doesn't seem like the place is neglected or anything — more like the kind of place where things just don't stop, where the whole place gets ground down a little every single day and night and there's never time for anything to breathe and recover.

And I can tell you this from watching the health department come in and give the meat section at the store a good going over: there's a level of wear and tear in hospitals that the inspectors would never put up with in the back room of the meat department. There are rules about how much things can be worn, because the grooves hold bacteria — and you'd think that if there was ever a place likely to have, grow, and shed bacteria like spores from a mushroom, it would be the emergency room in a hospital. But that doesn't seem to matter: the government isn't ever likely to call in its own inspectors on itself.

I pushed the cart out around the corner, left it right in the hall so that I could use it to block me from view if I had to, and started industriously cleaning away at nothing in particular.

That's the great thing about cleaning — nobody really has any idea why or what you're doing in any particular spot. How you picked it — whether you were told to go there, or whether there's a chart somewhere that says "you've reached the end — time to go back to the beginning." Fact is, if you hear a particularly interesting conversation, you can always push your mop and bucket over toward it, making it look as though that was the direction you'd always been intending to go. No one ever pays attention for long enough to see if there's any method in what you're doing. There is: you start at one end, finish at the other, but there's no real reason that one aisle has to come precisely after the one before.

All I really wanted to do was to keep working that far end of the hall — and maybe inch a little closer to the actual emergency room, hoping I could see Mary and the doctor together. Hoping that I could see if there was any clear connection between Mary and Patterson.

In the end, it didn't take very long. I was maybe fifteen feet down the hallway with the mop, moving far slower than I usually would, when the two of them, Patterson first and Mary second, came down the hallway from the other end, about twenty seconds apart.

They were walking with their heads down, a studious-looking distance apart, their faces set purposeful and serious before both of them turned right and headed into one of the examining rooms.

They didn't close the door or anything, just went in, each of them carrying a file folder. I was concentrating so hard on the doorway that I didn't see the nurse come around the corner and head right for me — at least, I didn't see her until she was right on top of me and saying, "Hey, we've been looking for you."

They had been calling me from down at the nursing station, actually waving their arms at me, and when I looked, I could see why: it looked like someone had been fighting with a chainsaw down there by the entry doors, and the floor was not just bloody, it was completely covered with blood, already darkening to rusty black blotches with long streaks in it where the doctors and nurses had been slipping around while they worked on someone.

I was stuck: back away down the hall, especially now that they'd sent someone to come and get me, and that would get everybody's full attention. Go and clean up, just do the job I do every single day, and I'd be taking the chance that Mary might walk right straight into me down there. As far as being inconspicuous was concerned, the plan was turning into a total bust.

You weigh the odds and decide what's the riskiest.

So I tucked myself in behind the cart and headed for the nurses' station and the blood, and hoped that Mary and the good doctor wouldn't choose that moment to come back out of the examining room.

But I also did it because I simply had to know.

Just as I passed the examining room door, I took one quick sideways look inside, and I can tell you, if Mary had been in my shoes, she would have known everything instantly.

Heck, even I knew it instantly, knew it absolutely for sure, and I'm not the most perceptive guy in the world.

They were back on to me, not even touching. But too close—the kind of comfortable, familiar close that two people have when they might just as well be touching. When, recently, they have been touching, when they know precisely how far they are from each other — and how close they are together. There's something about the way two people are when there's more to it than just friendship: there's a kind of joined air they seem to give off — and even with a quick glimpse, it was obvious that Mary and Dr. Patterson were living precisely in that space.

Perhaps it wasn't as obvious for other people, the people who had been working with Patterson and seeing Mary there week after week, month after month. Maybe, to them, the narrowing of distance between the two had been as unnoticeable as a glacial shift, a mile of ice that had spent months moving no more than a few inches.

To me, there was nothing glacial about it.

It was jarring, it was sudden, and it was absolute.

When I got up to the counter, one of the nurses hissed at me that they'd been calling for hours for someone from Maintenance, that it was about time I got there, that there were bloody footprints "from here to Diagnostic Imaging and back." I might be wrong, but I think it was the same nurse who'd checked me into the emergency room not that many weeks before. If it was, she clearly didn't recognize me.

I kept my head down, mopped and disinfected, almost forgot that my gloves and the cloth I used for the base of the walls had to go into a bag marked "biohazard," and I carefully looked absolutely no one in the face. It's funny where you go: I can start mopping and get lost in the whole darned thing — pushing the mop back and forth, watching the trails that each strand of mop leaves behind on the floor slowly dry up and disappear, seeing how every sweep back and forth leaves less on the linoleum and, at the same time, more in the bucket. There's a perfection to it, back and forth like the sweep of notes on a piano—not even, not regular, but patterned in a way that makes them, well, right.

Mary's legs went by four times, twice in both directions.

She gave no sign that she recognized me.

She gave absolutely no sign that she even saw me at all.

I didn't look up at her, didn't look at her face, but every time she passed I knew it was her. I suppose it's telling that she didn't realize, not even slightly, that it was me. I'm not sure if I was supposed to be angry about that, but I wasn't. There's a shuddering, definite fall to it, the loss of something you trust implicitly, as if you were an explorer and magnetic north had just decided to depart, heading west to spend a little time on the B.C. coast. The way you would feel as you watched your compass falling away to one side—the way you would know both that something was critically wrong and that it was absolutely beyond your ability to fix.

What I was—inside—was strangely out of balance and, in some way, a distant kind of cold. Like I had managed to finally put a whole bunch of stuff together into a precise and obvious order, but the real weight of that order hadn't sunk in yet.

It's strange, that hiatus between the blankness you feel and the knowledge you have that something much, much heavier is coming. Like seeing heavy clouds bellying up in the sky and knowing the storm will be powerful, long before the rain actually hits. And that there is no way of avoiding it.

I took the cart back downstairs on the elevator.

Pushed it back into the closet. Emptied all the water from the bucket into the big sink, and carefully wrung out the mop in the wringer. You've got to wring out your mop, no matter how tired and fed up you are. Mildew's only a night away, always. Leave it once and, after that, the whole next day, you can smell it, like it's trapped right there in your nose so you can't ever escape.

I turned off the light. Stood there just long enough to watch the green afterimage of the light bulb filament fade from in front of my eyes. Closed the door.

I walked home knowing it didn't matter when Mary came home, looking up and seeing the big clouds piling up grey in the night sky with the moon caught up behind them, the moon lighting the edges white and then vanishing from sight completely.

Knowing that, when she finally did come home, it wouldn't matter whether it was early or late.

Knowing inside, knowing precisely, that Mary had already departed.

CHAPTER 47

eggs
coffee filters
canned tomatoes
bananas, apples
masking tape
and Fuck You
You Cold Bastard.

Mary's handwriting. All of it clear and sharp.

I didn't keep that note. I won't forget it, though.

We shared buying the groceries the whole time we were married. We kept a notepad on the counter in the kitchen and the rules were unwritten and simple — if you noticed that we'd run out of something, you wrote it on the list and the next one who went to the store picked it up. And, to tell the truth, the person who actually went and got stuff was often whoever lost their patience and went first. It was like emptying the garbage: we just keep piling stuff in until the other person gave up, lugged it outside, and put a new bag in. At least then you got to have a little smile inside, for not hav-ing been the one to give up first. Small victories, but victories none the less.

When I got that "cold bastard" note, the house was quiet, summer quiet, and there were fine little dust motes hanging and turning in the almost-still air, the sunlight angling down through the kitchen in that kind of full light that's particular to June and early July here.

The house was empty and ticking gently, occasional, off-handed clicks and metallic clangs now and then like the fur-nace was embarrassed to be shutting down for summer and heading south, the radiators suddenly losing their brassy win-ter confidence. There was muttering from somewhere in the cheap seats, bubbles caught in transit, brass and aluminum playing the expanding and shrinking game that has no visible sign, but plenty of audible tone.

I still sometimes wake up from a sound sleep and think that I'm exactly, precisely there, that same room, that same day, that same hour. Then I look at my hands, my fingers, like I'm trying to be sure that I am still the same person I was before. I'm not sure. As if I could see proof in my own fingerprints.

The white rectangle of the notepad on the table, the pen next to it as if it had been set down on top of the pad and then allowed to roll slightly away. I don't want to keep repeating it, but every single word was important, like each one had its own particular weight both in what it meant, and in what it was tearing apart.

The last five words were inked heavily on the paper. I turned the page and, on the back, felt the ridges with my fingertip where the ballpoint pressed down hard on the capital *F*, the capital *Y*s, the *C*, the *B*. I saw the corresponding dents on the next page.

I don't think she was right about what she wrote—but I know exactly why she'd feel that way.

I can't find that list now.

I can't even remember if I put it somewhere or threw it away all at once. I don't know, maybe I lost it somewhere in the store.

I honestly haven't looked very hard.

I didn't see Mary again after that—it seems strange to say it, but it was like she found a way to simply extract herself from our genetic material, from the DNA of the house. Not many of her things were gone, but it was strangely as if she herself had vapourized.

One moment, she was there, the next, she wasn't—as definite a moment as the instant before a lightning bolt and the instant after, when the lawn furniture is all the same, the grass still the same length and the trees the same as they always are, the flash here and gone, but there's a particular smell in the air like hot, wet metal.

Not a trace anywhere in the house of where she might be going.

I didn't even bother to change the locks. There wasn't really a point.

Maybe she went back to Rabbittown, and then the gates

closed behind her like she was a princess coming back to the hometown castle, the world outside just cut clean off.

Or maybe she went west—you always hear about people who are heading out west for work, to change things or to forget things. I don't know why the police won't accept that sometimes people just like being missing.

After I reported her missing, there was a while when her family wanted to make trouble for me. They wanted to get me in deep, I guess, just to show how angry they were about the whole thing.

They told the police that even they didn't know where she was, and there was a while when the police would come by and talk to me regularly, me standing there with the screen door held open while they stood on the pavement right by my door, the heat rushing out in the fall, in the winter, asking me again if I had heard from her, and of course I hadn't heard anything. There was nothing to say.

Ask Dr. Patterson. That's what I told them.

Her family took it further than that, too. I was in the store—I can even remember where, in the aisle with the cereal and the dairy, dealing with the regular occurrence of dropped yogourt—and her brother Terry came barrelling straight down the aisle and got right up in my face, like he'd done so many times before. I don't know if he wanted to start a fight or whether he just wanted to get to me or what. He's a big guy, works with the city on a road patching crew, so you can guess he's pretty strong, with shovelling and raking the asphalt and with muscling that little steamroller they have down off the back of the truck and pushing it back and forth and everything.

He had his finger out, poking it at me, but carefully, without quite touching my chest.

"Where the hell is my sister?"

"How should I know?" I tried to keep my voice low, tried to be reasonable. "She left me. It's not like she's going to be reporting in or anything."

"Well, she'd sure as fuck tell us. And she hasn't. No one's heard a single goddamned word, and the last person who saw her was you."

I'm sure that's not true.

I mean, the second she left the house, someone had to have seen her, right? A cab driver, cop, I don't know. Maybe they just didn't know they'd seen her.

If anyone were to see her now, they'd know it.

The police had her face up on the news for weeks, me going through the wringer for not reporting her missing right away, so the fact is that she's probably moved out of the province. She always made her own decisions — she's headstrong like that — and if she wanted to go, she was just going to go. Maybe she got into some kind of trouble. I mean, she's got a temper, and that doesn't fly with everyone.

I don't know.

Nothing to do with me, whether the Carters want to rage or foam or whatever else they might want to do.

Like Terry.

There was Terry and he was still talking — well, he was

yelling — and I could see Morris, just over Terry's shoulder, making his way down the row, angling toward us.

Morris isn't a big guy — but he's got a uniform, black commando sweater with "Security" across the back in big block letters — and that seems to be enough to put the shoplifters off a little, and that's really why we have him.

He stands by the door out to the parking lot most of the time, doing his best to look like he's on the ball. There are four or five of them that rotate shifts, and every now and then they catch someone with a shirt full of T-bones or something, even though the store hardly ever goes all the way through the court process if they catch you and you won't plead guilty right away. Costs too much.

Morris is one of the smallest of them, a wiry little guy who used to be in landscaping until his back gave out. He bends to one side like he's still got a roll of sod balanced up there, waiting to unroll it on a patch of dirt somewhere or something.

I was sure all it was going to take was for him to reach out and tap Terry on the shoulder and Terry was just going to haul off and flatten him, right there by the Cap'n Crunch, every one of those stupid captains grinning out from their boxes, holding up their little swords and staring at the fuss.

Uniforms do different things to different people, and that's good, because Terry took one quick look at Morris and the air went right out of him. He turned back to me and said, "Don't think you and I are done, 'cause we're going to be all over you until we find her."

Then he put his hand in behind a row of cereal boxes and

just swept them completely off the shelf, the boxes bouncing with a hollow cardboard slap as they hit the floor, just something else for me to do, though at least none of them had burst open. And Morris looked at me with a "what the hell was all that about?" look, and I told him "it's personal, nothing big," and he slouched off to the door again to keep an eye on I don't know what.

I started picking up cereal boxes and putting them back. Not that it was really my job, but because it was sort of like it was somehow my mess.

You can understand why it is I keep looking over my shoulder now.

Not long after the racket in the store, two guys jumped me on the way home — never did see their faces and they didn't say a word, completely quiet except for their breathing. I had been walking, looking at my feet, and they caught me by surprise and gave me a good, careful working over with their fists until they knocked me down and started with putting the boots in.

Didn't ask me for my wallet. Didn't ask me who I was, and when one got tired, the other one would lay into me.

After they were done, it took me another half hour to get home, and you know how people will say sometimes that they get up in the morning and everything hurts? I know exactly what that's like, but I had to get up, because there was someone pounding on the door.

First thing in the morning, and Scoville and Hill were at my door, and the short one said, "Heard something happened to you," like it was all some kind of surprise, and did I "want to make a report?"

I did make a report, not because they were going to catch anyone, but because I could waste their time and keep them sitting there in the living room just the way they kept coming back and wasting my time.

The shorter one, he didn't stop smiling once. It was an evil, hard little smile, and it didn't look like he was even taking notes.

And we both knew what he meant by that.

CHAPTER 48

(St. John's, NL)—The Royal Newfoundland Constabulary (RNC) is seeking the assistance of the general public who may have witnessed an assault in the area of McKay Street in St. John's.

On Thursday, August 28, two men are alleged to have assaulted another man at approximately 11:30 p.m., as the victim walked home. Nothing was taken in the assault, but the RNC has not ruled out robbery as the motive for the attack.

The assault is believed to have occurred over a period of fifteen minutes.

The RNC is continuing to search for the alleged assailants and is seeking the assistance of the general public.

If anyone has any information pertaining to the incident, they are asked to contact the RNC at 729-8000 or Crime Stoppers at 1-800-222-TIPS (8477).

"It still doesn't take much to fuck up a court case," Dean said, "so back off, Jim."

"It doesn't take much for guilty guys to walk, either, even when you do everything right," Scoville said.

"What did you tell them?" Dean asked.

Scoville spread his hands out, as if Dean were supposed to be looking for blotches of dirt there on his palms. "I was just up in Rabbittown, doing a follow-up interview like we're supposed to, asked if they'd heard anything new, maybe mentioned a couple of things. Never said they should do anything about it. But it's probably not bad to knock him a little off balance."

Dean leaned back in his chair and rubbed his forehead.

"Chief's going to have a fit if any of this ever gets back to him. Think how it would look in the press. We'd be disowned, hung right out to dry. And our guy didn't look any more off balance than he ever does."

"He's got to know we're onto him."

"I don't think that matters. He doesn't care what we know — he cares about what we can prove."

Scoville scowled. "Maybe we should bring him in, make him go over the whole thing down here, and maybe this time we can get him to slip up somewhere."

"Not going to happen. He won't slip."

Scoville nodded resignedly.

Dean looked up at the ceiling, the off-white ceiling that never seemed to change. He thought about the way things can shift all at once.

"He can't keep going like this. Something has to happen eventually," he said.

"You are a fucking optimist, Dean."

CHAPTER 49

August 30 — The big news: I figured it out. He's
the guy from the grocery store — the cleaner. His
shirt says his name is Walt — I took a chance getting
close enough to read that. I don't think he saw me
though — if he did, he certainly didn't react. They all
have names on their shirts, and those uniforms — I
don't know if he really works for the store itself.
Probably they contract a cleaning company, but I
don't know who it is or who to contact. Probably the
store would be a good start. Or maybe the police — it
would be great to let Constable Rick Peddle know
just how wrong he was, even if I just get voicemail
again. Three days and I'll be gone anyway, so maybe
I'll call the store before I go. Just to give them a
heads-up that there's a stalker on their staff. I mean,
he won't be creeping me out any more, but maybe
telling them about it will keep him away from the
next woman. I'll already be gone. I was at my parents' last night, and what a fuss. You'd think I was
leaving the planet, not the city. They said they'd take

Bo, and then when I actually brought him over, Mom was all over it like she was going to back out, complaining about the litter box and where she was going to put it, and then Dad went off on one of those stories about what they used to do with unwanted cats when he was a kid, and I know it's not about Bo at all, it's that they're just trying to put up any roadblock they can think of. I'm doing the last of the packing now: almost everything's gone to Mom and Dad's or else been given away, and Mom says she'll come by with Dad afterwards and give the place a good going-over.

CHAPTER 50

Mango
cilantro
parsley
bread
peppers

Sometimes you want to cook something different. Sometimes you're just looking for a change. Sometimes that change walks right up to you and smacks you in the face.

There are racks of magazines at the front of the store, and they're always in a mess. People do two things with them: some pick them up and fling them on the belt, nonchalant like they've got better things to be doing when really they can't wait to get home and dive in. Other people snatch them up right there at the checkouts, reading as much as they can while they're waiting, like they were absolutely right in helping themselves, like it was a big free handful from the salad bar or a bunch of grapes they're allowing themselves to finish before they even get to the lane with their toilet paper and onions.

When the groceries are in the bags, it's the freeloading readers who stuff the magazines back any which way, not really caring whether they're in the right place or not. Sometimes they just leave them on the end of the checkout, a little more dog-eared and a little less likely to be purchased by anyone else.

Eventually, I'm the one who puts them back in order, me or one of the stockers, but usually me.

Glamour on *Glamour*, *Good Housekeeping* slapped right back onto itself, back into the same kind of order the magazine loves so much. Then there are the soft-papered tabloids, the ones no one admits to reading, the corners always curling down even before anyone's gotten around to pawing them over, the ones with the big stark front page photo of someone's cellulite sticking right out in your face. I guess you get to feel all right about everything in your own world when you're looking down on someone else.

So many of them.

The food magazines with cake decorations and six-layer recipes that only the most seriously masochistic would ever bother to try. Glossy magazines, the pictures on the front always drawn from a collection of bright electric colours that hardly look like they could exist in the real world.

Fashion and sex tips and cooking—all stacked up like their own particular set of commandments.

I found that latest list right near the doors, and then I just happened to be cleaning up at the checkout, and it was yet another cooking magazine in the wrong place. Right on the cover, just like on the list, there was a grilled bread, mango, and pepper salad, and it didn't look like it could possibly be all that hard. The way they have it on the cover, the way it all just stares right out at you, almost pornographic.

I know, the whole idea just sounds stupid, me at home fighting with grilling bread and carving up mangos, but when I saw it there on the cover, the mango bright and slick-shiny in the camera lights, it just seemed like something worth doing. Worth trying; worth tasting.

The list was already in my hand, a crumpled piece of lined yellow notepaper, just the corner of the page torn off, the words written in black Sharpie so that the ink had gone right through the paper and I could hold it up under my nose and still smell the solvents.

Me, the magazine, the list, and a quick trip back through the store at the end of my four-to-twelve shift, few enough items so I could dart through the express lane, pay Sandy, who gets half a smile on her face when she looks at me and sees what it is I'm buying, and then I headed home.

It was me the next afternoon before work, alone in a big house making a recipe for four.

Sun streaming down outside, plenty of blue sky up there and I had the mangos all peeled out of their skins and lying in the bowl and I could smell that odd turpentine smell they have and all I could think is that there's no way you could look at them and not start thinking about sex. The lustiness of them, fleshy and wet and inviting, and, at the same time, I was thinking that I couldn't imagine that cilantro was going to work. Because it's one of those few tastes you can really smell coming—just hold some while you're cutting it, just get a hint of it in your nose while you're piling it in the bowl, and your mouth is already getting around the shape of it.

Smelling it, I felt for a moment like I was almost in someone else's kitchen, like I could close my eyes and be taken right there, maybe someplace bright like Alisha's—not that I could ever go back there now. Not now. Somewhere else: somehow, it got into my mind that I was in one of those narrow walk-through kitchens where the cabinets all run down one wall, the fronts of them all panes of glass set in white frames, so you can see every single dish and glass and plate.

I just kept doing it, drawing it up there in my head. Make a place, put myself in it—just an average place where friends get together, that easy handoff where everyone knows everyone, where everyone fits together and all the work gets done without ever seeming like work.

In my head, there was a nice narrow counter with two deep white enamel sinks, the old ones that are always stained with iron or just plain hard and regular use, and it actually looks good on them. Narrow enough in the room that I'd always be just squeezing by someone if they're standing by the sink, familiar if you know them well enough, but with the chance of awkward if you don't. Close.

The kind of house where it's just fine that pieces of the baguette have been torn off the loaf in chunks and left there on the breadboard, salt in a shallow bowl with a single silver spoon instead of in a shaker, a place where there's a big solid pot of chilli on the back burner of an older-model stove. And the stove doesn't even look dated: somehow it manages to pull off classic. Empty wine bottles already lining up by the sink and plenty of dishes in the midst of piling up, lots of noise from the living room where people are talking loud — and maybe it's the smell of the cilantro that's doing it, but I was trying hard to remember if it was someplace that I had ever actually been.

Thoughts darted in: something about little kids on the floor and folk art and a guitar was catching at the edges of my memory, and I was almost sure that it was winter in the place I was trying to remember as much as imagine, because even though the kitchen was warm, there was that strange feeling that cold was hanging out there, right there in reach, ready to just come in and hang up its hat, sit on the couch with its feet up while you start to shiver. And it was long enough ago that I was different.

It was nagging at me, like it was something that I should be able to place absolutely immediately. But I couldn't remember it clearly, and even though I couldn't, I started thinking that I missed it keenly: the people, the noise, the being part of it all.

Being part of something. Being able to fit.

There was a hard knock on my front door, because the battery's dead on the cheap doorbell I bought, and by the time anyone figures out that it's not working — because no one's coming up the hall to answer it — they're already pissed off.

I was right at the very back, in my kitchen in my T-shirt with no belt on, my pants tucked in under the overhang of my belly, and I wasn't anywhere ready for company. That's funny, hey? Me. Ready for company.

No one ever comes to the house to visit except new pairs of Seventh-day Adventists now and then, and they usually manage just one visit before they decide there are greener pastures for missionaries, greener pastures where there's a heck of a lot less swearing going on and probably a lot better chance of a good clean salvation.

But there were people at the door for me, all right.

When I came down the hall, heading toward the glass front door to answer their knocking, I saw they were filling up the whole doorway outright, like they could block every scrap of daylight.

Solid, square men, and if you'd seen them, you would have been like me, you couldn't have helped but feel that there was something that made them look like they had popped right out of the exact same womb. Once inside the house, they filled the hall right up, too, one of them looking around like he was taking inventory, sucking it all in like he might need it again later, the other one doing all the talking.

The police wanted to talk to me again, and I have to say that I wasn't really surprised about that. They're just doing their jobs, and this is a job they apparently don't believe is done yet.

Two guys stuffed awkwardly into suits like they were on their way to a high school graduation they were actually too old for and probably wouldn't mind missing. I wondered fleetingly if the whole Criminal Investigation Division bought their suits at the same place, if there was a special police discount or a particular store that guaranteed ill-fitting to match their generally churlish attitudes.

They asked me to come down to the station for a formal interview. That was new.

I told them no problem, but I'd drive myself unless they were arresting me or something, because I didn't want the neighbours looking out the windows and seeing me in the back of one of those all-too-obvious undercover cars. Like the lack of hubcaps is supposed to make the cars go faster or something. It reminds me of the kids who never seem to get past putting sticks in their bike spokes to make more noise.

Take one look at those cars and you know what they are right away, and I didn't want the whole neighbourhood whispering back and forth, coming to their own damned conclusions in there behind their windows. There's enough of that already.

Bad enough that the police rig had been parked out there for half an hour, the two of them standing in the front hallway until they finally got around to telling me they want me to come to the station. Maybe they were thinking that they were getting my wind up, but really, it's a lot simpler than that: the reason I kept looking around is that I was wondering just exactly what I was supposed to do with the peeled mangos. Could they stay on the counter, or should they be in the fridge? Maybe that's a stupid thing to be worrying about when the police are at your door, when you should be thinking about who the best possible lawyer is, just in case.

Sunny outside, early fall, but it was like everything had changed around lately, like the seasons got confused somewhere. Spring here goes on and on now, a forced march designed to break your heart, but fall just can't make up its mind, flipping back and forth. Summer one day, cold rain the next, and it's never really clear day to day just what you're going to get. September, and there are raspberry plants shooting up high and throwing out brand new flowers all over again when they should be getting ready to die back.

They're the neighbour's raspberries: she planted them and then they came through the back of her yard into mine, claiming any freshly turned soil. She cut hers down, said they didn't bear enough fruit, and she asked did I want her to come over and cut down the ones in my yard as well?

I told her no, because the fact is I kind of like how they just keep trying to force their way along, new shoots marching out every year trying to take over a little more terrain. They'll cover every piece of open ground fast. Sometime, the runners are going to meet the maple seedlings in the middle of the yard, and there's going to be some kind of plant battle, stem to stem, at least until I wheel out the mower again and cut them all down so no one wins but me. And then the war's going to be postponed for another year.

When I got out to my car, they were sitting in front of me in their rig, their heads silhouetted against the back window, and I could see that those big lunkheads perched on their shoulders were just about exactly the same size — and maybe the one driving was looking at me in the mirror. Or maybe he wasn't, it was hard to tell, but the fact was that neither of their heads moved even an inch when their car pulled out and away. No signal, but I used mine.

When they got me in the interview room, the lunkhead twins left and it was two other guys. Guys I've seen before. One round, one tall. Scoville and Hill. Again.

Hill says I'm not being charged with anything and thanks me for coming in, "just a few questions for you and you can be on your way," all of it spilling out flatly like he's said it twenty thousand times before. Probably he has, for everything from drug cases to stolen bikes.

Hill tells me to call him Dean and do I want a cup of coffee and what do I take in it? Maybe a ginger ale? I've seen him lots before, a couple of times away from the force at one of the rinks, on skates with a hockey stick in his hands, no nonsense and standing straight up at the blue line in a not-very-friendly recreational hockey game, giving off an air of "just give it a try" the way some guys seem to do with absolutely no effort at all. He's also been around to talk to me plenty before; he's the one they pick to do the nice "take a little friendly advice, would ya?" line.

It was like they had no idea that anyone watched television or anything, or else just figured that we're all so hopelessly lame and eager to please that we're going to fall for it anyway. A nice clean glass of water right there on the table, as clean as if it was polished, not a mark on it, but I wasn't going to give them the satisfaction of having me touch it and leave marks for them to do whatever with.

Scoville hadn't offered his first name, hadn't said much of anything, and he was sitting with his back against the wall right there by the door like he could move half an inch and that would be all it would take to stop you from going anywhere. Like there wouldn't even have to be a closed door in the place, just him and his chair and his chin and haircut. He had his arms crossed across his chest, and I couldn't help but think that he was pretty much a cartoon character, and that inside his head, he must be telling himself to keep that stern look on his mug for as long as he possibly could, because that's exactly what the book says to do.

Then Dean came back with the coffee I didn't really want in a paper cup, and he said he was sorry that there wasn't any creamer left, but he put some whitener in if that's all right. There was one of those brown plastic stir-sticks angling up out of the coffee, and I could see he'd really stirred it, because the stir-stick was slowly bouncing around the inside rim of the coffee cup in the fading whirlpool like it was trying to get away but didn't really have anywhere to run to.

They had a lot of questions.

It was a small room, no distractions, not much in there to put your eyes on to take you away from exactly where you were, and it occurred to me that it was meant to be exactly that, that the person being interviewed was the only thing that's supposed to get any attention at all. It was all beige and the walls had fabric on them. Like carpet, almost, and it sucked in the sound. Like it was supposed to suck the words right out of you, too, make them come streaming out like you're some kind of magician and they've got a hold of your magic scarves and just won't stop pulling. Three chairs, one table, one empty wastebasket. I checked the wastebasket the minute I came in.

They had questions about a girl who went missing years ago, a girl named Lisa, and then some more about Alisha, whose house has been empty for two weeks now—"You're surrounded by women no one has heard from," the short one, Scoville, said. And most of the questions were about Mary at first, and they didn't seem to have a heck of a lot of interest in listening to the answers I was giving them. I was telling the whole thing, telling them what I could—about Mary leaving and about how I know Alisha by sight because she comes around the store sometimes but nothing more than that. Stuff they could pretty much prove anyway, stuff they probably knew already if they had all their ducks in a row.

Did I like fishing? "Yes."

"Where?"

"Cape Shore. Southern Shore. I move around."

"Got a cabin anywhere?"

That's a little too close. "No."

I was thinking, the thing to do is to stay as close to the truth as you can, but don't give them stuff that will make them head off in new directions. Don't give them any of the stuff you have trouble explaining to yourself, the stuff they can railroad you with. Because they like to solve stuff, and they don't care if they've got the right guy or not. As long as they've got someone.

Had I ever been in Alisha's house? That stopped me for a second. I weighed it real quick, thought there would be too much explaining: "No."

"Sure about that?"

"Don't even know where she lives."

Scoville piped up, changed direction. "You keep grocery notes for years," at the same time making his eyes big like saucers in a way that means he thinks I'm a nut job, and then he started talking about Mary's note. "You said right from the start she left a note, and you didn't keep it? You keep grocery notes for years—boxes of 'em, we've seen them all—but you expect us to believe that you didn't keep that one?"

I shrugged.

"And you think we should believe you when you say you can't remember just what day your wife left?"

He let that question hang there in the air, and I was skittering it around inside my head like there had to be a reasonable answer hiding in there somewhere, like maybe he's right and the answer should just pop to the surface like a cork. But it didn't.

"Well, I don't," I finally said, and even to me, that didn't sound sensible. It sounded petulant, like I should have been sticking my lower lip out when I said it, and that's not what I wanted it to seem like at all. The tall one, Hill, it was clear that he didn't like that answer at all, his mouth pursed up a bit like he'd tasted something sour.

Doesn't matter now: it was what it was.

It's like they were only hanging on to the words they

wanted to hang on to anyway — anything else was just going to get tossed out.

He shrugged, and his arms were still right there over his chest, and even Dean was throwing off an air then like he didn't believe me, though he was pretending to want to.

"Tell you what I think," Scoville said. "I think you know a lot more than you're saying. What do you think of that?"

The questions just battering back and forth from different directions. First about one thing, then about another. Try to get me off balance, I guess. And I could see where it was going, the two of them willing to keep talking all day, trying to push me along. Willing to just sit there, if that's what it took, leaving the room filled up with empty space where no one's saying anything at all so that you feel like you have to start talking, just so everyone will have something to listen to.

Scoville threw other questions out, too.

Dean looked down sometimes, like he was embarrassed the other guy was so blunt.

"What was it? What started it?" Scoville said. "I know guys like you. She wouldn't do what you wanted?"

Waited after that. Didn't say anything else for a while. Like at any moment, I'm supposed to start filling in the big old empty space with words.

"You're a strange one, Walt. You know it, I know it." He looked at his fingertips, looked back across at me. "Everybody knows it. You've got some former neighbours who think you could be up to just about anything."

I shrugged. Carefully.

Later, Scoville started going over old ground. "So your missus left you."

He said it really flat, like it was hardly worth saying, let alone believing. Looked at me, and then he was paying attention. Sharp.

"Betcha were mad about that," he said, and he was staring right into my eyes. "How mad were you, Walt?"

Said my name like it was a swear word, spitting it out of his mouth like he expected to be able to look down and see it lying there on the floor in a little web of mucousy letters. I didn't know just how he managed to do that, but he did. Push, push. He just kept pushing.

Backwards, forwards, backwards again. Running right over my answers, starting another cycle of the same questions.

I don't get mad, I tell them, but that rolls right off. The room's warmer all the time, and I wonder whether it's our combined body heat, or whether they've turned up the thermostat, too. And then I drop Patterson's name again, but it runs right off them like they don't even hear me saying it.

At the end of it, I've got nothing left to say, what's there is all laid out, and you can see from their eyes that they're not convinced, that they've got some completely different idea of what happened. Like they're playing pin-the-tail, and I'm always going to be the donkey.

Then it goes sideways. The tall one, Dean, he puts a picture of Joy Martin's place on Signal Hill Road on the table in front of me.

"Know that place, Walt?" he asks, and I'm trying not to freeze up, trying to keep my face the same.

"No," I say.

"How about here?"

Another photo. A wide-angle shot of the cabin, all burned.

"No," I say again, keeping my voice level, wondering how they got there—how they connected it to me.

"Right," Dean says.

Then Alisha's house, front and back. Her bedroom window, from a very familiar angle.

"Don't know the place," I say, but I can tell I'm going to start sweating soon.

Then I realize none of it can be concrete. They don't have bones or witnesses or anything, or I'd be charged already.

So I tell them straight out, "You want to go on with this, go ahead. I guess I'll have to take my chances in court."

Right then, it's words coming out of me one after another, even though there's part of me that's busy thinking I'm braver than I should be, that I should know enough to slow it down. That I don't have anything I've got to explain.

"All this other stuff? It's all in your heads, boyos. Mary went back to her family. Or else she went out west. Either way, I've told you I've got no idea where she is now, and I don't want to know, either. You should be asking someone else, not me."

In my head, there's the absolutely clear sound of someone telling me to just shut up, but another part of me isn't listening.

"As for anything else you think I did, well, you can go on thinking it."

I know it's stupid. I know it's just like daring them to do something, to tell me they've got something else that puts me somewhere I've said I hadn't been.

I just can't seem to stop myself. The words come pouring out, and it feels good.

"So maybe if there's nothing else you guys have to say, nothing else you have to ask me about, maybe you can just go ahead and let me go. I've been helpful—I've come in here and I've told you everything you wanted to know, and I haven't been snuffling about 'where's my lawyer' and 'why are you picking on me' or any of that."

I straighten up.

"I've got stuff to do —I've got a job I'm supposed to be at. A job I've had for years. Night shift tonight—but you guys have to know that already, if you know so damned much about me."

When I get up to leave, they just sit there, watching me go, and they don't say anything. Don't try to stop me. This, I think, this is the point where, if they actually have anything solid, they get out handcuffs and tell me that I'll be staying in lock-up for a while.

But they don't.

When I'm going though the door, Dean gets up from where he's sitting and walks me down through the hall to the front of the police station and out past the security, a couple of cops sitting there waiting for the people out on bail to come in and sign the book before heading on their way again. I push the big glass door open with the flat of my hand.

"Don't think we won't be talking to you again," he says, and even Good Cop sounds a little bad now. In its own way, it's the scariest thing that's been said to me yet.

He doesn't stop me from going through the door, doesn't stop me from heading out into the sun, and I can't help myself, can't help but turn back and give him a little wave, a little kind of half-salute.

So close, and yet so far. That's what I want it to say, that's what I really want to say, even if it would just end up making more problems for me.

Outside, it's sunny, and I find myself wishing I hadn't driven there, because suddenly, I just want to walk.

I want to walk fast, want to feel the stretch in the muscles of my thighs as I push forward, that nice clean feeling almost like the muscle fibres inside your legs are tearing themselves apart, but in a good, reconstructing kind of way.

They say you have to tear muscle to make it come back stronger. I really think that has to be true, that when you push things right to their limits, they go ahead and set new limits for themselves.

The leaves will be changing before long, the last of summer falling off the trees so they can wait for spring to come around fresh and start all over again, and even if I did walk, there'd still be enough time to get to the store before my shift.

And the mangos are out on the counter at the house, probably still sweating those great round drops of mango juice that bead up right out of the flesh, so full and round and waiting.

CHAPTER 51

(St. John's, NL)—The Royal Newfoundland Constabulary (RNC) is continuing to investigate a series of missing person cases, and will hold a press conference at 10:30 a.m. on Friday morning, Sept. 15, to provide media with an update on progress in the investigation.

Dean stood, watching Walt leave, watching the glass door swing closed. Scoville came down, flopped into a chair in reception. "Well?"

"You know it. I know it. Never in Alisha's house?" Dean looked again at the glass door, at the clear single handprint backlit on the glass. "Call Ident and tell them to get down here. We'll see if that says otherwise—and we already have the prints they found at her place. We can charge him with break and enter to start. Stalking, maybe."

Scoville nodded.

"Did you see his face when we showed him the photos? Get some forensics guys lined up, and we'll take ourselves a trip to the country. Finally, a few cracks in Mr. Ice. Won't be long now."

Scoville stood up slowly, smiling.

"Maybe after that," Dean said, "we'll dig around in his backyard a little."

"No one's ever looked there?" Scoville was incredulous.

"You know the rules. You need less to dig through someone's possessions than you need to dig up their yard."

CHAPTER 52

Zuchini
Soup — chicken broth
Bread
Banans
cheese

Comparing the handwriting on the notes, I know every one that's hers. Too many things the same, even some of the misspelled words. Always *banans*. It's like fate telling you "hurry up, hurry up, I'm here again."

It was like a dream, really, the way everything moved slowly and looked wrong, like there were problems with the light or the angle you're looking at the room from.

Like I felt she was standing in a doorway, looking across the room, while, in real life, there isn't a doorway where she was standing at all. As the confusion clears, it was just me at one end of the kitchen, her at the other, the furniture all gone so that the place looked completely different, barren. Her two suitcases were by the front door, and the diary had to be in one of them. Won't be anything new in it, probably. It had only been a day since I'd been through it last. I mean, it's always in the top dresser drawer. But there was enough already in that last entry: that she saw the guy.

That she saw me.

"It's all right." I said the words because I thought I should be saying something, because we couldn't just keep standing there, silent and staring at each other.

I said it with my hands held straight out in front of me so that she could see my palms, so that she could see my hands were empty. As if they were harmless, as if things are always what they seem.

"It's all right. It's only me." The car parked out front, waiting, a chance I had to take. I didn't like that, but there wasn't much choice.

She looked at me like she'd never seen me in her life before, but also like she was looking right through me and could see who I really was. And I couldn't have that.

The lights in her kitchen have always been too bright for me.

It's not my fault; that's what I was thinking. None of it.

I didn't even see her, not on the day she says she spotted me. And call my boss? The store? The police? I don't think so.

I keep my eyes still, drop those lids, try not to show anything on my face.

CHAPTER 53

Lisa, who was looking for a cabin
Mary, who no one will ever find
Alisha, who shouldn't keep writing

It's my list. In my own handwriting.

The notepaper is real soft, folded and unfolded until it feels almost like cloth now. Each name in different ink.

It's not anywhere you'll find it, Officers.

Hold on.

The cops are at the front door. Banging. Again.

ACKNOWLEDGEMENTS

For those who have believed in this book and helped me through all the times I wanted to give up on it, thank you. For those who did not believe, thank you as well, because you've helped make it a better book as a result of your doubts.

At House of Anasi, thanks are due to my familiar and expert editor Janice Zawerbny and to Sarah MacLachlan, a publisher who's shown she's willing to take a chance or two. For the eagle eye of copyeditor Linda Pruessen — I owe you several crucial debts.

Sincere thanks as well to the toughest of agents, Shaun Bradley of the Transatlantic Agency. We live to fight again.

The Canada Council for the Arts and the Newfoundland and Labrador Arts Council have provided that most necessary of things – financial support.

My sons Philip and Peter Wangersky have heard many things about this book, and have remained patient and thoughtful throughout the writing process.

To those who helped me collect hundreds of real grocery notes and want to remain nameless — you have my gratitude. Finally, for my wife and fellow writer Leslie Vryenhoek's constant support and exceptional editorial counsel, there are no words. Well, actually, there are two — thanks, love.

RUSSELL WANGERSKY is a writer, editor, and columnist from St. John's, Newfoundland. His five books include *Whirl Away*, a finalist for the Scotiabank Giller Prize and winner of the Thomas Head Raddall Award for Fiction; *Burning Down the House: Fighting Fires and Losing Myself*, a memoir of his years as a volunteer firefighter, which was a *Globe and Mail* Top 100 Book, won the BC National Award for Nonfiction, the Edna Staebler Non-Fiction Award; and *The Glass Harmonica* winner of the BMO Winterset Award. He works at the St. John's *Telegram* as the news editor.